ASHBURN

An Urban Fantasy Novel

Ashes Still Burn #1

M.W. LAYNE

Published by Writer Layne, LLC
Originally published 2019

Cover Art and Design by M.W. Layne

ISBN: 9798869068736

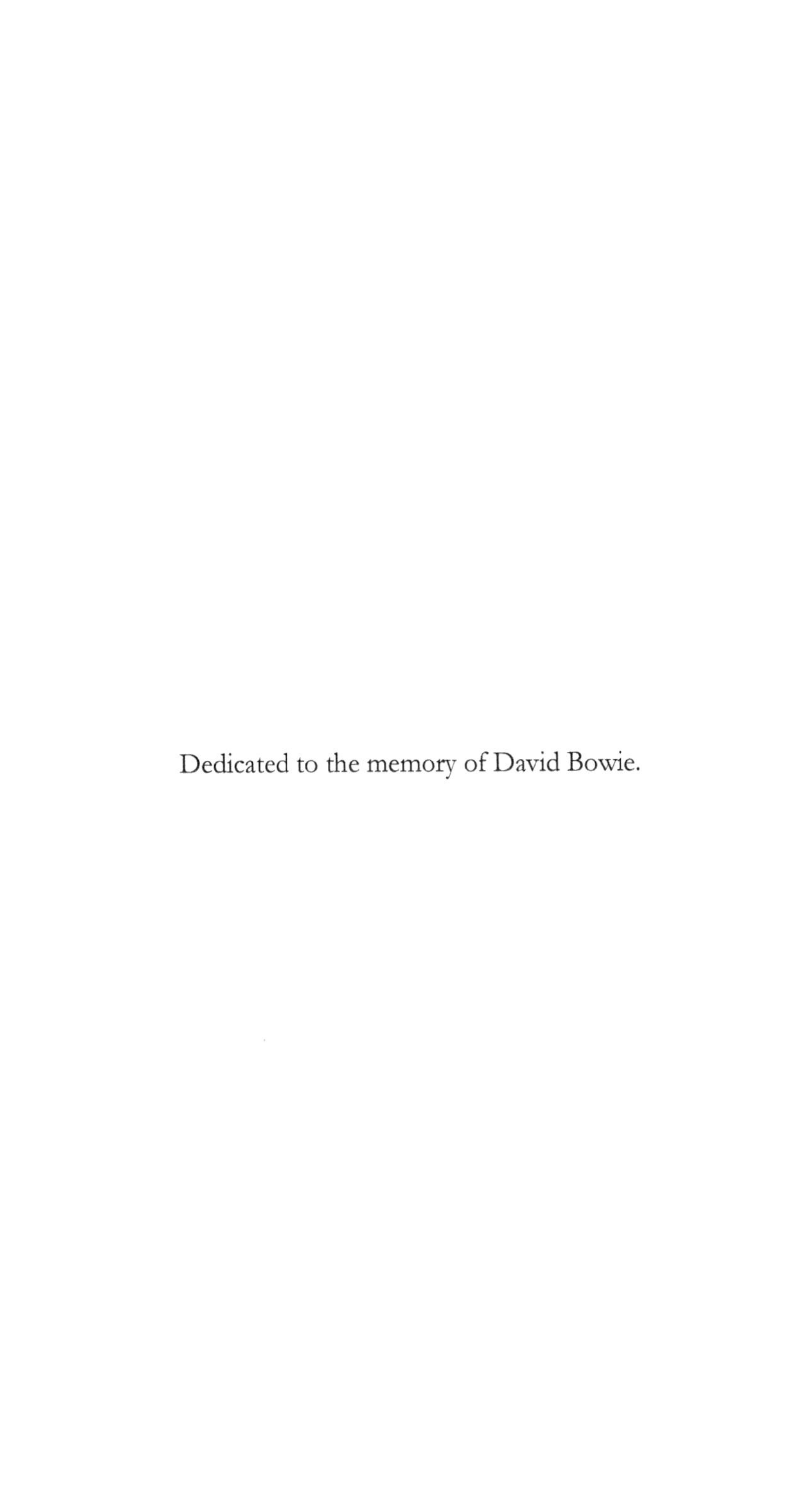

Dedicated to the memory of David Bowie.

OTHER BOOKS BY M.W. LAYNE

Ashes Still Burn Series:

The Demon Slayer of Ashburn (Book #2)
The Blood of Ashburn (Book #3)

Horror/Thrillers:

The Gate
Running Club: A Short Dystopian Thriller
Thirst: A Horror Short Story

ACKNOWLEDGMENTS

Thank you to my amazing set of Beta Readers for their help in making this the best book it could be.

Thank you, Mom, as usual, for being a great reviewer of my work. You always make the best catches that no one else finds. I appreciate your love and your critical eye!

Kristen Paul, thank you for your strategic insight into the story arc—what was working and what wasn't—and for your near-daily encouragement to keep writing!

Kevin McMahon, you've read each of my books, usually more than once, and as always, you had great comments and insights on this one. I can't thank you enough!

And then there was Amy Wade. Without you, this book would not exist in its current state. Thank you for being my Urban Fantasy expert and for all the conversations preparing for the writing of the story, during its execution, and as a Beta Reader after it was done. Amazing. I am eternally grateful!

Oh, and of course, a very special thanks to Ashburn, VA, my suburban home for so many years now. I might give you a hard time, but you're a good place to live. Thanks for having me.

I never knew Hell was green.
The grass. The money. Everything.
I thought it was red with bloody streams.
But not everything is as it seems.

From *Ashburn Blues*
by
David Steele

CHAPTER 1

MY NAME IS DAVID—David Steele.

Yes, that David Steele.
But, you can call me John.
At least for now.

CHAPTER 2

I REMEMBER SITTING up in bed, breathing hard, my skin covered in sweat. The morning sun forced its way into the bedroom through a break in the heavy curtains, as I tried to recover from my nightmare. My mental haze lifted like it was made of lead, as I sorted through what was real and what wasn't.

In my dream, I'd been a rock star performing in front of a sea of demons who were all trying to steal my soul.

The rock star part was true—or at least it had been for about two weeks in 1981, right before the launch of MTV—back when a singer's voice counted more than his looks.

As far as being at a concert, well, I was in a bed instead.

Also, the last time I'd checked, I was dying of lung cancer.

I took a deep breath, bracing for the agony that usually followed. But for the first time in a long while, I didn't cough anything up—no blood and no bits of thick, rotten, black goo.

Best of all, I wasn't in any pain.

My lungs were clear, and I smiled. But only for a second.

I scanned the bedroom, searching for my favorite Gibson electric, but it wasn't there. Sure, I was awake, but something was wrong.

When I rubbed my eyes to clear them of sleep, the room came into sharper focus. This wasn't my bed. Waking up in a strange place was something that happened every once in a while, especially when a woman wanted bragging rights for sleeping with *the* David Steele, the famous one-hit wonder.

But this morning was not that.

I held my hand in front of my face. My long, aged fingers that could still pull a seven-fret spread without effort were gone. Instead, my hand was covered in the smooth skin of youth, with digits that were crooked in places, like they'd been broken and left to heal on their own.

"What the hell is going on?" I said out loud even though there was no one there to answer.

Then I heard something—a deep, menacing growl rising up from the floor and growing louder, moving closer.

For a second, I thought I'd fallen asleep again and was having another nightmare, but I wasn't that lucky.

Frantic, I searched the bed, feeling around for something I could use as a weapon, but all I could find was a pillow. I held it against my chest, even though a few inches of down feathered softness wasn't going to protect me from much of anything at all.

Still, it made me feel safer.

I held my breath and peeked over the edge of the bed, searching for the source of the monstrous sounds that were growing louder. When I saw the shadow of a creature walking across the carpet, I exhaled in relief.

It was a dog about as tall as my knees, with short, thick, grayish blue-and-black mottled fur and a dense area of black on one side of his face that made him resemble a pirate with an eye patch.

I laughed, feeling foolish but also relieved—until he bared his teeth, and the hair along his spine stood on end. That, plus the way the animal glared at me with glowing, crimson eyes convinced me that it would not to be a good idea reach down and pet him.

I'd owned dogs all my life. I even used to take my dog, Rocky, to my shows. But the evil thing that was inching closer was only part dog and a lot of something else altogether.

I clutched my pillow-shield tighter and stared, wide-eyed at the animal, waiting for it to leap and attack.

"Who's a good boy?" I whispered through clenched teeth. With a flex of his haunches, the dog launched into the air and landed at the foot of the bed, straddling my feet.

I scooted away from him, until my back pressed against the

headboard, still holding my useless pillow in front of me. The dog crawled closer, leading with his razor-sharp teeth. His growl grew louder and more intense with each step. When he was close enough for me to feel the hot exhale of his breath, he lifted a front paw and pushed against my pillow harder than a dog his size should have been able to do. Still waiting for him to attack, I gathered my courage and prepared to push him away the instant he made his move.

Although I was afraid and at the animal's mercy, a spark of rage welled up inside me, and my fear gave way to anger.

I felt my lips pull back as I showed my own teeth, matching the dog's snarl with one of my own. It was a ridiculous gesture, since I posed no real threat to him. But whether I was acting on instinct or had simply lost my mind, for a moment, I felt like I was the most dangerous creature in the room.

The dog didn't seem to agree, and as the seconds ticked away, we both glared at each other. After what felt like forever, the rage in his eyes dimmed to mild distrust but then rekindled as he moved his snout close enough to almost touch my nose. I took an inadvertent whiff and raised my eyebrows at the stench of the animal's breath.

Someone needed a bath and a dental cleaning, and it wasn't me.

The dog edged closer and sniffed my neck, then sat down on top of my stomach. With his tongue lolling out of his mouth, he scanned the room, suddenly bored. When he turned to focus on me again, his eyes were big and brown, and I had to resist the primal urge to pet him.

The two of us waited in silence until he wagged his tail a few times, then used my crotch as a launching pad to jump off the bed.

His dismount was a little painful on my end, but on the positive side, he hadn't tried to eat me—yet.

As an extra bonus, even though I hadn't had a single drop of coffee, I was wide awake.

As I shifted my weight to get out of bed, my hand touched something silky—a tiny pink thong buried in the covers. I arched one brow and left the panties where I'd found them, wondering who they belonged to and if she was still around. Maybe the night had been better than I remembered.

I stood up, still wary of the dog, but he only watched me as I surveyed my dimly lit surroundings. The bedroom was normal by all definitions, with a nightstand on either side of the bed and piles of books stacked on most horizontal surfaces. A wicker laundry basket stood in the corner, with a load of dirty clothes surrounding and on top of it. A wooden dresser sat next to a free-standing, full-length mirror, and of course, a large flat screen TV was mounted on the wall. The room had all the basics of modern-day living, but not a single piece of art, a family photo, or other personal item to give the place any personality or warmth.

The dog shot me a glance, then trotted over to his fluffy bed on the floor and started chomping on a large bone he held steady between his two front paws. As I looked closer, I was pretty sure he was munching on a human shin bone. I didn't want to think about how he'd gotten ahold of it, but seeing it made me think of my own legs, which were walking without effort for the first time in months.

With my heart doing a drum roll, I positioned myself in front of the mirror and faced my reflection—only it wasn't me who was looking back.

I stared at a complete stranger in the mirror and tried to stay calm. Don't get me wrong—I was amazed and happy to be alive and healthy again, but I hadn't planned on waking up in someone else's body, and it was more than a little stressful.

The good news was that I was young again and in amazing shape. Also, my new face was everything my old one had never been— square-jawed and handsome. In fact, if I'd seen the guy in the mirror walking down the street a month ago, I would have hated him on principle alone.

The bad news was that my hair was buzz-cut short, and the only thing I was wearing was a pair of tighty whities for underwear, but I could fix that.

As I made my way to the window, I stretched my new limbs and my neck. I squeezed my fist and grinned as the muscles in my forearm popped.

With one hand, I parted the bedroom curtains and squinted at the sudden glare from the outside world. It was still early in the morning, but the day was already too bright for me. As my eyes adjusted, I looked out at a scene so foreign to me that I could barely speak. I'd seen photos of such a place—I think in National Geographic and maybe once on the news—but I never thought I'd experience it firsthand.

I wasn't in the city anymore, where I'd lived most of my life. Instead, I'd woken up in the suburbs somewhere.

I swallowed hard, and the dog wedged his block-head between me and the curtain so he could look outside, too.

Down below, two fit, middle-aged women in brightly colored clothes jogged past an oversized rubber trash can and a street sign that read *Ridgeway Drive*. As their feet slapped the sidewalk, the sprinkler system next door hissed to life, barely missing them with its lazy spray. I pressed my nose to the window and checked up and down the street, but all I saw were houses—lots of them—with each being nearly identical to the other.

I closed the curtain, and the room sank back into blissful darkness. I sat on the edge of the bed and reminded myself that I was alive, and that even though something had gone very wrong, I should have been ecstatic.

But I wasn't.

"None of this was part of the deal," I said. The dog's ears went flat against his head. "Not this body. Not this dog. And not wherever the bloody hell I am right now."

I laughed at my pitiful reaction. Why did I care where I'd ended up or what I looked like? I'd beaten cancer and cheated death—things that never happened to real people in real life. I laughed again and felt truly grateful—not to God or to any of his angels, but to a dark creature named Ahriman—the demon who had saved my life.

CHAPTER 3

*F*IRST THINGS FIRST, as my dad used to say.

I went to the bathroom, splashed cold water on my face, and sat on the edge of the unnecessarily huge tub to plan my next move.

My top priority was figuring out where I was, but first I needed some clothes. Unfortunately, the best I could scare up was a pair of tan khakis and a white polo shirt. The good news was that I found a pair of clean boxer briefs, which were a thousand percent better than the Homer Simpson tights I'd woken up in.

I dressed then checked myself in the mirror, shaking my head at my uncomfortable, preppy outfit. I looked more like a nerd on his first day of school than a rock star, and I wasn't a fan of the look.

I hope you're enjoying this, Ahriman, I thought to myself as I threw the tighty whities in the trashcan and left the bedroom.

On my way down the stairs, the dog followed right behind me, so close I was afraid I was going to step on him. Down on the ground floor, I checked out the living room, the dining room, and the kitchen. It wasn't as modern as the studio I used to live in back in the city, and all the cabinets and furniture were made of light wood, like someone had spent their life's savings at Ikea to furnish the place. After rifling through the coat closet, the bathroom, and the laundry room, I finally found what I was looking for—the door to the garage.

But as I went to open it, the dog whimpered. Even though I wanted to get out of there as fast as possible and back to my home, I looked down at the pup's face with its eyepatch of black fur and sighed.

What can I say? I'm a sucker for animals.

"What do you need?" I said. "Doggie want some breakfast?"

His tail wagged furiously. I'd hit the jackpot on my first guess.

The pantry was mostly devoid of food and didn't hold anything dogs would be interested in. It was, however, filled with plenty of wine and bottles of liquor. The fridge was mostly empty too, except for a dozen bottles of what looked to be home-made red wine that shouldn't have been refrigerated in the first place. I closed the refrigerator and touched the handle to the freezer door.

When I did, the dog barked so loud, it made me jump.

I reached in and pulled out a rack of ribs that were frozen solid. There was no way I was going to wait for them to defrost, but they'd melt eventually, so I set them down in his food bowl with a heavy *thunk*.

"Sorry boy," I said. "You're going to have to wait a few hours before you can eat those."

The dog didn't seem to mind at all, and he started licking the block of ribs like it was a giant meatsicle.

I turned to leave, but the dog's whimpers stopped me again. When I turned around this time, he was standing at the back door, begging me with his big brown eyes, barely able to contain his excitement as his tail thumped repeatedly against the floor. *Whap. Whap. Whap.*

"Okay, I get the message."

As I walked past his food bowl, I noticed it was empty except for a single smear of red, and I laughed, wondering how the crazy dog had managed to hide his breakfast so quickly. When I picked up the leash hanging on the wall, he went absolutely ape-shit, jumping up and down and grunting like a pig. I'm sure he would have loved a walk, but when I looked outside, I saw the backyard was fenced-in, so I opened the door and let him outside to do his business.

With the dog taken care of, I made sure the back door stayed open then snagged a set of keys hanging on the laundry room wall and headed for the garage again. I was hoping to find some American muscle waiting for me—maybe a Camaro or an old Mustang. What I got wasn't as good, but it was what I expected in the 'burbs—a brand new, pearl black, Audi A6, complete with a six-speed stick shift.

I hopped in, clicked the garage door opener, and backed out into the morning air, squinting at the harsh sunlight reflecting off the fog that had settled in.

Within seconds, I was rolling down the street, trying to figure the quickest route back to civilization. I turned on the car's GPS, but without knowing my destination, it wasn't much help. So, I switched it off and decided to rely on blind luck instead.

I quickly discovered that one of the problems with the suburbs was that there weren't a lot of unique landmarks. Each house I passed was equally spaced from the next, and every driveway had a similar high-end luxury vehicle or two parked in it. The only way I could tell one home from another was by the color of their mulch, their choice of garden statue, and whether they'd had enough money to pay for workers to relocate a decorative white granite boulder to their front yard. All in all, it looked like someone had built a house, hit the *duplicate* key a million times, and called it a community.

"What a bunch of sheep," I said before taking a left at the next street. With no clear path in mind, I hung a right and then another before coming to a stoplight at a four-lane road.

I flipped a coin in my head and decided to take another right. *What the heck.*

As I revved the engine, getting ready to turn, a dozen men and women in shorts and fluorescent shirts appeared on the sidewalk on the other side of the street. They were running at a good clip, two abreast through the foggy morning air. The reflective parts of their gear glowed so brightly, I had to squint more than I already was when I looked at them.

I shook my head and squeezed my eyes shut before opening them again. I wasn't sure if what I was seeing was real or a trick of the sunlight, but I was pretty sure their feet weren't touching the ground as they ran. That was weird enough, but what really confused me was when they collectively gave me the middle finger as they passed by.

Maybe they were just a bunch of health nuts who didn't like my German car with its crappy gas mileage, but getting dissed so early in the morning by a bunch of strangers was still a sucky way to start the first day of my new life.

"I thought runners were supposed to be nice," I said, shaking my head as I made my turn.

I gave the car some gas and sped away, taking a left at the next stoplight onto another main road. Within a minute, I passed two almost identical strip malls where the main differences were the names of their grocery stores and of their Chinese restaurants. However, the next shopping center had a Moon Dollarz, and I was tempted to stop for a much-needed dose of caffeine, since my adrenaline fix from the dog was wearing off. But when I saw the sign for Dulles Airport, I forgot about my java fix and took the on-ramp to the toll road instead.

With one hand on the wheel and the other on the stereo tuner, I searched for a decent song until I found a station blasting a favorite from the Clash. I leaned back with a grin and pressed the pedal down hard. The Audi responded beneath me, slammed my body into the bucket seat, and in seconds I was cruising 90 miles an hour in the left lane, while still in fourth gear.

Not bad.

Joe Strummer screamed at me through the car's speakers, wondering whether he should stay or go, but I wasn't experiencing that dilemma at all. I couldn't wait to make it to the airport and get my ass back home. Sure, I'd be in someone else's body, but that was better than the alternative.

As the car shot down the highway, I tried to smile, but the muscles in my new face were tight and gave way grudgingly, like the guy who owned my body before me hadn't used them very much.

A few months ago, I hadn't been laughing much either.

I'd been sick for a long time, with the cancer and the treatments eating away at me more and more each day. I wasn't going to make it much longer, but I didn't want to die. I mean, no one ever *wants* to die, but I *really* didn't want to. Not because I was afraid of death, but because I wanted a second chance to do things right and to prove to the world I wasn't just another blip in the history of music—that I was more than my one hit song, the annoyingly popular *Yeah, Yeah, No, No, Maybe*.

But the big C wasn't a nice mistress, and she wore me down, until I was living full-time in a hospital bed set up in my living room-turned-studio. I tried to play guitar once or twice and struggled to jot down some lyrics about how shitty I was feeling. But the chemicals the nurse pumped into my veins took away more than just the pain. They stole whatever energy I had left, and I could barely stay awake, much less do anything creative.

The doctors couldn't help me, and I didn't believe in God, so prayer wasn't an option either. I had no hope at all until Duane introduced me to Ahriman.

I started to relive that painful memory, but a red Hyundai almost ran into me, blowing its horn loud enough to wake the dead. The sound snapped me out of my daydream in time to see the sign for the airport exit coming up fast.

But before I could merge into the right lane, the surrounding air erupted louder than a stack of exploding Marshall amps. And the next thing I knew, I was cruising close to 100 mph on the other side of the road, heading in the wrong direction.

I swerved onto the shoulder, kicking up a cloud of gravel, trying to keep from plowing into a line of slower moving cars.

I had no idea what the hell had just happened, but I merged back into traffic, hunkered down, and took the next exit. I kept my foot off the brakes and sped around the cloverleaf until I doubled back and slingshotted across four lanes of traffic, headed for the airport once more.

It wasn't long before I saw the sign for Dulles again, and like a vinyl record that kept skipping at the same place in the same song, I heard another loud bang before the car was pointed in the wrong direction again.

This time I gunned it and neared 110 mph, threading my way between the other cars on the road like they weren't even moving.

I passed the exit for the Moon Dollarz and read the sign.

Ashburn.

That was the first time I knew the name of the place where I'd woken up that morning.

As I cruised along, the roadside markers counted down the miles to a place called Leesburg, which I'd never heard of before either. But since my plans for the airport weren't working out, Leesburg was my new destination.

I made it five miles before I ran into another loud boom, and once again the Audi was heading back toward Ashburn proper.

I slammed my palm into the steering wheel, and the inside of the car shook.

I shouted an incomprehensible curse above the tune blaring from the speakers. The guy in the song was angry about being stuck in a hotel in California and not being able to leave. I nodded in agreement, feeling his pain.

I looked up at the sky, certain that Ahriman was out there somewhere, laughing his ass off.

When I saw the Ashburn exit on my right again, I slowed down. I wasn't having any luck getting out of town, and I needed somewhere to collect my thoughts and to think things through.

I also needed some caffeine, pronto.

A few minutes later I pulled into the strip mall and parked in front of the Moon Dollarz.

I eased my way out of the car and shuffled across the parking lot like a zombie in need of a fix.

"Admission's free," I muttered as I opened the door to the coffee shop. "But you gotta pay to get out."

CHAPTER 4

T HE PUNGENT SCENT of roasted java made my mouth water instantly and brought back plenty of memories slinging espresso shots as a barista one summer at a local coffee shop trying to compete with Moon Dollarz. The job had paid crap, but I had plenty of energy and wrote some innovative speed metal ballads that year.

Smelling coffee beans wasn't as good as drinking them, but it was a start. Like I'd done so many times before at my local Moon Dollarz, I got in line and stared at the shelf of pastries and drooled over the sugar-laden goodies while waiting for my turn to order.

The franchised coffee shop was the same as it was in every other city, but smaller, and most of its dozen customers wore running clothes or expensive casual wear and slurped syrup-sweetened dessert drinks while the latest catchy but crappy pop song infiltrated their ears.

The cute girl working the espresso machine moved like a robot more than a human, but she was quick and knew her drinks. Person-by-person, I inched forward until I was face-to-face with the cashier.

"Would you like the usual, sir?" he said in a shaky voice.

I almost asked him what he was talking about before I remembered I wasn't in my regular body anymore. As far as the kid knew, I was the same guy who probably came into his shop every day and ordered the same thing. But just because I was stuck in a new outer shell didn't mean I had to be a slave to the last guy's taste buds.

"Give me a grande of whatever's brewing," I said. "As long as it's high-test."

The kid cocked his head, confused.

"Make sure it has lots of caffeine," I said, not even attempting to explain my reference. Normally I was more of a snob about my java. It needed the right beans, the right grind, and the right ratios, but just as important was the water. You'd think using filtered water wouldn't make that much of a difference, but it really does. But on that morning, I was happy to have any kind of coffee at all.

He gave me a quick nod that was more like a bow before writing my order on a cup and handing it to the barista girl.

"This is just a coffee," she snapped as she tried to hand the cup back to the cashier. "Get it yourself."

The cashier glanced at me, then whispered in the girl's ear. To my surprise, I could hear every word they said as clear as day.

"That's *him*," he said through gritted teeth. "Make a fresh pot and do it quick."

When the cashier turned back to me, I checked the back pocket of my khakis and sure enough—no wallet. I searched my pockets, hoping to find some cash, but I was dead broke.

I cursed myself for not looking through the house for money or a credit card before I left, and I started to shake—not because I was angry, but because I was afraid I wasn't going to get the stimulant I desperately needed.

I sized the kid up and wondered how well he knew the guy who used to own my body. I was about to ask him if he could put it on my tab, but he looked away.

"What can I get for you today, ma'am?" he said to the woman next in line.

"Listen…Elvil," I said, interrupting him as I read his name from the badge pinned to his shirt. "I'm a little light on funds right now."

He held up a finger to the customer who'd started to place her order and leaned over to me. I met him half-way, even though I had no idea why we were being so secretive about coffee.

"As always, there is no charge for your drink, sir," he said.

I stepped to the side and tried not to act confused while the girl started to brew my coffee.

The irritating pop song that was playing overhead ended, and another one took its place. I hated it as well.

The song began like most popular tunes, with a strong beat and a stylized singing voice altered by a computer to be pitch-perfect. The singer was comparing the woman he was in love with to a goddess. After the second line, another track joined in, fleshing out the melody with a chant that sounded like Tibetan monks praying. The singer kept crooning above it all while I rubbed my neck and frowned.

The kid behind the register must have seen me cringe, because even though he'd finished helping the woman and was on to the next guy in line, he turned his full attention to me again.

"Did I do something wrong?" he said.

I shook my head.

"It's this song."

He gave me a fake laugh and continued to ignore the man who was still trying to place his order.

"I love it, too," the cashier said with a huge smile. "Did you hear what happened? The guy who sang it died last night, right before it came out. It's already being played every hour on the radio, and the video has a million views. Sucks for him, but pretty cool, too, right?"

I felt a strong urge to make the cashier a mix tape filled with real music and shove it down his throat, but I reminded myself of a few things. First, I didn't plan on being in Ashburn long enough to make a mix tape for anyone. Also, it was probably illegal to wedge a cassette tape down his throat. And lastly, it would have been a wasted effort, since I was certain he had no idea what a cassette tape was.

As the song drilled its way into my brain, I tilted my head, listened more closely, and raised my eyebrows when I realized it sounded like my voice on the recording.

My head spun as I reached out to the cashier.

"Let me see the CD case," I said.

His eyes opened wide.

"The song's on my phone," he said. "I've never even owned a CD."

Of course he hadn't.

"Tell me the name of the singer."

As he fumbled with his smart phone, a guy with a deep voice spoke up behind me.

"You already know his name."

I turned around and saw a tall, refined-looking man in a black suit, with a pointed chin and a wry grin. It had sounded like he was standing near me, but he was sitting at a table in the back of the store.

"The artist's name is David Steele," he said. "You remember him now, don't you?"

The monster lifted his shot of espresso and motioned for me to join him.

I'd never seen Ahriman in his human form before, but I recognized his smell at once—a pungent combination of burnt coal, charred flesh, and sandalwood. It wasn't a scent I could ever forget.

Before I knew it, I was in front of his table, rattling off the words Duane had taught me that fatal night when I'd first summoned the demon.

"I command you, Ahriman, Avestan Angra Mainyu, the destructive spirit, the loathsome one, Druj, the lie, son of Ahura Mazdā, brother to Spenta Mainyu. I command you to do my bidding and release me from this unholy place."

That stopped the bastard in mid-espresso sip. He moved his hand to his chest and winced, and for a second, I thought everything was going to be all right.

Then he laughed so loud that the rest of the customers should have run away en masse. They should have at least been staring. But no one moved or looked up from their drinks.

"Thank you for that," Ahriman said with a smirk. "It's not often I have a chance to have a good laugh. Everyone is usually so serious in these matters. Now please, have a seat and join me for a drink. We have a few items to discuss."

Stunned, I sat, not understanding why the demon wasn't under my power. I'd used the right names, but I hadn't been standing in a protective circle. Maybe that was it. I opened my mouth to try again, but a cup of steaming coffee appeared on the table in front of me with the name *John* scribbled on the side of it.

I glanced behind me at the cashier, but he was at the register, taking someone else's order. I took a sip of the hot, black liquid as the chorus for the song started up again. Several of the people in the shop sang along mindlessly.

When the world ends
With a wound like a whisper
When the world ends
Through the pain I will miss her
When the world ends
It will break like a blister
When the world ends
All my blood will go with her

The words were utter crap, and they sure didn't sound like they belonged to a hit song, but the beat was infectious, and even my traitorous foot started tapping along without my consent.

"It's only your first day, John," he said, pointing at the name on my coffee cup. "It's normal for things to be rough as you adjust to your new surroundings."

"Who the hell is John?"

"John Starling is the one who gave up his body for you."

"Tell him I'm very grateful to him and to you as well, for whatever that's worth to you, but my name is *David*. And I'm not having a hard time adjusting to anything other than being trapped here against my will."

Ahriman clapped his hands together and let out a roar of a belly laugh.

"You really don't remember everything yet, do you?" he said. "Worry not. I have no doubt your full memory will return soon."

As soon as he said that, images from my past poured into my head, but none of them were good.

CHAPTER 5

I REMEMBERED A sense of freedom when the doctors stopped trying to save my life.

They didn't say it, but I could tell by the way they acted when I was around. Discussions turned to ways they could make me comfortable instead of different approaches for fighting the disease. They'd given up, but I kept looking for a way out. Whenever I could stay awake long enough, I searched the web, looking for any possibility, no matter how slim. I'd already been through all the legal experimental drugs, so I started thinking outside the box—way outside the box. I tried yoga, energy work, acupuncture, even becoming vegan. Nothing worked. Eventually, I turned to a long shot—a glimmer of ridiculous hope that came in the form of Duane—the little brother of my drummer, Mark.

I liked Mark more than most people. He'd stuck by me even after the money stopped pouring in and was always there to lay down a beat for one of my new songs. But his brother Duane was strange—the kind of guy who wore silver pentacles for jewelry and only wore clothing that was black. At first, I thought Mark was kidding about Duane wanting to help, but he convinced me that talking to his brother couldn't hurt.

Turned out, he was pretty wrong about that.

Duane showed up one afternoon with his mop of hair falling across his forehead and his hands in the back pockets of his skinny black jeans. We talked for a while, and he did his best to offer me hope.

"I can introduce you to someone," he said. "A spirit, actually. His name is Ahriman, and he can help, but he wants something in return."

I remembered laughing when he said that, right before I coughed up a load of blood. When I finished rattling and hacking, Duane was still there, still looking serious but also afraid.

"I don't believe in ghosts," I said.

"He's a spirit—not a ghost. And you don't have to believe," he said. "Not for this."

"Where is he?" I asked—my voice raspy from coughing.

"You have to say *yes*, first," he said. "Then I'll teach you how to call him."

Duane turned away, like he was listening to someone I couldn't see or hear.

"He says he can't wait to talk to you."

Well, that shut me up. I still figured the kid was full of crap or certifiably insane, but I was dying anyway, so I said *yes*.

I memorized the words he taught me. I didn't understand any of them, but I'd always been good at remembering the sounds of things. The hard part was making the circle. Circles are harder to draw than you'd think. Duane guided me, but I was the one who had to make the shape and the ancient symbols surrounding it, and it took me three times to get everything right. After the preparations were complete, with Duane by my side, I tried to call the spirit, but nothing happened.

After an hour, the candle burned down until it was black, Duane went home, talking quietly to himself, and I fell asleep.

I opened my eyes in the middle of the night to the smell of burning. As I peered into the darkness of my studio, I saw a dark shape that wasn't quite human sitting on its haunches at the foot of my bed. He had the form of a large man with deadly sharp horns protruding from his forehead, and he reeked of dead animal.

"I summoned you," I said in a shaky voice, wishing Duane were there so I could punch his face until it fell off for not telling me Ahriman was a large, putrid demon. I'd never seen, much less met, a demon before, but it turned out they were a lot like pornography— hard to define, but obvious when you saw one.

Ahriman stared at me with fiery red eyes before speaking in a gut-rattling, profondo voice.

"Death seeps from your pores," he said, sniffing the air. "I can smell it."

"Are you here to help or give me compliments?" I said, still nervous, but trying to assert myself. I was the one who had done the summoning after all.

"I have the power to save your mortal life and grant you a new beginning, if that is your desire. I only ask one thing in return for my services."

"And what's that?" I said.

Ahriman told me what he wanted, and I laughed until I coughed up more blood—not because what he asked for was funny, but because it wasn't worth all that much.

In exchange for saving my doomed life, he wanted to write my next set of songs—my comeback album, he called it. That was it. A few songs in exchange for my life.

I thought he was nuts, but he was right about death being close, and I figured either eternal darkness or something worse was waiting for me on the other side. With nothing to lose and everything to gain, I agreed to his offer. As soon as I said *yes*, Ahriman closed his eyes, like he was savoring a bite of his favorite food. When he opened them again, I felt better—not cured, but better—healthier for the first time in a while.

"I'm still sick," I said.

"When you have honored your obligations fully, I will heal you fully," the demon said. "You have my word."

"I won't die from cancer?"

"You have my bond," he said with a deliberate nod. "You will not die from this cancer or from any other human disease—ever."

"Then let's do this," I said. "My life is in your hands."

No sooner had the words left my mouth than Ahriman crawled up my bed, quicker than any natural being could move, and he lay down on top of my chest. I turned away from his stench, trying not to vomit as he scratched at my torso with his ragged claws.

I looked back in time to see his twisted face unhinge, his jaws opening like a shark preparing to devour its prey. I waited for his attack, but in a blink, he was gone, and I was alone.

That's what I thought, at least.

It turned out Ahriman was still there, but he'd entered my body and had become a part of me. He was inside me, closer than my own shadow and twice as dark. For lack of a better explanation, and because there was no other way to say it, I had been possessed by a demon.

But it wasn't anything like what I'd seen in the movies. My head didn't spin around. I didn't breathe frosty air from my lungs. And I didn't float.

"Things are going to be okay," I said to myself, as I swallowed hard and closed my eyes. "I'll get through this."

And after a minute or two, I felt stronger and my head cleared enough for me to think straight.

But my stomach turned to knots as I felt Ahriman forcing me, compelling me to get up and making my legs move without my consent. I slid from the hospital bed, shuffled over to my chair, and picked up my Les Paul. I plugged it in, turned on the amp, slung the strap over my shoulder, and started playing.

My fingers danced and skipped across the fretboard with skill developed from a lifetime of practice. But the chords and the notes weren't mine. The demon was controlling my hands, and the music they made belonged to him.

Next, my foot started to tap out a beat. But it was the demon's rhythm, not mine.

Finally, my voice erupted in words and lyrics I'd never heard or even imagined before, but those were his too.

Everything was.

It went that way for nearly two hours, and near dawn I wrote down the music to our first hellish collaboration. I didn't like the melody or the lyrics, but most of all, I hated that someone was using me to create their own music. It felt unholy.

As much as I despised every moment, the next couple of months were filled with creativity and productivity I hadn't known since I wrote my one and only hit single. With the demon driving, we came up with song after song in the early morning hours of each night, until a new album started to form from a dozen new tunes.

And to be honest, I didn't like any of them.

I'd spent my entire life going from job to job, playing crappy clubs at night, trying in my off-hours to recreate that lighting in a bottle I'd once held. And now someone or *something* else was using the talent I'd built up and earned over the years—bastardizing it to write utter trash I would never have put out under my own name.

I was sure the demon could hear my thoughts about the music, but I openly fantasized and hoped for the songs to fail anyway, even though I knew it would be my name on the album and not his.

All I wanted to do was finish the album, start my new life, and of course make Ahriman pay one day for everything he was making me go through.

I knew he could hear those thoughts, too, but I just didn't care.

CHAPTER 6

AHRIMAN SNAPPED HIS fingers.

"If you are finished with your daydreaming—" he said.

I blinked, as his pointed face came into focus. In his human form, he didn't have horns, but it was still unnerving as hell sitting across from him.

"Duane told me names were important," I said. "They give humans the power to command demons. And I used your names—all of them—just like Duane taught me. Why won't you obey me?"

"Names *are* the key to controlling beings of power," he said. "But demons do not share their true names with just anyone. *Ahriman* and all the other names you used for me—none were my true name. They were only attempts by human beings over the millennia to understand that which their kind was never meant to grasp."

"They worked before," I said. "I used them to summon you."

"You called me," he said. "But you did not summon me. I came to you of my own free will, John."

"Stop calling me that. My name is David."

"Lesson number one," Ahriman said, before sipping his espresso with a grin. "Your name is John Starling now. His is the body in which you reside, and his is the name by which people in Ashburn will know you. Hence, while you are here, you will be *John*."

"You can say that all you want if it makes you happy, but I'm not John, and you can't make me tell people to call me that."

"Lesson number two," he said, ignoring me. "You are here to serve a purpose—to work off your debt—and you will remain in Ashburn until you have done so in full."

"I already paid you," I said, unable to keep the tension from my voice. "I kept my end of the deal. I let you write my album. That's what you said you wanted, and that's what I gave you."

"Once again, you did not let me do anything," he said, fixing me with his dark gaze. "I demanded a price, and you accepted. As such, it was a fair trade. As far as my album is concerned, have you heard that it debuted at the top of the charts? Not a bad showing for my first creative endeavor, wouldn't you agree?"

"If you're so happy with it, that's great," I said. "So what's the problem?"

"Your music paid for only part of what you owe."

"That's ridiculous," I said. "What about your end of the bargain? I was supposed to live and to be able to write and play music again."

"And you *will* make music again, my boy, if you decide to do so. You could write a song right now if you wanted. No one is stopping you. You could record your new song and sell it, if anyone would buy it, of course. But not as David Steele."

Ahriman raised his finger, silencing the question I was about to ask.

"You cannot record as David Steele any longer, because as your barista friend mentioned, David Steele is dead. You are no longer *he*, and *he* is no longer *thee*. After all, you cannot be someone who is no longer alive."

I calmed my breathing and tried to let go of my anger and frustration. It didn't make any difference to me what some asshole from Hell wanted to call me. I knew who I was, and once I returned to my studio, I could make all the music I wanted, and I could release it under my name. I didn't look like David Steele anymore, but I was still me, and I knew how to write a killer song. Maybe I'd become a recluse—living in seclusion, so no one would see me. As long as people liked my music, I wouldn't care.

"You can call me John, if you want," I said, "but I'm not going to work off some made-up debt to you. I kept my part of the deal, and I don't owe you anything."

Ahriman slammed his hand down on the table.

"You are so correct!" he said. "You did come through for me, and the album is doing oh so well. Your once-famous name, combined with my natural instinct and talent—it was a match made in—well, not in Heaven. And for that, I truly am grateful. However, the fact remains that you do have an outstanding debt, and you have no choice but to pay it."

I wanted to say something stupid and non-effectual, but even through my confusion and rage, I knew I had no say in the matter and no real alternatives. It wasn't like I could take him to Hell's court and sue him for breach of contract. To help keep my own mouth shut, I forced myself to take a sip of my coffee. The pungent liquid shot past my lips and landed in my churning stomach, but I remained silent.

"Ashburn will be your home for the next ten years," he said, "during which time you will work for me."

A decade was a long time. My situation was going from bad to worse.

"I'll figure a way out of here a lot sooner than that," I said.

Ahriman tapped the tabletop with one of his knuckles and thought for a few seconds.

"I am not pleased with the way our relationship is unfolding," he said, stretching his neck violently to one side. "However, never let it be said that I was not fair and honorable in our dealings. I do have a reputation to maintain after all. As such, I will make you an offer only this one time. If you would rather not spend the next ten years in my servitude, I will place you into another body—one that is dying of cancer, to be fair. You will live out your last days as a human, and you will soon be free of this life and of me, forever."

I hated him, but he'd made his point. A decade above dirt, working for a demon in the suburbs and pretending to be someone else was better than an eternity of darkness and death.

"Why here?" I said, looking for a way to at least improve the course of my fate. "There's plenty of sin and corruption in big cities."

"Because this is where I need you," Ahriman said, as if he were explaining a simple concept to a three-year-old child. "Ashburn is a special place. It is where I relocate supernatural creatures who mean me harm or who are dangerous to humans and their world."

"There're more things like you here?" I asked.

"There is nothing like me anywhere," Ahriman said, with a sneer. "But yes, Ashburn has its fair share of demons, forgotten deities, spirits, and other assorted foul creatures. We're all different sides of the same coin, really. Did you know the word *demon* comes from the ancient Greek word, *daimon*, which meant god or god-like?"

"Fascinating," I said, not meaning it. "And what exactly do you expect me to do here in this magical land to pay you back?"

Ahriman raised his eyebrows and pulled his head away in mock surprise.

"I see the problem now. You have misunderstood me," he said with fake enthusiasm. "John sacrificed his body and gave up his life here as my faithful servant—for you. You will work for me, but John is the one to whom your debt is owed."

"How can I owe a dead man?"

Ahriman picked at something under one of his black fingernails.

"He was one of my best servants, you know—a lesser demon, but faithful and hard working. John played an important role here. He kept the peace and enforced my commandments."

Now it was my turn to laugh.

"I've held a lot of strange jobs in my life. I've been a barista, a pet sitter, sold books door-to-door, and even done some private investigating, but I'm no enforcer," I said, with an exasperated breath. "I don't even like following rules."

Ahriman smiled, like he was laughing at a joke I couldn't hear.

"Do not be so quick to dismiss yourself. I would not have chosen you if I were not certain that you have the skills to succeed here. You will assume John's identity and his role with no one being the wiser, and you will ensure the supernatural beings of Ashburn continue to obey my commandments.

"They are very simple and based on common sense, really. My first commandment is the most important. No supernatural being leaves Ashburn. Ever. Including you. I have, of course, put in place precautions to ensure compliance from my supernatural guests. Some of them have insisted on testing my boundaries in the past, but none have ever succeeded. John made sure of that, which is why no one here liked him very much. It's also why they will not like you either."

He held up a finger, silencing me again before I'd had a chance to interrupt.

"Additionally," he said, "no supernatural creature may kill, annihilate, or in any other way destroy another—which they *will* try to do on occasion—nor may they harm or kill any member of Ashburn's human population."

"Of course," I said, trying my hardest to make sure Ahriman heard the sarcasm in my voice.

"Lastly, Ashburn's supernatural community must remain a secret from humans. If you discover anyone breaking this or any of my other laws, you must resolve the situation promptly. Just remember, thou shall not leave; thou shall not kill; and thou shall not tell. Simple."

I nodded, not because I was agreeing to do what he demanded, but because I wanted him to stop talking.

"There *is* one last item," he said. "But it is more of a guideline, and it applies only to you."

"I can't wait," I said, my head throbbing.

"I advise you to smile, be happy, and enjoy your new life. Second to me alone, you are the ruler of this town."

The pained look on my face must have been obvious, because Ahriman set his glass down, and frowned. His movements were correct and practiced, but I could tell his sympathetic expression was manufactured.

"You do not seem happy," he said.

He was right. I wasn't happy. Because working as a demon's enforcer was very far down on my list of things I wanted to do for the next ten years.

"What if I refuse to work for you? Maybe I can't leave, but I don't have to play your game either."

Ahriman became very still, and all attempt at levity left his face.

"But you do. I am not *asking* for your cooperation. I am giving you a command."

"And if I don't obey?" I said, despite the lump in my throat.

He leaned in close and whispered a word I'd never heard before but which was immediately both intimate and familiar. My brain didn't know what was going on, but my gut did, and fear spread through my limbs and numbed my fingers.

Ahriman stood straight and adjusted his suit jacket.

"That," he said, "was your name. Your *real* name. With it, I could order you to tear out your own heart, and you would do so without hesitation. You *will* be my enforcer here in Ashburn. You will feel compelled to do so, even when you don't wish to. And if you work against me in any way, you will die—permanently."

I remained silent, and Ahriman nodded, satisfied that he'd made his point at last.

He had.

"Do not worry," he said. "Very soon, the job will become second nature to you. Until that time, I will return to monitor your progress, beginning with next Monday, at which time I expect to find you settled in and performing your duties."

The conversation was over as far as he was concerned, but I needed more answers.

"How will I make them listen to me?"

Ahriman exhaled loudly.

"Everyone in Ashburn feared and obeyed John. As long as they continue to think you are him, they will be afraid of you and obey you as well."

"Why were they afraid of him?" I said.

"For many reasons, but mostly because he knew their true names—just as I know yours."

"What if I can't stop someone from breaking one of your laws?" I said.

Ahriman's face grew dark.

"If you fail me, I will take corrective measures," he said calmly. "And they will not be pleasant. I am capable of inflicting vast amounts of misery over the span of ten years."

Without another word, Ahriman turned and left me alone in the Moon Dollarz, imagining all the horrible things a demon like him could do to me with nothing but time on his hands.

"I'm still not John," I whispered to myself.

I downed the last sip of my black coffee, then got up to leave. By the time I made it outside, Ahriman was gone, but a tall brunette with a shapely body wrapped in a tight red dress almost ran into me when I stepped onto the sidewalk.

When she saw my face, she seemed surprised and frightened at the same time.

I started to say something awkward and probably not nearly as funny as I thought it was, but before I could embarrass myself, she stepped in close, gave me a crushing hug, and kissed me.

"I'm so relieved you're alive," she said softly in my ear. "I thought he had destroyed you."

I wasn't quite ready to thank Ahriman for being his prisoner in suburbia, but as I recovered from the best kiss I'd ever had, I started to think that being stuck in Ashburn might at least have a few perks I hadn't thought of before.

Then again, I'd been wrong plenty of times in my life, and for some reason, this felt like one of them.

CHAPTER 7

"WOULD YOU LIKE help opening the store?" the woman said with a smile that made my mouth dry and my pulse race. "Since we'll be a few minutes early, maybe we can go in the back and have some fun before someone shows up."

I tried to say something witty, but all I managed was a noise that sounded like something was stuck in my throat. She looked at me with narrowed eyes, trying to figure out what was wrong with me, and I couldn't blame her.

Thankfully, she gave up and started strolling down the sidewalk, with me doing a double step to catch up with her.

I still didn't know her name, but I had a feeling she was John's girlfriend, which technically made her my girlfriend as well—at least as far as she was concerned.

A few steps later, I realized I had another problem. I didn't know which shop was mine, so each time we approached a storefront, I walked slower and followed her lead.

We passed a salon and spa with a chalk sign outside that advertised a sale on Botox. Thankfully, she kept walking.

Next up was the ABC store. For a moment, my hopes rose, but she moved past it as well. I walked faster to keep up with the strides of her long legs.

In quick succession, we passed a store called Enchanted Scrapbooking, a grocery store, a children's martial arts studio, a gym called The Box, a place filled with nothing but mailboxes, a pet store, a store decorated completely in pink called Ms. Fancy, and of course, a Chinese restaurant.

And still, John's hot girlfriend continued on.

Next up was a running store, then an Indian restaurant, and finally a used bookstore. The sign painted on the window read, *Ancient Pages*. Finally, a store I'd actually shop in. When the woman stopped, I exhaled with relief. I'd always loved books—reading and collecting them—and if I had to own something besides a music store, a bookstore would be next on my list.

The woman in red turned, waiting for me to unlock the door.

I reached into my pocket, took out the key to the Audi, and noticed there was another key on the same ring.

"Are you going to let me in?" she said, with a devilish grin.

"I'm on it…babe," I said, cringing at how stupid that word sounded coming out of my mouth.

Thankfully, the key fit the lock.

Once inside, she flicked on the lights but left the sign turned so the *Closed* side was facing outward.

The store wasn't large, but it was comfortable and had been designed to resemble someone's personal home library, with a few cushioned reading chairs, a small secretary's desk, and an oriental rug. The shelves were over-stuffed with books, most of them spine-out and covered with a light patina of dust.

Inhaling the intoxicating and heady scent of old paper and dust was bliss—the opposite of what I'd grown used to in the antiseptic sterility of the hospital and my studio toward the end of my life.

"Are you coming?" the woman said, beckoning me with a curled finger to the back of the store.

Before I could get far, she pulled me behind a shabby set of curtains that separated the front and back of the store. It afforded the tiny back room the smallest amount of privacy, and within seconds, we were kissing again.

And it was good.

But as most of my body surged with excitement, my chest tightened with anxiety. I may have looked like John, but I wasn't him, even if she didn't know that yet. It was tempting to go with flow and enjoy myself, but the annoying voice of morality wouldn't shut up.

I started to pull away, in a half-hearted attempt to do the right thing, but she kissed me harder as the passion between us heated up and her groping turned more physical. The hotter things became, the more I felt a darkness rising inside me—a lust fueled by animal cravings at a level I'd never before experienced.

The next thing I knew, the voice of reason in my head stopped talking, and my instincts took control.

Before I could let loose, I heard a woman's voice through the fog of hormones, calling to me from the front of the store.

"Are you back there, John? I need to speak with you immediately."

I looked at John's girlfriend in time to see her face distort into a savage snarl, complete with sharpened fangs and glowing red eyes. My eyebrows raised and my libido sunk as I switched from passion to fight-or-flight mode.

My heart slammed against the wall of my chest, confusion and fear filling my veins. But as I watched, her face softened again, and she was once again beautiful. She stood tall and adjusted her dress, then her hair.

"You'd better see what she wants," she said with her arms crossed in front of her chest. "You know she won't go away. She never does."

CHAPTER 8

I ADJUSTED MY polo shirt and stepped out from behind the curtain, with John's girlfriend by my side. There in the middle of the store stood the perfect picture of a high school librarian with the morning light shimmering off her tightly wrapped bun of blonde hair. Her form-fitting skirt ended below her knees, and her blouse was buttoned up to her neck, making it look like she was bound by her clothing instead of wearing it. She was attractive in a snooty way but seemed like the kind of person who would punish me for something I hadn't yet done.

"I don't think we're open yet," I said casually as I checked to make sure my zipper was closed.

The woman looked past me and glared at John's girlfriend.

"Good morning, Sybil," she said in an icy voice. "John and I need to speak in private—about business."

Sybil tilted her head and gave the woman a tight smile.

"We were about to conduct some business of our own when you interrupted, *Oizys*. Don't you have something better to do, like handing out fines to people for putting their trash cans out too early?"

Oizys chuckled. Her mouth spread into a smile that grew larger and larger until it seemed too wide for her face.

"Sadly, maintaining a neat and tidy neighborhood is as close to godliness as I will ever get," she said. "The fact that I enjoy my work is simply icing on the cake."

The last thing I wanted was to stop kissing Sybil, but I needed to slow things down until I could sort out my moral dilemma, and Oizys provided the perfect excuse. Besides, as Oizys stood there with her hands on her hips, she seemed deadly serious about needing to talk with me.

"I'm sure it won't take long," I said with a sigh.

Sybil leaned in and kissed me on the lips. She lingered longer than was appropriate, and I got the feeling she wasn't kissing me as much as she was claiming her territory—a point not lost on Oizys.

"I had a long night and need to sleep," Sybil said to me. "I'll meet you at the concert later, like we planned. Don't make me wait too long."

I didn't know what concert she was talking about, but I nodded and watched her strut past Oizys on her way out the door.

"You're nicer than usual," Oizys said. "You look different too. Maybe it's because you're not wearing those ridiculous goggles for once, although I'm not sure I like the new you."

Before I could figure out how to respond, she moved closer and sniffed my neck, just like the dog had done earlier. I wasn't sure whether that was the way supernatural beings greeted each other or if it was just an Ashburn thing. But when I leaned forward, ready to take a big whiff of her neck, she turned away and sat down in one of the store's plush reading chairs.

"I have information that will interest you," she said, crossing her legs.

I bobbed my head, pretending to understand what she was talking about, while she tapped her foot, waiting.

It was a Mexican standoff, and I knew I'd be the first one to cave. After all, I had nothing to offer, whereas she possessed news I evidently couldn't wait to hear.

"You win," I said. "What do you want to tell me? Did you figure out a way to leave town?"

Subtlety had never been my strong point.

"There's no need to brag, just because you can leave this place whenever you wish."

I tried hard to suppress my smile, but inside I was ecstatic, because if John knew how to leave Ashburn, that meant it was possible. All I had to do was figure out how he did it. For the first time that day, I was hopeful.

"I'm stuck here like the rest of us," I said, holding her gaze. "If I could leave, I would."

"I don't believe you," she said. "But I do believe someone else has also figured a way out of here and that they're going to attempt an escape any day now."

I didn't care if every supernatural entity in town left Ashburn and moved to the beach. But I didn't want them leaving before me. Ahriman never said what he'd do to me if someone broke out of Ashburn on my watch, but he knew my real name, and that meant I needed to be careful.

I hadn't been in my new job for even an hour, and already I had to deal with something I wasn't prepared for.

"Who is it?" I asked.

"If I told you," she said, with an evil grin, "I'd be ratting out one of my fellow inmates, and although I don't mind compromising what ethics I still have, doing so doesn't come cheap. I would expect you to compensate above and beyond our normal arrangement."

"How much do you want?" I said, remembering I still didn't have any money.

"It's not like you to make jokes, especially when discussing something this serious," she said. "You know what I want from you."

"Humor me, and tell me anyway," I said.

"I want you to owe me—to be in my debt."

"Consider it done," I said. "Now, tell me who it is."

She was silent for a moment before speaking.

"Give me your demon bond, first."

I didn't know whether giving my demon bond required a special hand shake or a magic word or a pony, but I'd role-played stranger things in my Dungeons and Dragons days, so I decided to wing it. I closed my eyes and counted to three while I pretended to be contemplating something deep and mystical. When I opened my eyes, I looked at her as intensely as I could.

"My bond is given," I said.

To my surprise, she accepted my vow with a smile. In hindsight, her reaction should've been my first clue that owing her a favor wasn't a good idea. That being said, once I was in her debt, she kept her promise and told me everything.

"One of my human homeowners—the Voodoo priestess I've told you about—she's up to no good," she said with a smirk. "Marie Lacroix received tickets from authorities twice in the last few weeks for sacrificing livestock in her living room—chickens, I believe. She was offering more gifts to those damn ancestral spirits of hers again—her *loa*. She told the Sheriff it was all an innocent part of her religion, but I'm sure she was asking for a favor from them. And there's only one reason she'd need the power of her loa—to break through Ahriman's spells that keep us here."

She crossed her arms, waiting for my reaction.

"You figured all that out because she killed a few chickens?" I said.

"The animal sacrifices make it easier for her to attract the loa's attention. If she's bonded with the right ancestor and curried his favor, she may have figured out a way to leave Ashburn. Voodoo spirits are notoriously clever and love to meddle in the affairs of the living."

"But she's a human."

Oizys glared at me, exasperated.

"You're trying my patience today," she said. "Yes, she's human, but she has supernatural power, and Ahriman will be angry if she escapes."

"How long before you think she'll try it?" I said.

Oizys scrunched up her lips, acting like she was trying to remember something, but I could tell she was faking it—trying to build the drama—making me wait.

"My administrative assistant has been watching her house, but he hasn't learned much yet. Her residence is protected by a web of Voodoo spells and charms, and her front door is guarded by a nest of zombies working her garden."

"Did you say she has zombies for gardeners?" I asked. "As in the undead walking the earth, eating human flesh and brains kind of zombies?"

Oizys shook her head and gave a half smile.

"Why are you treating me this way today, John? You know very well that a Voodoo priestess would own Haitian zombies to do her bidding."

Oizys stood up, then handed me her business card with an address written on the back of it.

"Regardless of which creatures are in her employ, I know you'll handle this appropriately, as you always have with matters like these in the past."

"I'm grateful for the tip," I said. "But other than me owing you a favor, why are you so concerned about her escaping."

Oizys glanced at her shoes.

"I do not like when residents disobey my rules."

I nodded, although I knew she was hiding something.

"If you let one person get away with something, I find there's often a domino effect, and then it's nothing but work, work, work to get everyone back in line again. That being said, I will leave you to your business. I'm sure you will want to deal with the priestess as soon as possible."

"Absolutely," I said as Oizys turned and hurried out the door, leaving me in a wake of blissful silence.

I stepped to the window to make sure she was really gone. As her pink VW Beetle pulled away, I shook my head at her MAKUHRT vanity plate.

With the shop to myself, I checked out a few books on one of the shelves. I'd always been a big reader of fiction—all the way from fantasy to the classics—but I didn't recognize any of the titles I picked up, which meant they were either very rare, very expensive, or both.

After a few minutes of poking around, I found the religion section and pulled out a book called "The Serpent and the Rainbow: A Harvard Scientist's Astonishing Journey into the Secret Societies of Haitian Voodoo, Zombies, and Magic."

I slouched in the reading chair and made it about half-way through the first page before my eyes started to close, so I set the book aside for later. Closing my eyes, I took a deep breath and tried to process my day. I'd woken up that morning, alive but trapped in a demon's body and stuck in the suburbs of Ashburn with no way to leave for the next ten years. And to top it off, I was being forced to act as Ahriman's enforcer—a job for which I was highly unqualified. I needed to sit for a while and get my head straight, but as soon as I closed my eyes, I felt a tugging in my gut, a spell-driven compulsion I couldn't control or resist to look into the Marie Lacroix matter right away.

I shut off the store lights and stepped outside onto the sidewalk. The sun was higher in the sky, and the shopping center was alive with a constant flow of European luxury performance cars, oversized trucks, and SUVs.

When I turned to lock up the shop, I noticed a petite Asian woman in front of the Thai restaurant next door, standing only a few feet away from me.

She bowed her head without looking at me.

"Good morning, David," she said in a sweet tone that was familiar and alien to me at the same time. "I have many names, but you may call me Rose. You would honor me if you were to join me for a meal when you find the time. You are always welcome in my restaurant, and the food is quite good I assure you."

"That's very nice of you," I said with a disinterested smile as I turned the key in the lock.

A fraction of a second later, I realized Rose had just called me David, but when I looked up, she was gone.

CHAPTER 9

M Y STOMACH YELLED at me to visit Marie, but my brain wanted to find Rose. I put my face to the glass door of the Thai Restaurant and tried to spot her walking around inside. But the place was dark, and the chairs were turned upside down, resting on the tops of the tables.

I stepped back and read the sign—*Bangrak Thai*. I had no idea what *Bangrak* meant, but the fact that its owner knew who I was left me unsettled and curious. Unsettled, because I was paranoid about supernatural beings and names. Curious, because if she knew who I was, maybe she knew other things as well, including how to get out of Ashburn.

I decided to take her up on her offer as soon as possible, but first, I had a job to do. As soon as I was in the car, I pulled out the business card Oizys had given me and punched Marie's address into the car's GPS.

Soon, I was cruising through the streets of Ashburn, and my brain wandered to my fantasy of becoming a mysterious, recluse musician, putting out new songs on a regular basis while living a life of secrecy and shunning public adoration.

As I thought things through, I wondered if I'd be better off starting over from scratch, with a whole new identity. Maybe not being David Steele anymore was a blessing in disguise. For one thing, my new face was younger and, in all honesty, better looking than my old one. The best part of it was that I'd no longer be known as the guy who sang the *Yeah, Yeah* song. For the first time in decades, my music would be free to stand on its own again.

I smiled as I reached over to turn on the stereo, but as I passed another shopping center, a sign featuring a golden harp superimposed on a musical staff caught my eye. And at the bottom of the sign was a single beautiful word.

Music.

Normally, visiting a music shop called *Music* would be as bad as buying a can of soup labeled *Soup* or shopping at a store called *Store*. But the place probably sold guitars, and I was seriously in need of one, so I pulled into the parking lot and decided the Voodoo priestess could wait a little longer.

When I walked in, I realized at once what I'd found. It was a music store, as advertised, but it was mostly there to serve the needs of young students and the beginner hobbyist who had more money than common sense.

Bins of sheet music filled the middle of the store, and black instrument cases of every size and shape teetered in sloppy stacks in the back corner. But the walls were what interested me. That was where the guitars were. I didn't have to get very close to see they were the bottom-of-the-line student models. But they had strings, and I was willing to bet they made a sound when strummed. And anything would be an improvement over what I currently had for a guitar, which was exactly nothing.

As I looked them over, trying to pick out the best of the worst, someone behind me cleared his throat. I turned around and saw a short, pudgy man with light brown skin and a bushy black mustache standing behind the counter. His substantial eyebrows shot up and his eyes widened when he saw my face. I didn't know why, but he looked at me with equal parts surprise and fear, the same way Sybil had when I first ran into her outside the Moon Dollarz.

"Mind if I try one?" I said, nodding toward one of the guitars on the wall.

"You may do whatever you please in my store," he said as he straightened items on his counter that didn't need straightening.

I pulled down one of the Fender imitations, knowing it wasn't going to be a high-quality instrument. Touching the thing confirmed it. The weight was off—too light to be a real Telecaster. The pickups were cheap, and the neck was a little bowed.

But for only a hundred dollars, it would give me what I needed—except for one tiny problem I kept forgetting about. I still didn't have any money.

The expletive that shot from my mouth made my new friend jump, but he recovered quickly, as I sat down and decided to give the guitar—and John's fingers—a try.

A chill ran up my spine as I plugged the pseudo-Tele into an amp and tuned the strings. What if I couldn't play? My mind knew what to do, but that wouldn't matter if my fingers wouldn't do their part.

The next thing I knew, my new fingers were dancing across the fretboard like they'd been playing for years.

I sighed, closed my eyes, and lost myself in the notes and chords I was coaxing from the instrument. I didn't even pay attention to the G string as it started to slip out of tune. It was enough that I was making music again—my first song since the start of my new life.

While I was playing, the store owner didn't utter a sound. Instead, he gave me one of the greatest gifts a man could give—complete silence. When I finally took a break and looked up, he hadn't moved at all. He was just staring at me as he wrung his sweaty little hands together.

That's when I remembered what Ahriman had said about the supernatural residents of Ashburn being afraid of John. Given the look on the store owner's face, I began to suspect he was one of *us*.

Regardless of who or what he was, I still didn't have any money to pay for the guitar, so I handed it back to him with a nod.

"Not bad for the price," I said. "I'll be back for it later, if you can set it aside for me."

I turned to leave, but the owner held up his hand.

"Your playing was masterful," he said. "I did not know you were a musician. I keep instruments of higher quality in the back, you know—my personal collection—if you would like to see them."

"That would be great—" I said before snapping my fingers like I was trying to remember his name.

"It is all right," he said. "I thought that because of last week, perhaps you might remember my name, but I understand. You are a very busy and important individual. I am Enkimdu, but you may call me Chaz."

"Are you sure?"

"I am very sure of my name."

"Not what I meant," I said, pursing my lips. "I was talking about your guitars. I wouldn't mind seeing them if you have a minute."

He smiled and led me to the back of his store, chatting with me as we walked.

"You will love my axes," he said. "They are works of art."

I stopped my eyes in mid-roll and forced myself not to laugh at the fact that he'd just referred to his guitars as *axes*.

Much like the bookstore, the back of the music shop consisted of a small office with a cluttered desk, a computer, and two filing cases. The only things missing were the guitars he'd promised to show me. Before I could say anything, he produced a rusted key and touched it to the wall. From nowhere, a door appeared.

Chaz unlocked the door, and we stepped into a hidden room of enormous size. I raised my eyebrows and stared at the stunning collection of guitars. Some of them were top-of-the-line models from the major brands while others were clearly handmade by master craftsmen who made custom instruments for either very special or very rich players. I gave a low whistle and looked at Chaz with increased respect. At the same time, I wondered how he could afford all his beautiful guitars. It certainly wasn't from the profits he made selling sheet music and renting tubas to kids.

I reached over with care and picked up a tiger-stripe green PRS with the brand's standard mother-of-pearl inlaid birds running up and down its neck.

"Let me hear what you got," I said, handing it to him. He grinned and plugged the guitar into an old Marshall amp, like he was handling a religious artifact. Once the amp started to hum, his fingers began moving across the fretboard.

He started slowly and simply with a series of perfectly formed chords and followed them up with arpeggios, plucking each note in one chord before moving on to the next. He gradually increased his speed and added complex riffs, bending strings and holding notes and playing with all his heart.

I'd seen plenty of better guitarists in my life. I used to be one of them. But Chaz was good. Really good, especially for a guy in the suburbs running a store called *Music*.

"Where do you play?" I asked. "You must be in a band."

His hand stopped moving, and his cheeks turned pink.

"I practice here when I have time and sometimes at home."

"You've got real talent," I said. "You could find a band if you wanted to. Maybe even start one up yourself."

He shook his head and averted his eyes.

"Perhaps I would, if things were different. But not many bands perform only in Ashburn."

My instinct was to tell him he could be anything he wanted—that he should never limit his dreams. But he'd just confirmed my suspicion—that he was one of the supernatural beings trapped here, just like me. And like me, there would be no world tours for him any time soon.

Still, he was being a damn good sport about showing me his collection, and I could have spent the rest of the day talking music with him. But the compulsion to check out the Voodoo priestess was real, and I couldn't ignore the twitch in my stomach much longer.

"These are making my mouth water," I said as I stood to leave. "But I have some business I have to take care of. Maybe I could come back and we could jam sometime."

Chaz nodded as he placed the PRS back in its stand and opened an ancient, dusty hard-shell case. He pulled out an acoustic guitar that was as beautiful as it was unique. It was unlike anything I'd ever seen, made of unstained walnut with archaic letters and symbols inlaid in gold up and down the neck.

He looked at it lovingly, then held it out to me.

Touching another man's favorite guitar was almost the same as feeling up his wife, so I shook my head and kept my hands by my side. But he nodded at me in reassurance and inched it closer, tempting me.

When I wrapped my hand around the wooden neck, Chaz smiled.

"I forged it myself," he said with pride.

Even though I'd never heard anyone talk about making a guitar like he was forging a weapon, my impression of Chaz increased again. I held the instrument in my hands, feeling the cool dampness of its wood. He'd taken good care of it and had stored it in the proper humidity. Its balance was sublime, and the frets were of the highest craftsmanship. Maybe Chaz rented and sold cheap stuff to the public, but he had a future in making custom instruments if he ever wanted one.

He nodded again, encouraging me to try out his creation, so I did. I'd spent a lot of my younger years playing electric guitars, but later in life I'd fallen back in love with the simplicity of an acoustic. As my hand glided across the strings of Chaz's baby, I realized I'd never played anything like it before.

Its tone was bright and perfect as my right hand strummed a few chords before I went into a few riffs from some of my own songs. Faster and faster, the fingers of my right hand plucked the strings without effort, while my left hand landed without flaw every time, nailing each chord precisely. It was so effortless, it was as if the guitar knew what I wanted to play before I did.

"This is amazing," I said, taking a break, and catching my breath. "I don't think I've ever played its equal."

A mini-spasm rolled across Chaz's forehead and his left eye twitched involuntarily as his mind calculated his next move. After a lengthy pause, he spoke.

"The instrument is yours now. A gift from me."

"No one gives something like this away for free," I said, shaking my head.

Chaz took a deep breath.

"It is yours now. I only ask that you would be kind enough to provide me with a favor in the future if I am ever in need, and if you feel the value of the gift warrants it."

And there it was.

First Oizys and now Chaz. Both placed a lot of value in John's favors. The idea of being in debt to another supernatural being didn't excite me, but my hand refused to loosen its grip on the guitar. So I gave up.

"I give you my demon bond that I am in your debt," I said as I again pretended to know what I was doing.

I placed the guitar back in its case and looked at Chaz. I didn't want to push my luck, but since he was being so generous, I decided to ask.

"Any chance I can score some light gauge strings, a couple pads of blank sheet music—and some picks?"

Chaz smiled and led me from his secret room, back to the main store.

Within a few minutes, I had a fresh ream of sheet music and a bag of picks in hand, but no strings.

"You will not need new strings," he said. "Ever."

That was an outrageous claim to make, but something about the way Chaz looked at me made me think he knew something I didn't, so I didn't argue.

"Is there anything else you require?" he asked with a smile.

Behind him on the counter, I saw a stack of dark blue tee-shirts sporting the phrase, *I Love Rock and Roll* in white letters, but with a red heart icon where the word *Love* should have been.

"I'll take one of those in a Large."

Soon, I was out the door, stowing my new gear and my sweet tee-shirt in the trunk.

I looked back, and saw Chaz standing outside his store, waving at me like a father watching his kid get on the school bus for the first time.

I nodded back, hopped in the car, re-engaged the GPS, and continued on my way to find Marie. It turned out she lived close by, and in less than five minutes I pulled up in front of her house.

As Oizys had promised, the trees in the front yard were filled with prayer flags and offerings to the loa spirits—bits of hair, pieces of candy, wooden masks, and a feather from a black bird hanging from a tree branch.

Also as Oizys had claimed, six gardeners—in straw hats and baseball caps—worked slowly but steadily at pruning bushes that were already well-shaped, pulling weeds that weren't there, and rearranging chips of mulch in the garden.

When I got out of my car and set foot on the driveway, one of the workers, a man with dark ebony skin, turned and glared at me. As the sun broke through the clouds, the light hit his face and reflected off his milky white, lifeless eyes.

I tensed, ready for him and his crew to come after my brains in true zombie fashion. Instead, the gardener ignored me and turned back to his imaginary weeds. With his head down, no one could tell the difference between him and one of the living, but now that I knew what he and his crew were, a song started to form in my head about a dead guy who tended a garden where the crop was human souls. Each time he harvested a spirit, he'd send it on to the land of the living, then return to his never-ending task. The imagined chords and drums to my new song started to kick in just as I knocked on Marie's front door, ready to meet my very first Voodoo priestess.

CHAPTER 10

A N EXOTIC WOMAN with latte brown skin and curly black hair opened the door. She was barefoot and wore a simple but form fitting cotton dress covered in a faded flower pattern. Her wild hair spilled over and covered one eye, and the smell of rum followed her.

"May I help you?" she said in a light Cajun accent. She hesitated for a second as she glanced past me to the lead zombie in her gardening crew.

"I'd like to talk for a minute or two if you have…a minute or two," I said.

It wasn't my most brilliant opening line, but sadly, it wasn't my worst either.

She flashed me a coy grin before turning away and leaving the front door open behind her.

It was no surprise that the layout of her house was almost identical to John's. The main difference was that her place was decorated. Her living room was furnished with a black leather couch and a matching love seat. And the kitchen was functional and well-used, overflowing with cooking tools, utensils, dried herbs, hanging pots and pans, and a large wooden cutting board.

She crossed her arms, waiting for me to explain why I was there.

"Hope I didn't interrupt anything," I said, clearing my throat.

"Like sacrificing a chicken?" she said.

"Or a goat," I said with a shrug, my voice trailing off. "I don't discriminate…"

"Goats are offered only at Easter," she said in a tone that was suddenly serious. She shook her head, like I should have already known that somehow.

"I'd ask you to join me for lunch, but there's only enough meat for one. What did you want to talk about, John?"

"Have we met?" I asked, surprised she knew my name.

"Not in person, but everyone knows who you are."

She stepped closer and, yes—just like everyone else in Ashburn—she sniffed me. She exhaled like she was cleansing her palette and cocked her head to one side.

"I assumed you wouldn't look like a demon. None of you do. But you don't smell quite like one either. You're part demon for sure, but something else too. Something that dominates your *ti bon ange* enough for my gardeners to let you pass—and for my charms and wards to not stop you dead in your tracks."

I felt my shoulders relax even though I hadn't realized they'd been tensed. If she was right, maybe I was only a demon on the outside but still a human where it counted.

"You don't have to explain what you are to me," she said. "We all have our secrets, and since you made it into my home safely, I can only assume you don't mean me any harm."

She stepped closer, and I tensed up, excited but wary.

"If you're not here to hurt me, then why *are* you here?" she whispered, like she didn't want someone else to hear her question.

Maybe it was her magic or maybe I was just a sucker for a beautiful woman, but even if I'd wanted to lie to her, I don't think I could have at that moment, as the truth came rolling out of my mouth.

"Someone told me you're going to try to leave Ashburn, and I'm here to see if that's true and to stop you if it is."

She paused, then laughed so hard her shoulders shook.

"I don't have any plans to go out today," she said. "But I was thinking about visiting the mall tomorrow, if that's all right with you."

"You can do that?"

"Of course," she said as she plopped down on her couch. "I love shopping."

She motioned for me to sit next to her, but I wanted to keep my focus, so I sat in the love seat across from her.

"I meant the leaving Ashburn part. How do you plan on accomplishing that?"

"I'll probably drive. I go whenever and wherever I please because I'm not like you. I'm a human. I stay in Ashburn because I have roots here, not because someone is forcing me to."

"If you're a human, who told you—"

"No one told me anything," she said, cutting me off. "Most locals don't suspect anything about who and what their neighbors really are, but not all of us are blind to supernatural activity. To me, this town reeks of demons and gods and angels and other things—like a supernatural barn yard."

"Oizys says you have power and that you're in the same situation as the rest of us."

Marie rolled her eyes when I mentioned Oizys.

"Things are starting to make sense now," she said. "I know who Oizys really is—a mid-level demon who lives off of human suffering, especially from the residents in her community. Perfect choice for someone to lead the homeowner's association if you ask me."

"I'll give you that, but you need to convince me you're not working with the loa to help you escape. Then I'll leave you alone."

"Do you even know what a loa is?" she said, her face devoid of humor.

"I know they're the spirits of your ancestors," I said, leaning forward in my seat. "And that you've been killing a bunch of innocent chickens with no intention of eating them. I'm sure your loa appreciate it, but it won't put you in very good standing with the local vegan Meetup group."

"In Voodoo," she said, "we believe in the one god, *Bondye*. But unlike the Christian deity, our god does not interfere in human affairs. He leaves us alone, and we leave him alone. To feel close to Bondye, we worship the spirits who serve him—the spirits of our ancestors— the loa. They watch after us and guide us. Offering them the lives of the animals is an essential part of my religion, especially as Saint John's Eve approaches to mark the beginning of summer."

"How does killing a bird bring you closer to your dead relatives?"

She hesitated before answering, but the tremble in her hand told me I was getting under her skin.

"Before I kill an animal, I pray and I ask the loa to come to me. When I make the sacrifice, I offer myself to them, and if I am fortunate, one of them accepts my invitation and possesses me. While the loa is inside me, I gain its strength, and it is able to do things it can only do while in a mortal body. The spirit eats the offering—the animal's body and its soul. The loa uses my mouth and my teeth, but it gains the nourishment and strength from the life energy of the animal—not me."

"One of the loa possesses you?" I said. "Like a demon?"

Finally, we were talking about something I had experience with.

"It is a very different thing," she said. "The loa are strong, but they are not demonic beings. And unlike your victims, I am their willing host. I welcome their spirits into my body."

She went on for fifteen minutes about the details of the ceremony she'd performed the week before. At one point, she compared being possessed to a sexual experience, which got my attention, but otherwise, I spent the time scanning the living room as she talked. There was one wooden drum in the corner, three bags of cornmeal on the floor, and faint remains of at least a dozen red splatter marks on one of the walls. I took a gentle sniff of the air with my new nose and was certain the marks were made from blood.

On the mantel above the gas-powered fireplace, six glass jars were lined up on a shelf, filled with various items such as strips of clothing, strands of hair, and an occasional tooth. Everything in the jars was covered in a fine yellow-orange powder, and each jar contained a small wax carving of a person. Those were strange enough, but what stood out the most in the living room was a framed ink drawing hanging on the wall above the mantel—an illustration of a man wearing a black top hat and a tuxedo jacket with his face painted white to resemble a skull. He wore mirrored sunglasses with one lens missing, and his one exposed eye seemed to peer into my soul. In his left hand, he held a glass of booze while his right hand clutched a staff with a skull mounted on top of it. It was the first thing I'd seen in Marie's house that fit my preconceived notions about Voodoo and dark magic.

She must have noticed me staring at the drawing because she

stopped talking and cleared her throat.

"That is the Baron—one of my most powerful ancestors. He watches over me and is with me at all times."

"Have you ever been possessed by him?"

"Is there anything else you wish to ask me before I have my lunch?" she said, ignoring my question.

I shrugged, not wanting to be a pain, but I was still afraid she was going to make a break for it the second I left her alone.

"You still haven't convinced me that you're not trapped here like the rest of us—that you can leave whenever you want."

She stood up and went to the kitchen where she pulled out a small piece of white paper from one of the cabinet drawers.

It was a receipt for a drum she'd purchased in Sterling only a few days ago.

"You could have faked this," I said. "Or ordered the drum off the Internet."

She stood in front of me, her closeness making my legs weak. I didn't know if she was trying to use her magic on me again, but I had to concentrate and focus on every word that came out of her mouth to understand what she was saying.

"I can get in my car and leave Ashburn right now. If you'd like to come along for the ride, you're more than welcome."

She offered me her hand, but I didn't take it. Nothing would have made me happier than to get in a car with her and go. But whether she could do it or not, Ahriman's spells wouldn't let me leave. I was sure of that.

"Let's assume you can do what you say," I said. "Then what's up with your zombie army out front? I don't think Oizys likes it when she can't check up on her homeowners in person."

I wasn't sure if I'd asked too many questions or if she was finally ready to eat her lunch, but she gestured for me to stand.

"As you are aware, Ashburn can be a dangerous place—more so than it appears on the surface. Many of the worst creatures in this town, including Oizys, don't like the fact that a human knows what is really going on here. Think of my gardeners as my home security system."

"Do they ever get a day off?"

"They don't need one. It's more of a permanent career than a job, and they're happy to serve me."

I studied her face, looking for any sign of deceit, but I found none. Either her magic was incredibly strong, or she was telling the truth.

As I walked toward the door, I wondered why Oizys would send me after Marie if there wasn't anything there to discover or something to stop. Maybe Marie was telling the truth and Oizys was the one planning to escape. She could have tipped me off about Marie to distract and keep me occupied. A part of me didn't know who to believe, but Marie was a human and Oizys was a demon, and demons weren't exactly known for their honesty.

Before I left, I turned around and motioned at the jars on the mantel.

"Those are interesting," I said.

She touched my elbow with her hand, and the sensation made my head swim, but I stayed my ground.

"They are my Kanari," she said after she saw that I still wasn't leaving. "Some call them soul jars."

"As in, they contain people's souls?"

"Only the ti bon ange," she said. "The part of a person that determines who they are—their personality."

"And those belong to the men working outside?"

She looked at me but didn't answer.

I didn't need my heightened demonic senses to see that she was hiding something. But like she said, we all had our secrets. And as long as hers didn't hurt me or break one of Ahriman's commandments, I didn't need to know her personal business.

"You're not going to make one of those jars for me, are you?" I said with a laugh, trying to ease the tension between us. "I like my personality the way it is."

"Not unless I need to," she said as she opened the front door and let the sunlight spill into the foyer.

When I stepped outside and stood on her Welcome mat, I thought of one more thing I wanted to know.

"I don't mean to be nosy, but you seem like a nice enough person—"

"Such a heartfelt compliment," she said with a sarcastic tilt of her head.

"How did you end up becoming a Voodoo priestess? Did you apply for the job or hear about it from a friend?"

She paused before letting out a short burst of laughter.

"I wasn't expecting you to be this funny. But no, I didn't have an interview or send in my resume. I was born into the church. The day I came into this world, my destiny was set."

"Never had a choice?"

She grinned.

"Everything's a choice. It's just a matter of degrees. But I'm doing what I was meant to do, and I find happiness in that."

I shrugged and nodded my head. In some ways, she and I were completely different, but we were both stuck doing what we had to, and that made me like and trust her a little more than I was prepared for. I mentally placed her into the *probably harmless* category and moved Oizys into my *danger, danger, beware* file.

"Any chance you'd be up for a meal sometime so we can talk more?" I said.

My abrupt statement surprised her as much as it embarrassed me, but she recovered quickly and answered.

"I don't know how safe that would be for me," she said. "But feel free to ask the next time you're hungry—for food. You know where I live."

CHAPTER 11

I SAT IN the car outside Marie's house with the motor running, even though I wanted to go back to John and Sybil's house, raid their stash of liquor, and play my new guitar.

But Ahriman's magic was working double time, making my left hand twitch—urging me to find Oizys and see why she'd sent me to Marie.

I eased the car forward and drove down one street after another, thinking about what Oizys had said about John knowing how to leave Ashburn. I was far from being a psychologist, but if the way out of town used to be in John's brain, maybe it was still there as a ghost memory in mine, waiting for me to find it.

With that small hope dangling in front of me like a supernatural carrot, I turned the nav off, took a deep breath, and let my instincts guide my steering.

The first thing I discovered was that Ashburn proper had grown so large and overpopulated, a single name wasn't enough to contain it. Instead, it was divided into several large, distinct neighborhoods, including Ashburn, Ashburn Village, Brambleton, Broadlands, and Ashburn Farm. Of course, I never saw a village or a farm, and the land itself was anything but broad. Mainly what I encountered were a lot of busy people, expensive cars, and enormous houses.

On the positive side of things, the town had several Moon Dollarz strategically placed in each neighborhood. And from what I could tell, they were always packed. Even the kids ran on designer coffee in

Ashburn, most of them hooked on caffeine long before they were old enough to drive.

When I was a kid, coffee was something my dad drank to help him stay awake on long family road trips. I never touched the stuff until I was in my twenties and needed to stay awake for a show.

Maybe it was because of all the caffeine, but Ashburn's sidewalks and walking paths were filled with endless streams of runners and walkers. They exercised alone, in groups, with dogs, and even while pushing baby strollers. And of course, I ran into plenty of cyclists who wanted to be treated like cars until it wasn't convenient for them.

After two hours of getting lost, twilight was settling in, and I gave up thinking I'd magically remember the way out of town. Instead, I started looking for familiar streets and tried to figure out how to get back to John and Sybil's house. Still lost, I turned a corner and saw an old stone building that was distinctly out of place among the rest of the town's McMansions. But what really got my attention was that, as I approached the building, I could hear the vibrations of live music in the air.

I slowed down when I saw an immense crowd of people just off the side of the road, gathering at the top of a large grassy hill next to the old house. My heart rate revved when I saw the unmistakable glow of stage lights coming from the bottom of a sloped field tucked away just outside the tree line.

Daylight was almost gone, and I was dead tired, but I always had time for music. Plus, Sybil said she was going to meet me at a concert, and I doubted Ashburn had more than one of those going at a time.

So I took a right into the parking lot and pulled into one of the last open spots. Hopping out of the car, I followed the crowds of homeowners dragging their coolers and fold-up chairs as they slogged toward the base of the hill to listen to the band. They were playing a cover of a popular reggae song by Bob Marley, and I laughed, wondering if Mr. Marley ever thought his music would be played in an affluent suburb like Ashburn.

As I walked by the old two-story stone building on my right, a coldness passed through my bones. I stopped moving, stunned by the sudden drop in temperature, but the crowd swept me up in their flow and carried me away. The chill left me when I glanced back, wondering what was inside the historic structure.

I was close enough to see the concert venue—a fenced-off grassy slope filled with people listening to live music in the warm spring evening. Hundreds of parents sat on blankets and beach chairs, drinking from plastic cups and handing out snacks to members of their brood who ran around as if possessed by sugar demons.

It wasn't Woodstock, but it was better than nothing, and as I looked past the two off-duty police officers pulling overtime as gate security, I saw the band. There were five of them on stage, producing a sound that barely required three people. They mimicked the movements of rock stars, and their facial expressions tried hard to say *bad ass*, but their untucked designer tee-shirts, freshly purchased baseball caps, and ironed cargo shorts left no doubt that they were suburban dads.

At the entrance to the field, a sign warned of the consequences of bringing glassware onto the lawn, while overhead a banner read, *Hump Day in the Styx*. I laughed out loud at how appropriate the sign was, given Ashburn's supernatural reality.

The herd pushed me forward, and when it was my turn to get my hand stamped, the off-duty cops glanced at me with the combination of surprise and fear I was starting to expect.

One of them stamped my hand without a word, and I passed through the gate and entered the chaos, stepping over and weaving around blankets, boxes of white wine, and abandoned sippy cups, as I searched for a place to sit. Just as I found a piece of open grass halfway up the hill, the band finished their song and went straight into a Jimmy Buffett classic.

I wasn't surprised at all.

I sat on the ground and studied the band and its gear while the crappy but catchy lyrics about attitudes and latitudes washed like sandy water through my ears and threatened to leave a nasty headache in their wake.

As suspected, the band had the nicest consumer-level gear on the market. Shure mics and Marshall amps, probably turned up to at least 5—the highest the neighborhood HOA probably allowed. And their instruments. I had to admit, a couple of them made my mouth water. One was a vintage Telecaster with original Fender pickups and a custom tremolo bar, just like I had back home in my studio. The bass player was trying to maintain a mellow groove on an '89 Rickenbacker with signature head stock. And of course, the drummer was surrounded by all manner of percussion, including a mounted cowbell, chimes, and toms of every size, all built around a nice five-piece walnut kit.

Watching them perform reminded me of the gorgeous custom acoustic waiting for me in my trunk, and I smiled as I imagined myself playing it. My happy daydreams were interrupted a few seconds later when I heard a commotion and a familiar voice coming from the lawn directly in front of the stage.

There at the center of everything was Sybil. She was dancing like the seductress she was and dressed to kill, wearing a tight, small black dress that accentuated her long legs and her figure. Five drunk guys jostled around her, each desperate for her attention. Watching her dance was like watching a witch cast a spell with her hips. I envied the man who'd be going home with her that night.

Then I realized I was probably the lucky guy I was thinking about, and I swallowed hard, my throat suddenly dry.

I sat mesmerized by Sybil's undulating curves and her hypnotic moves. The guitarist flubbed a few notes of his solo. When I looked up, he was staring at her, too.

Half-way through one of her gyrations, she spotted me. With a snap of her fingers, the men paused in their orbits, and she headed up the hill, marching directly for me.

"There you are," she said, stopping to pose in front of me, with her stiletto-heeled feet shoulder-width apart and one hand on her hip. "I told you not to make me wait—now I'm ravenous."

Suddenly, the day caught up with me, and I felt a gnawing in my stomach.

"Anywhere around here we can get some food?" I said as I stood up and stretched my back.

As soon as I asked, I knew I'd screwed up.

She cocked her head, leaned forward, and wouldn't you know it, she sniffed me—a tradition that was starting to annoy me.

"How about our regular place?" she asked slowly.

And there it was. She was testing me, and I was about to fail because I had no idea where our regular place was or if we even had one.

Backed into a corner, I decided to pivot—something I'd learned during that month in the 80s when I was popular and had to give interviews daily. If you don't know the answer to something, change the topic and answer a different question.

"Wherever we go, the first thing I want is a stiff drink," I said.

It was an obvious dodge, but it brought a smile back to her face.

With her pack of want-to-be lovers drooling a few yards behind her, she leaned in and kissed me.

While we kissed, the band finished their song, and the hairs on the back of my neck stood on end as I heard the first notes to a pop tune I instantly recognized.

I pulled back from Sybil and looked up at the suburban dads on stage as they performed a horrible cover of the horrible song that had dogged me throughout my life. And as if that wasn't bad enough, middle-aged homeowners all around me stood up and started clapping and smiling as they screamed the words to *Yeah, Yeah, No, No, Maybe* as loud as they could.

"Come on, babe," Sybil said, grabbing hold of my arm and pulling me toward the exit. "I know how much you hate this song and everything else this wanker ever wrote."

I scrunched up my eyebrows. Yes, it was true I loathed the song that had brought me so much fame, so little money, and so many headaches. But I was the wanker who'd written it, and I was allowed to hate it. The fact that John hadn't liked it made me defensive and angry, and I fought the urge to defend it to Sybil.

Thankfully, she pulled me away before I could say anything. As the two of us moved through the crowd, her fan club followed us. Without even thinking about it, I turned and snarled at them, which stopped them in mid-step.

They looked at me, confused and afraid, then turned around and shuffled away in the opposite direction.

As we neared the exit, I heard a familiar voice. It was Oizys chiding a young couple with a baby. She was going off on the mom, pointing at the glass bottle the woman was holding and wagging her finger. The mom was in tears, the baby was screaming, and Oizys looked like she was in bliss. Meanwhile, the distraught husband tried unsuccessfully to catch the attention of the police officers, hoping they would come to their rescue.

They didn't.

As we walked past them, Oizys saw me and broke away from the young couple. Sybil and I walked as fast as we could, blowing past the old building on our left and stepping into the parking lot.

"We need to talk," Oizys called out as she chased us.

Reluctantly, I stopped. Sybil groaned.

"Tell her it's not a good time," Sybil said. "Or you can let me take care of her. I promise I won't leave much of a mess—nothing the animals won't clean up before morning." Even with my heightened powers of observation, I couldn't tell if she was kidding.

"Leaving so soon?" Oizys said, finally stepping up next to us. "Did you not like the concert?"

"It was fine," I said as *Yeah, Yeah's* chorus rang out through the night air.

"How did things go regarding that matter we spoke of earlier today?" Oizys asked me. "I hope you weren't too hard on the poor girl."

"I'm not working right now," I said, avoiding her question. "And I'm hungry. Maybe you could stop by the store tomorrow if you want to talk."

"I knew it," she said, shaking her head. "You did nothing at all. This is something we need to discuss right away."

"He's coming with me," Sybil said, grabbing my arm. "Go find your own date."

Oizys ignored Sybil and addressed only me.

"You know this is in your best interest," she said as I sighed and caught Sybil's eyes.

"Just give me five minutes," I said.

Sybil released my wrist and strutted over to a picnic table to wait.

"Make it quick," I said to Oizys, and she smiled, relishing my frustration like a tasty snack.

CHAPTER 12

I FOLLOWED OIZYS and her tightly wound hair to a paved path that led into the woods. After twenty yards, the path turned to packed dirt, and the trees blocked out the moonlight from above and the lights from the concert.

Oizys slowed down and turned to me as we walked along, side by side.

"You didn't take care of the priestess," she said. "I can see it in your face."

"I talked to her," I said, looking around as we moved.

Suddenly I was concerned about being alone in a dark forest with a demon who got her kicks from other people's suffering.

"She's not going anywhere," I said. "She's just a Voodoo woman who likes killing chickens in her spare time. I've done worse things—trust me."

Oizys stopped and backed away, revealing a micro expression of fear she couldn't conceal, taking my words as a threat.

"How do you know she's not going to leave?" Oizys said more calmly.

"Because she's a human. She can come and go when she wants."

"Do you have proof of that?"

I crossed my arms, my answer already prepared.

"She had a receipt."

Oizys didn't respond at first, but even I thought Marie's explanation sounded pretty lame when I said it out loud.

"I thought you knew all about that woman," Oizys said. "She is a human, but she's also a high-level priestess in the Voodoo church. More importantly, she's connected heavily to the loa. Trust me, she's trapped here and trying to get her spirits to help her escape. That's why she's been increasing the number of blood sacrifices she's making to them."

"The receipt was from a music store in Sterling," I said, my words sounding even dumber the second time around. "I saw the drum in her living room. And she said she was raised here."

Oizys took another deep breath.

"I know you have a tough job and it can't be easy working for—*him*," she said. "And I am well aware of the sex magic a Voodoo priestess has at her fingertips. But you're usually not that susceptible or gullible. Don't you think it's possible her priest or a member of her congregation gave her that drum and the receipt? Her church is in Sterling. Near a music store. Doesn't that sound more plausible, given the fact that my assistant has been watching her for the last month and she hasn't left Ashburn even once?"

I'll admit, I felt a little stupid when she put it like that. But on the other hand, I also wasn't surprised I sucked at being a demon's enforcer.

"I've expended quite a bit of energy making her life as miserable as possible," Oizys said. "If Marie could have, she would have left a long time ago."

Unfortunately for me, that made a lot of sense.

I threw my hands up even as the gnawing in my stomach began. I wanted to tell Oizys it was my first day on the job and that she should give me a break, but I couldn't. Instead, I clamped down on my anger and kept pretending I knew what I was doing.

"I'll keep an eye on her and talk to her again. But let me ask you a question first."

That caught her by surprise.

"Do *you* have any plans to leave Ashburn?"

"What a ridiculous notion," she said. "I have everything I need here. I can't kill anyone, which makes life a little boring at times, but inflicting misery on my herd of humans more than makes up for that. Ashburn is where I find the meaning in my life—it's the key to my satisfaction."

"And also where you get your power," I said. "Maybe enough power to escape if you really set your mind to it."

She straightened her posture and glared at me.

"My job satisfies me, but it doesn't allow me nearly enough power to leave, even if I wanted to."

She moved closer and over-enunciated her words.

"Did you at least remove the charms in her yard and get rid of those pesky zombies? With them gone, I could take care of this without your help."

I scratched my chin.

"Having a charm-free, zombie-free yard isn't one of Ahriman's commandments."

Her face turned a deep red, but I cut her off before she could say anything.

"Don't worry," I said. "I'll look into it, like I said, in case you're right."

"No matter what happens, you still owe me," she said with hesitation. "You cannot break your demon bond once it is given."

"You mentioned that about a thousand times already," I said as my anger rose.

I blinked, and in that instant, she was gone.

Alone in the dark forest, I headed back the way we'd entered. After fifteen minutes of following the trail, I figured I should have made it back to the parking lot already. My heart sped up, but I forced myself to stay calm and to continue following the trail. Finally, I saw a light through the trees.

When I emerged from the trail, I was greeted by silence and a nearly empty parking lot. The concert was over, and only a few stragglers hung out around their cars, slowly loading blankets and sleeping kids into their vehicles, while the band loaded their gear into two SUVs. I cringed when I saw Sybil standing at the picnic table in exactly the same place I'd left her.

"That was longer than five minutes," she said, tapping her foot, with her arms folded across her chest.

I looked behind me, but the trailhead was gone. Before I could explain, Sybil started yelling at me.

"You know perfectly well that time passes differently in those woods," she said. "I've been patient with you tonight, but I'm about to lose my mind. We only have a little time before the bar closes, and I'm beyond famished."

I held up my hands, surrendering, as we walked back to the car without speaking.

As we pulled out of the parking lot, a group of runners darted past us and raised their middle fingers in unison.

"Assholes," Sybil said in a whisper as she smoothed out her dress.

I wanted to ask why the running community seemed to hate me so much but decided to let it go for the time being.

The drive to the bar took all of two minutes, and luckily for me there was only one neon sign still lit across the street—the only place open for business at that time of night besides the gas station.

When we got out of the car, I patted the pockets of my khakis and cursed.

"I keep forgetting my money."

Sybil grabbed my arm and opened her mouth—about to say something. Instead, she shook her head in silence and pulled open the door to the Broadlands Pub. The instant we stepped inside, I was greeted by loud, classic rock, the heady smell of freshly fried bar food, and a thick bouncer who was at least a foot taller than me.

When he saw me, he nodded and stepped aside.

"Good evening, sir," he said, dropping his human guise long enough to show me a razor-sharp set of fangs and red eyes that burned like embers.

I did my best to keep my poker face as I nodded and walked past him into the bar. I hoped my exterior looked calm, because inside, I was completely freaking out.

CHAPTER 13

W E SAT IN the back of the bar at a table with a glossy wood finish that stuck to my elbows, like it had never been fully cleaned. And even though no one was smoking, the place smelled of stale ashtrays, reminding me of being backstage at a concert.

But that's where the similarities stopped.

Instead of hot groupies, old roadies, recovering addicts, and musicians, I was surrounded by middle-aged males in tight designer shirts hoping to get lucky and women wearing impractical heels and showing more cleavage than they actually had.

At the bar itself, a few people sat with stacks of quarters by their sides, popping coin after coin into the bar-top video game machines. Their eyes were as big as poker chips, and most of them looked like they hadn't moved in hours.

All in all, it was the type of place I used to hang out at when I was starting out in the business—the kind of bar that paid half the door cover for three sets of someone else's songs. But there was no band there that evening. It was karaoke night instead, and I cringed, waiting for the next drunk person to indulge in his or her fantasy of being a star.

Thankfully, it was only a few minutes before a smiling blonde server showed up. She smiled and leaned across the table so we could hear her above the crowd.

"Something to drink to start you off?" she said, looking first at Sybil and then at me.

I waited for Sybil to order, but she was busy checking out the waitress to speak.

"Maker's Mark, straight up for me," I said.

I looked at Sybil, but she remained silent, staring.

When the server left, Sybil looked at me and grinned.

"I thought you were hungry," I said. "And thirsty."

She raised her eyebrows, scanned the bar, then turned back to me.

"I am definitely hungry," she said, then got up and walked away.

She's lucky she's hot, was all I could think as I watched her disappear into the mass of bar-goers.

The server returned with my whiskey a minute later, which was one of the oddest things I'd witnessed all day. Drinks from a crowded bar never came that fast.

My face must have shown my surprise, because when I looked up, the cute blonde was smiling nervously.

"I told Frank to make it as fast as he could."

I studied her, trying to figure out if she was another one of *us*, but my gut told me she was human.

"Be sure to thank Frank," I said. "And thank you, too. What's your name?"

The server blushed and straightened her posture, showing off her considerable chest in the process.

"Hillary," she said. "But people call me Hills."

I nodded and took a sip of the whiskey. It burned a hot trail down my throat, straight to my stomach. It was pure bliss—so good I closed my eyes and sighed.

When I opened them again, Hills was still there.

"Do I have to pay as I go?" I asked, suddenly hoping Sybil hadn't gone far.

Hills giggled nervously then shook her head.

"They didn't tell me you were funny," she said with a lopsided grin. I studied the lines on her face, and she muttered something underneath her breath.

"What was that?" I asked.

She leaned forward, her chest close enough that I finally realized why her nickname was *Hills*.

"I said I'm new here," she said, whispering directly into my ear. "But the owner told me how to treat you—that everything's on the house," she said. Then she pulled back a few inches and stared at me with her soft blue eyes.

She was oozing sexuality, and having her that close sparked something in my gut—that same dark flame I'd felt with Sybil in the back of the bookstore. If it had been simple lust, I would have recognized it, but it felt like something deeper and more sinister.

"I asked him if he really meant *everything*," she said, still looking into my eyes.

She swallowed hard and smiled.

"He said *everything* meant *everything*."

I took another sip of whiskey and then one more for good luck.

When I didn't respond, she started to leave, disappointed.

"Maybe you should bring me another one of these," I said, holding up my glass.

Piercing the noise of the bar, a drunk businessman started singing *Smoke Gets In Your Eyes* in a key in which it was never meant to be sung.

"Make that two, if they're on the house. I have a feeling I'm going to need them."

She smiled and hurried away.

"I thought only rock stars and actors got that kind of treatment," I murmured to myself, shaking my head.

When I threw back the rest of my drink, I tasted the nuances of the alcohol more clearly and distinctly than I ever had as a human. The fire water tasted better, more intense, and I could almost smell the wood of the barrel it had been stored in. But it wasn't hitting me the way alcohol usually did, and I was still stone cold sober.

I leaned back and observed the steady influx of customers. Within half-an-hour, all the tables were filled, and the din in the bar kept getting louder, until I could barely hear Hills when she showed up with my drinks and some food I hadn't ordered.

"The owner said to bring this. He said you'd like it," she yelled over the karaoke singer's clunky voice.

The cheese sticks and french fries she placed in front of me weren't fine cuisine, but they looked and smelled like heaven to me at that moment.

I took a swig of Maker's Mark and watched Hills walk away. The drink tasted as good as the first one, but it still wasn't having the desired effect on me. With a shrug, I dug into my food and mulled over the Marie situation.

She'd seemed honest to me. A little weird, but truthful. But as much as I wanted to trust my instincts with her, I kept hearing Oizys in my head, telling me the Voodoo priestess was playing me for a fool. By the time I was on my second cheese stick, I was starting to wonder whether or not Marie had really asked her loa to help her escape.

Once the thought started bouncing around in my head, the compulsion spell kicked in and my stomach started churning, trying to force me to do my job right away.

"You can rumble all you want," I said to my stomach. "But I'm not doing anything about Marie tonight."

The gnawing inside me persisted anyway, forcing me to think about Marie while I gritted my teeth and shoved more fries into my mouth. In the end, I made up my mind to visit Marie again the next day, and once I did, Ahriman's spell relaxed its hold on me and let me finally relax.

As I chewed the last french fry, a middle-aged couple stepped up to the karaoke mic and started their rendition of Meat Loaf's *Paradise by the Dashboard Light*. I closed my eyes and cradled my head in my hands, preparing for nine minutes of hell. When I did, I could hear all the conversations going on at the bar at once, like they were all speaking directly into my ears.

Most of the discussions were in English, but the guttural voices I heard weren't human. They were deep and gravelly and the words they formed sounded more like animals growling than people speaking. At first, it was all just a jumble of words and noises, but I found that if I focused on one conversation at a time, I could make sense of what they were saying.

"Remember that one guy who made his pentagram out of sugar?" one of the voices said. "Too bad for him that he had mice. They ate through his lines, and I marched right up to the twit and had myself a nice dinner."

"Those were the good old days, Ren—back before you had the

bright idea to check out Virginia. Worst decision of my life, following you that day."

I looked up and scanned the tables until I found lips moving in sync with what I was hearing. Ren was a stocky man in his late 40s, and his friend had black hair that hung past his ears and a thin face. When they noticed me looking at them, they dropped their human guises momentarily, just like the bouncer had done, and bowed their horned heads with reverence.

At least Ahriman had been honest about one thing. Ashburn really was filled with demons.

I tuned in to another conversation where three guys were arguing about the best way to torture John for eternity. One guy preferred the idea of a beast from Hell eating John's genitalia every morning until the end of time. Unfortunately, that meant he was talking about a monster eating my manly parts over and over again, and that was definitely not cool.

After hearing that, I tried to keep eating, but I was suddenly wary of my surroundings—watching for anyone who looked like they wanted to fight me or worse. I paused mid-cheese stick, looking around, but as far as I could tell, no one was paying any attention to me.

Then I spotted the three young guys hunched over their beers, sitting at the far end of the bar, giving me the stink-eye.

Unlike the other tables, this bunch looked like they were humans. They weren't saying anything, but they glared at me with blatant hostility. Two of them were huge but otherwise unremarkable. The third man was tatted-up heavily on his arms and neck and wore several pieces of polished silver jewelry. He also wore sunglasses, which didn't look nearly as cool as he thought it did in a dark bar.

I kept watching them watch me until Sybil sat down and started rubbing my thigh with her hand. I started to ask her if she knew who my three admirers were, but when I turned back to the bar, they were gone.

"What's wrong?" she said, staring with disdain at the remaining crumbs of fried food on my plate.

"I was thinking about Marie, the Voodoo priestess I spoke with earlier."

"And who is Marie, exactly?" she said, forcing a smile.

I finished my second Maker's Mark, making her wait on purpose. I had the feeling John hadn't been very patient with her, and I was afraid being too nice might give away my secret.

I set my glass down and contemplated it for a few seconds before responding.

"Her name is Marie Lacroix, and Oizys thinks she's planning an escape. But when I spoke to her, she said she was a human. A Voodoo practitioner, but still just a human. And I believed her."

Sybil narrowed her eyes at me.

"Did you lose your goggles?" she said.

"I forgot to wear them," I said, not knowing what she was talking about and hoping she wouldn't notice.

"I've never heard of her," she said. "But I don't trust anything Oizys says. Get your goggles, bust into this Marie's house tomorrow, and take a look at her for yourself. That's the only way you'll really know if she's one of us or one of them."

She had a good point, although first I had to find the magic goggles she was talking about. Before I could learn more about them, Hills showed up wearing street clothes and a huge smile

Sybil must have seen my reaction. She grinned and nodded toward the server.

"I think you already know Hillary," she said, crossing her arms. "She's new here, but Ramond said she could get off work early and come play with us. She lives in Sterling, but I told her she could stay with us tonight."

I looked at Sybil, but she stood up and took Hillary by the arm.

"Are you coming?" she said to me.

I wasn't sure what was happening, but I didn't need to be asked twice. Together, the three of us headed for the exit, past my favorite bouncer, and into the parking lot.

Once we were outside and headed for the car, I clicked the key fob and popped open the trunk.

"Tell me you didn't buy another guitar," Sybil said as we neared the car.

"You're a musician?" Hills asked, coming up from behind me and grabbing me around my waist. She pushed the front of her body against my back and looked over my shoulder at the guitar case in the trunk.

Despite being a ridiculous question to ask someone with a guitar in his trunk, I nodded and opened the case, ready to show off my new six-stringed friend.

But before I could do that, Hills squealed, and I smelled the stench of stale beer as someone hefted me into the air and slammed me down hard onto the parking lot asphalt.

CHAPTER 14

W HEN MY FACE hit the parking lot, it didn't hurt as much as
I thought it would.

I sprang to my feet, worried about Sybil and Hills, but they were both gone. Maybe they'd been kidnapped, but that didn't seem likely. Sybil wasn't the kind of demon who was easily made to do something against her will. The only other possible scenario I could think of was they had run away and left me alone to face my attackers. Maybe Sybil was testing me, wanting me to prove to her I was the real John. Or maybe it was just the kind of shit demons did to each other.

Either way, I felt angry and abandoned. When I turned to face the guy who'd just tossed me, I recognized him and his sunglasses from the bar. His jewelry glistened in the light of the parking lot overhead lamps as he snarled at me.

One of his two friends was as big as a professional football player, and he stepped to me and took a swing with a fist the size of my head. Before I knew what was happening, I'd moved out of the way faster than should have been possible. Mr. Muscles overextended his punch, tripped, and face-planted into the pavement.

I looked back at the guy wearing the sunglasses and his remaining pet mountain and I smiled.

I'd never been a great fighter, but I had a feeling that was about to change. John's body was a serious upgrade from the one I'd been stuck with all of my life. I flexed my muscles and prepared to go into full-on demon attack mode.

At least that was my plan before the guy with the sunglasses landed a fist in my stomach that bent me in half and sent me to the ground puking up mozzarella sticks and french fries.

Before I could get back to my feet, all three of them started kicking me and stomping on my back. Not only was I hurting—I was also confused and not very impressed with my so-called demonic powers.

With no better plan, I covered my head and waited out their onslaught. They must have worn themselves out pounding me into the asphalt, because instead of going in for the kill, they backed away, breathing hard and giving me time to get to my feet.

"You're making a big mistake," I said, hearing how empty my words sounded.

Mr. Sunglasses touched a circular silver pendant hanging from around his neck with a stylized face in the middle of it that was sticking its tongue out—a monster as best I could tell—maybe even a demon. He smiled at me, arrogant in his safety while his two gigantic friends stood on either side of him.

"I have a message from Marco," he said in a distant voice. "Ashburn is our town. Your services are no longer required."

I spit blood onto the ground and tried to ignore the fact that it was black.

"I couldn't agree with you more," I said, coughing and forcing myself to take a deep breath. "If you can get me out of this piece of shit suburb, I'll leave right now, and you can have it all to yourself."

"You have been warned," he said, before he signaled his two friends to attack.

As they closed in, I thought about making a break for it—about taking off as fast as I could and hoping none of them were in the running club.

Out of nowhere, the opening guitar riff from Footloose wormed its way into my head and started playing on repeat. Don't ask me why. Maybe because I identified with the spiky-haired kid in the movie who wanted to get away from his small-town blues. Or maybe it was because Footloose was the perfect music for a dance—or a fight.

While I was jamming along with Kenny Loggins in my head, one of the big guys reached out to grab me, and on instinct, I tried to push him away.

When my open hand touched his chest, it was like receiving the most intense static shock you could imagine. After a huge *pop*, my essence poured out of me like water and into my attacker's body.

For a second, I was disoriented as hell. I'd spent all day getting used to John's body, and now I had to deal with someone else's. The difference this time was that the person who owned the body was still in there with me. I could hear what he was thinking and see his thoughts and memories like they were my own. It turns out, his name was Paul, and Paul was more than a little freaked out that I had taken over.

Through his eyes, I looked down at John's body sprawled out on the pavement. Without my soul to animate it, John's shell was useless. But Paul's human body was just what I needed as Mr. Muscles bore down on top of me. His name was Buddy, and before I knew what was happening, I'd made use of Paul's highly developed fighting instincts and slammed a muscled forearm into Buddy's windpipe.

Good ol' Buddy fell to the ground, cursing and screaming, confused about why his friend had just clotheslined him.

Mr. Sunglasses' name was Miguel, and he wasn't worried one bit about Paul or Buddy's safety. Instead, he came at me with a wide-bladed wooden sword that was studded with razor-sharp black stones. Paul's body reacted with the speed of a trained fighter, but it wasn't fast enough to fully dodge Miguel's swing. When the wooden sword sliced into Paul's right leg, Paul's spirit bellowed in agony. But even though his blood was spewing onto the parking lot, I didn't feel a thing.

Call me a jerk, but I really didn't care about what happened to Paul. With the freedom of recklessness that comes from risking someone else's body, I lunged at Miguel and tried to overwhelm him with pure force.

I backed him up across the parking lot, but I made a wrong move, and Miguel spun me around and threw me into the rear gate of a Ford F150 truck. I could hear Paul scream in my head as his face bashed into the vehicle. But I still felt fine, so I pushed away from the truck and went for Miguel again.

The only problem was that Miguel must have figured out what was going on, because he started moving straight for John's body.

I closed half the distance between us with two lumbering steps, but I had no idea what I was going to do once I caught him. I needed a weapon, but nothing in the parking lot seemed a fair match for Miguel's brutal sword.

Over to my right, I saw the open trunk of the Audi. I dashed over to it, pulled up the floor of the trunk where the spare tire was, but couldn't find a crowbar. And I was out of time. The only thing of any substance I could swing was my brand-new guitar.

I glanced over in desperation as Miguel neared John's body.

With a curse on my tongue, I lifted the guitar from its case—its wood cool in Paul's beefy hand. I held it by its neck like a club and bolted for Miguel.

I reached him just as he raised his wooden sword above his head like he was about to chop a log in half with an axe. When I slammed the guitar into the back of Miguel's head, the instrument shattered into several pieces, but he dropped his weapon and fell to his knees, cradling the back of his head. Still holding what was left of the guitar neck in my clenched hand, I lashed out with a horizontal swing. When the jagged end of the guitar neck connected, blood splattered from the side of Miguel's face, covering his silver bling and showering the parking lot with blood and broken teeth. The blow knocked the sunglasses from his face, and I could finally see his wide-open, crazed eyes. He rolled away, and I followed him, ready to hit him again.

Before I could catch Miguel, Buddy tackled me, and with Paul's leg still losing blood and not working all that well, I collapsed to the ground, pulling Buddy down with me. I tried to push him away, but he felt like dead weight on top of me, and when I looked into his eyes, they were lifeless. When I rolled him off me, I saw that the jagged end of the guitar neck had pierced his chest.

Like I said, I'd never been much of a fighter, but I'd never been a killer either. The same as everyone else in America, I saw death all the time on TV and at the movies. I'd read about death, sung about death, and for all intents and purposes, I'd even died myself. But seeing Buddy's lifeless body and knowing I'd been the one who made him that way hit me harder than I expected.

Through my shock, a part of me knew I still had to deal with Miguel. When I turned to look for him, he'd backed up against a car tire and was trying to get to his feet.

I grimaced and extracted the guitar neck from Buddy's corpse, then stumbled over to Miguel.

He stopped trying to get up, frozen. Suddenly, his crazy eyes returned to normal, like a fog had been lifted from his brain, and he started to howl in pain.

"Don't kill me, man," he stammered as he struggled to hold it together. "I don't even know how I got here. I swear to Santa Maria, man."

Since my arrival in Ashburn, I'd been able to read people's expressions like a second language. And as I peered down at Miguel trying to shield his face from me, I believed him.

Evil and hatred had dripped from him only moments ago. But now he looked like a guy who'd just woken up from a nightmare only to realize his reality was worse than his dream.

I lifted the jagged, red-stained guitar neck to Miguel's throat, letting him know I could finish him if I wanted.

He started shaking, and a tear travelled down his ripped-up cheek.

"Why did you try to kill me?" I said. "And who the hell is Marco?"

"What are you talking about?" he said. "I don't even know who you are."

He looked past me at John's crumpled body.

"Oh shit, is that John?" he said, his eyes wide open in surprise and shock. "You better hope that asshole is dead, because if he's not, you don't have a lot longer to live."

I moved the edge of the jagged guitar neck away from Miguel's throat, then turned and walked over to John's body.

Behind me, I heard the slapping of footsteps as Miguel bounced from car to car, careening away from me into the darkness.

I knelt next to John's body and pressed my open hand on his chest. Just like before, I felt a quick snap of static electricity before my essence poured out of one body and into the other.

Back inside John's shell, I felt safe again—at least for the moment.

When Paul's spirit reclaimed ownership of his torn and beaten body, he screamed so loudly I had to cover my ears.

CHAPTER 15

P AUL PASSED OUT within seconds—the pain too much for him to handle. If I'd been smarter or meaner, I would've woken him up to get more answers, but I was too tired to care. Instead, I wiped the bloody guitar neck with his shirt and tossed it in the trunk before starting up the engine and heading back to John and Sybil's house.

I kept the stereo quiet as I navigated the streets of Ashburn on autopilot. Before I realized where I was, I was turning into the driveway. It had been a long and hard first day on the job, and even though I had more questions than answers, I tried to look at the positive side of things. I was still alive, my new body was strong and healthy, Ahriman's spell was leaving my stomach in peace, and there was a comfortable bed, a hungry dog, and possibly two hot women waiting for me inside.

That put a smile on my face, but I was still annoyed about Sybil and Hills abandoning me back at the bar. Maybe it had been another one of Sybil's tests—one where I could either prove I was really John or die in the process. But Miguel said he'd been delivering a warning from someone named Marco, which seemed to let Sybil off the hook. Even so, that still didn't explain why she hadn't stayed with me, and I was ready to give her a fair amount of shit as I entered the living room.

Then I saw Sybil and Hillary sitting on the couch, cuddled up, without any clothes on.

I was still angry, but not as much, because you know, forgive and forget—that's what my dad always said.

"That took longer than I expected," Sybil said.

She tilted her head toward the dog sitting on the floor at her feet.

"Shadow was starting to get worried about you. I hope you had a good time, at least."

I glared at her through narrowed eyes, then shook my head. I didn't know what the hell John did for a good time, but it seemed my definition of enjoyment was a lot different than his.

"I was hoping you would have stayed and watched," I said, trying to guess at how John would have reacted.

Hills started rubbing Sybil's shoulders and kissing her neck.

"I didn't want our new friend to get hurt," Sybil said. "Besides, watching you teach a few humans a lesson didn't seem like it would be worth it."

Maybe John made a habit of beating up gang bangers, but if dispatching those three was supposed to have been easy, I had a steep learning curve ahead of me.

My moment of introspection was interrupted as things between Sybil and Hills heated up. Both of them were stunning in their own right, but together, they were irresistible, and the looks they were shooting my way told me I was welcome to join them whenever I wished.

I started to take off my shirt, trying to get into the spirit of things. While I struggled to get my head out of the polo shirt's neck-hole, unwanted thoughts about Miguel and the mysterious Marco entered my head. I also wanted to know why humans had been able to hurt me so easily while I was in John's body.

"The head guy, Miguel, gave me a warning," I said as I threw my shirt to the floor.

Sybil sighed loudly, frustrated that I was ruining her fun by talking too much. She stopped kissing Hills and held her at bay with one hand.

"What kind of warning?" Sybil asked.

"He said Marco was tired of working with me and that my services were no longer required."

Sybil let out a burst of laughter.

"Marco and his little gang of *Olmecs* wouldn't be anything without you. He's the one providing services to you—not the other way around. We'll talk to Marco about Miguel the next time we see him.

But for now, why don't you stop thinking and come join us."

"He seemed like he really meant it," I said as I unzipped and stepped out of my khakis. "But he was also pretty confused at the end of the fight. Said he didn't know what he was doing there."

Sybil went back to licking Hillary behind her ear, and the young woman's moans and euphoric squeals confirmed she was enjoying the attention.

Sybil looked up from ravishing Hillary as I stepped toward the couch.

"Are you going to join us or not?" she said.

"Come on," Hills said, with her own version of a devilish grin. "Think of it like practice for Sunday. Sybil invited me to the party, too. You Ashburn people really know how to have a good time."

I raised my eyebrows at Sybil, but she closed her eyes and shook her head.

"Get down here, now," she said with a sudden tone of authority in her voice.

I stepped forward in my boxer briefs and socks. Before either of the women could comment on my sexy attire, I put one knee on the couch and leaned in closer to them.

I kissed Sybil deeply and didn't resist when Hills joined in and started kissing me too. I could still hear that voice of morality in the back of my head, telling me that I was deceiving Sybil because she thought I was John. But the voice was much quieter this time. I was just about to dive in head first when Sybil pressed her hand against Hillary's chest and turned to me.

"The first time I saw you looking at her, I knew you wanted her," she said with a snarl.

I backed away as razor-sharp talons grew from the ends of Sybil's fingers and her eyes glowed a deep crimson red. Without breaking eye contact with me, she shoved her hand deep into Hill's chest, then pulled it out with a wet, sucking sound. I watched as Hillary's eyes and mouth opened wide when she saw Sybil holding her still-beating heart.

I tried to speak, but I had to close my mouth to keep from throwing up.

Hillary's body went limp and fell to the floor, and Sybil held the young woman's shining slick heart out to me as if she were offering a freshly picked apple.

Through the fog of my disgust, I knew she was testing me again, and that I had already failed.

Sybil stood up and shoved the heart closer to my face, insistent. I shook my head and backed away.

"I didn't think so," she said as she tore off a giant chunk of the organ with her fangs and chewed.

"I can explain," I said, backing away. But before I could say anything else, Sybil was all over me, and not in a good way.

Thankfully, John's muscle memory kicked in. My hands shot up on their own and held the she-demon at bay as she frantically tried to reach my jugular with her teeth. My vision turned into a dark tunnel with her in the middle, and in the background, Shadow barked and growled.

"Tell me who you are," she said, spitting Hillary's blood at me with each over-enunciated word. "Because you sure aren't John."

To emphasize her point, she hit me with the oldest fighting move known to women—a knee to the groin. And it hurt like hell.

I groaned, and thankfully she paused in her assault just long enough for me to lunge at her with all my strength.

Surprisingly, that turned out to be quite a lot, as I slammed into her body and sent her sailing across the living room and into the kitchen. I followed after her while Shadow whimpered and barked behind me.

Before I could close the full distance, Sybil was on her feet again and snarling mad, and that's when I realized my big mistake. I'd sent her into the room where all the sharp things were kept. Sure enough, in a flash she grabbed two chef's knives from the counter and threw first one and then the other at me with blinding speed.

The stainless-steel blades sliced through the air, but my reflexes were supernaturally quick, and I easily dodged the first blade. But I wasn't fast enough to avoid the second knife as it sliced into my left arm. It didn't hurt much, but it drew thick, black blood from me that oozed from my wound. By the time I looked back up, half a dozen steak knives were flying through the air faster than the first two.

I didn't even try dodging them. I just dropped to the floor and covered my head.

Only two of the knives grazed me, but when I raised my head to see where Sybil was, her foot came up hard and hit me under my chin. As I rolled across the floor, something strange crossed my mind.

Even though she was kicking my ass, it turned me on for some reason. Half of me wanted to clobber her, but the other half wanted to take her upstairs and have hot demon sex as soon as possible.

I shook my head and tried to clear my vision as I got to my feet.

"If you can calm down for a minute, I can explain everything," I said.

"You smell like him," she said, moving closer to me, like she was stalking her prey. "But you don't fight like him, and you sure don't know how to use his powers. If you did, I'd already be dead."

"Maybe I don't want to kill you," I said, walking backward. "Have you thought of that? Maybe I just want to talk."

She leapt into the air and came down on me hard, body slamming me, then wrapping her legs around my torso, preparing to hit me again. I glanced over and saw Shadow sitting on the couch with a bored expression on his face as he watched us *play.*

"You weigh more than I thought," I said as I reached up and placed my open hand on her chest, deciding to try the only power of John's I knew anything about.

Maybe it was because my adrenaline was pumping and my anger was running hot, or maybe it was another example of John's muscle memory, but for whatever reason, my hand landed directly on one of her magnificent breasts.

I closed my eyes and tried to jump into her body the same way I'd done with Paul.

Turns out, my little trick didn't work on her at all. It only made her angrier.

She pulled back her clawed right hand, ready to slice my face to ribbons. I reached around and pulled her hair backward for all I was worth. Her head snapped back, and she screeched at me, as I used my leverage to flip her onto her stomach and pin her with my knee in the middle of her back.

I was breathing hard, but at least I had her under control, if only for the moment. I desperately tried to think of something I could do to maintain my advantage. And then I remembered something Ahriman had told me—about the leverage John had over the supernatural beings of Ashburn; he knew their true names. And even though I didn't have that information, I was hoping Sybil hadn't figured that part out yet.

"I'll let you up as long as you stay calm so we can talk," I said. "If you don't, I'll use your name to send you somewhere a lot less pleasant than this house. Are we clear?"

"You know nothing of my true name, imposter," she said, her voice muffled by the carpet.

"You're right about the imposter part," I said. "I'm not John. But I *am* his replacement. Ahriman sent me to do his job, and he made sure I had the tools to do it. He gave me everyone's names, including yours. And I have no problem using it if I have to. It's your choice."

As soon as I mentioned Ahriman, some of the fight went out of her, and her body relaxed.

"Fine," she said. "If you release me, I promise not to eat your heart—yet."

I counted to three in my head then let go and backed away, almost tripping over Shadow, who had decided to be social.

After a few sniffs, Shadow walked over to his water bowl, took a few casual sips and returned to the couch, collapsing on one of its leather cushions to watch us some more.

Sybil, still naked, sat on the ceramic tile floor, with her back against the kitchen's center island.

"Ahriman replaced John?" she asked.

"That's what he told me," I said.

Sybil rubbed her forehead and exhaled hard.

"This can't be good," she said, without explaining what she meant.

"I agree completely, but here I am."

"You're too nice for this job," she said.

"I have my own way of doing things."

"Your way won't work."

"It won't have to for very long," I said, wiping sweat from my forehead. "Let me ask you, what's the one thing you wish you could do right now more than anything else?"

"Besides eating your heart?"

I nodded.

"Getting the hell out of here," she said.

"Then it looks like we have something in common."

"If you just want to escape, why did you take this job in the first place? And if you're in John's body, what happened to John?"

"Ahriman tricked me into this situation, as demons will do—no offense. As far as where John went, I have no idea."

"Not all demons are the same," she said with a scowl. "I don't trick people. I give men—and women—exactly what they want."

I nodded toward Hill's lifeless body.

"Is that what *she* wanted?"

Sybil shrugged and rolled her eyes.

"She got plenty of what she wanted before you showed up. After that, it was my turn—and I needed her heart to stay alive."

I shook my head in disgust, horrified there was nothing I could do to help poor Hillary.

"I just want to leave Ashburn and get back to my old life," I said as I looked around for my shirt. "If you want to help, I'll bring you with me. If you don't want to help, stay out of my way because I'm getting out of here as soon as I can."

"In John's body?"

"I'll work with what I have," I said.

"And you'll take me with you, if I help?"

I nodded.

She sprang to her feet and stood in front of me in her full, naked splendor. She approached me, but more slowly this time—her anger replaced with sensuality again.

"John told me he used to leave Ashburn all the time—said he'd take me with him one day if I continued doing what he wanted. I kept my end of the deal, but he never took me anywhere. I should have known he wouldn't."

She averted her eyes and looked down at the carpet.

"He had me do a lot of horrible things for him, you know? Even by succubus standards."

"I'm sorry about that," I said as my anger and my libido waned, and my humanity resurfaced.

"Don't apologize," she said. "It sounds wrong coming out of his— out of your mouth. And stop being so polite and nice. You need to act more like him—more like a demon if you don't want people figuring out who you really are."

She gazed into my eyes, trying to seduce me, but it didn't work. I knew she was only trying to distract me from the truth and that I'd hit a chord with her. She wasn't used to someone treating her nicely, and she didn't know how to handle it.

Instead, she fell back on what she knew best, moving into my space until her body was pressed against mine. The smell of iron from Hillary's blood mixed with Sybil's scent and filled my nostrils, making me lightheaded in both a good and a bad way as she kissed my neck.

I hesitated, but now that Sybil knew I wasn't John, my guilt about deceiving her was gone. Even so, I was still shaken up by Hillary's death.

"I'm not really in the mood after the whole eating the heart thing," I said.

Sybil looked deep into my eyes and grinned.

"Oh, I think you *are* in the mood," she said as her magic tugged at my insides.

I tried to resist her for about two seconds before her lips moved to mine. The next thing I knew, we were upstairs, kicking in the bedroom door, and falling onto the bed.

I raised my head from the mattress and looked in her glowing red eyes.

"Maybe we should shower first?" I said, since both of us were still covered in dried blood.

She shook her head.

"I like things dirty."

"What about Hillary?" I said.

"You want me to go get her?" she said, smiling.

I scrunched my eyebrows together and wondered if she'd just suggested bringing a corpse into bed with us.

"No," I said. "Remember, I'm not John. I was just thinking it doesn't seem right to leave her down there like that."

Sybil laughed dismissively.

"She's dead. She'll be fine. Now get to work and no more talking unless you have something sexy to say."

I moved to kiss her again, tentatively at first, until she drew blood from my back with her talons and the demonic part of me awoke in full force. Our bodies meshed, and I let my dark urges rise and take over my mind and my soul.

As we explored each other with increasing passion, Santana's hypnotic guitar started playing in my head, followed by the singer lamenting over a black magic woman who was trying her hardest to turn him into a devil.

Needless to say, I totally understood where he was coming from.

CHAPTER 16

W HEN I OPENED my eyes, I was no longer in bed with a succubus.

I was back home in my home recording studio. For a minute, I felt a surge of happiness, and then I realized Ahriman was with me, writing the lyrics and the music for my songs and seizing control over everything else—even the videos and the cover art.

For the last two months, all I'd done was play his notes and sing his words. It felt like letting another man sleep with my wife—well, ex-wife—and being forced to watch. I grumbled here and there along the way, but each time, Ahriman soothed me with dark promises and told me this wouldn't be my last album—that I was giving so little for so much—that I would soon be able to write as many songs as I wanted, after he'd taken my cancer away.

Like a mule following a carrot, I kept going, laying down track after track as Ahriman worked through me, using my hands and my voice like I was a puppet. Having him inside me, occupying the same space as my soul, was terrifying. There was nowhere to run or to hide because he *was* me, and I was him. The only difference between the two of us was that he was the one in control.

When the guitar and vocals for the last song were finished, I worked with Mark to refine the drum track until Ahriman was satisfied. He told me that rhythm was the key to the human heart, even as I saved the files to the hard drive and backed them up for the fourth time that night.

After we were done, I watched Mark leave, wondering if I'd ever see my drummer again. Before Ahriman came into my life, Mark had been the closest thing to a brother I'd had. As he said goodbye, I didn't know whether to thank him for hooking me up with Duane or to tell him how much I hated him for it. In the end, I didn't say anything, and it was probably better that way. After all, Mark had made the introductions, but I was the one who'd made a deal with a demon.

Alone in the house, I went back to work mixing the songs on the computer. Two hours later, I was still at the computer, sweetening the vocals and putting the final touches on the last track.

I listened to the finished songs all the way through and nodded, satisfied the album was at least produced well. The sounds were tight, but the lyrics—I cringed at the thought of them being published under my name. One of the songs, *Calling You*, was so filled with *oohs* and *ahhs* it reminded me of *Yeah, Yeah* and made we want to puke.

"I'm sure it'll be a big hit in the karaoke bars one day," I said out loud, although I knew Ahriman would've heard me just as well if I'd simply thought my words instead of shouting them.

I enjoyed taking a jab at the demon, but I wasn't a fan of what he did to my internal organs a second later. My body seized up, and I doubled over, dropped to the floor, and screamed.

After fifteen minutes, the pain receded enough for me to sit up straight. Soon after that, I felt strong enough to get back to work. That's how it was with him. Punishment followed by just enough comfort to be productive again. When I hit *save* for the last time and loaded a copy of the album onto a portable drive, I felt relief, but also fear. Ahriman didn't need me anymore, and even though I wanted him to leave my body, I was afraid he'd go back on his word and let the cancer fully reclaim me. From what I knew of demons, it wouldn't be the first time one of them had deceived a human. It was what they did best.

That night, I tried to sleep, but the anxiety and fear of possibly waking up with cancer riddling my body again kept me up most of the night. I finally dozed off sometime in the early morning, and when I awoke, I still felt okay, but Ahriman was still inside me.

I sat up in bed and heard his voice in my head.

"You have more work to do before you are free."

I closed my eyes, and a tear made from equal parts relief and dread escaped my left eye.

CHAPTER 17

I WOKE FROM my dream in the pitch black of the bedroom, gasping for air. The fire that had consumed me earlier had been quenched by Sybil. But as I reached over, expecting to feel her bare hip, I found only cold sheets. My first instinct was to be concerned about her, but then I remembered who and what she was and what she'd done to poor Hillary. It was the rest of Ashburn that needed to be worried—not her.

If she had enough energy to go out after the night we'd spent together, then more power to her, but I was still tired as hell and tried to fall asleep again, even though I couldn't get the image of Hillary's heart out of my head.

When I awoke the next time, it was late in the morning, but I was better rested and thankful for the lack of dreams. I glanced to my left and saw Sybil's naked back.

I turned on my side and took in the feminine strength of her shoulders as I replayed details from our night together. She'd been a true demon in bed, but there was something else about her—a dark humor mixed with a matter-of-fact way of looking at life that made me like her. After only one day of knowing Sybil, I was beginning to suspect John hadn't deserved her as his girlfriend.

As I watched, she shifted in bed, and I caught a flash of the side of her face. I was expecting her high cheek bones and her slightly too-large mouth that gave her that killer smile. Instead, I saw a face made of dark red reptilian skin and a mouth lined with rows of deadly sharp teeth, like those of a shark.

I remembered Ahriman's true form and the demonic faces from the pub, as my mouth went dry and my heart raced. All I wanted to do was get out of the bed and away from Sybil. The thought that I'd kissed those lips and wrapped myself around that inhuman body sent waves of nausea rippling through me. Then a fear struck me with the realization that my true form was likely just as hideous now that I lived inside a demon's body.

As I shifted my weight to get out of bed, Sybil opened her eyes and her face returned to its regular beauty.

"That was a long night," she said, her voice lazy and sultry. "I'm sorry I didn't wake you up for more fun when I got home, but I was exhausted."

Even though I didn't respond, the expression on my face must have told her plenty.

"I don't usually look like that," she said, turning away from me. "It's a good thing it's what's on the inside that counts, right? Isn't that what the humans always say?"

She laughed, but I could tell it was forced and fake. The truth was, she was embarrassed that I'd seen what she really looked like beneath the human facade she maintained while awake.

"It's not a big deal," I said as I slid out of bed and walked over to the closet, hoping to find something to wear other than khakis. Luckily, I came across a pair of faded jeans. Those plus the dark blue tee-shirt from Chaz's store, and I at least felt comfortable. It wasn't the rocker image I would have chosen, but it would do for the time being. Even so, if I ended up staying in Ashburn for very long, I'd have to buy some real clothes.

"Get some more rest," I said to Sybil as I got dressed. "I'll feed Shadow and make some coffee."

"Fine," she said, but she didn't mean it.

Half-way down the stairs, the memory of Hillary popped into my head again, and I took a deep breath, preparing myself for the horror that was waiting for me in the living room.

I breathed through my mouth as I continued down the stairs, but when I turned the corner, the living room was empty, and Hillary's body was gone.

At first, I thought Sybil had disposed of the corpse to spare me the experience. Then I heard a whine and a burp, and I saw Shadow sitting on the couch, licking his lips—the fur around his mouth and nose stained pink.

As I stared at Shadow, Sybil snuck up behind me and grabbed my ass, literally almost surprising the shit out of me.

"Nice outfit," she said, motioning toward the *I Heart Rock and Roll* message blazoned across my chest. I looked like a dork, but she looked great in her skin-tight dark jeans, a fitted black tee-shirt, and classic black-and-white Chucks.

"It's better than a polo shirt," I said.

She raised her eyebrows and shrugged.

"Suit yourself," she said as she plopped down on the couch next to Shadow and scratched him behind his ear. "I told you everything would be taken care of. You're lucky to have this little guy around."

"Do I want to know what he did?"

"Let's just say he already had his breakfast. Speaking of which, I think you'd better let him out in the yard pretty soon, if you know what I mean."

I *didn't* really know what she meant, but I opened the back door anyway. Shadow slid off the couch and waddled out the door, his stomach distended and his eyes half closed.

I watched as he slowly found a place in the yard and did his business. It was both disgusting and impressive, but there was no way in hell I was going to pick up his crap. It could sit there for the rest of eternity for all I cared.

After he was done, the three of us regrouped in the kitchen to make a pot of coffee. The good news was Sybil had a coffee maker, but her beans were pre-ground and had been stored in a can on the counter, where the sun had likely baked them and severely compromised their flavor.

Blasphemous.

"Do you have any purified water?" I said.

She shrugged.

"In the refrigerator door, but I don't think the filter's ever been changed."

I shook my head and ran water out of the tap. Five minutes later, the kitchen smelled of brewing coffee, or as I like to say, pure bliss.

"Do you even drink this stuff?" I said.

"Of course," she said. "I'm a succubus, not a barbarian."

That was arguable.

I looked down at Shadow, who was staring up at me with his leash in his mouth while his tail wagged back and forth.

"I just took you outside a minute ago," I said, before turning to Sybil. "What does he want now?"

Behind me, Shadow dropped his leash onto the ceramic tiles with a clank.

"It's hard to tell sometimes, but I'd say he wants to go for a walk."

"Maybe later," I said, and Shadow huffed at me.

Carrying our coffees into the living room, Sybil and I sat down, and I had a chance to think through my situation.

"When was the last time John left Ashburn?" I asked.

"He was a hard demon to keep track of, even for me," she said, shaking her head. "He didn't say much about his trips, and usually I found out about them after the fact. I think he kept things quiet because he didn't want Ahriman to find out."

"I can understand why he'd be afraid of Ahriman," I said.

She laughed.

"I didn't say he was afraid of Ahriman. John wasn't afraid of anyone, even when he should have been. He didn't want Ahriman to know he could leave town because he didn't want Ahriman to figure out how to stop him."

She looked at me with sadness in her eyes.

"I don't know why John didn't take his chances out in the real world or back home even. I would have."

"Maybe he came back because of you," I said. "You two were a couple, right? I figure the sex must have been amazing at least."

She grinned at me, then frowned.

"We had our moments," she said. "You're not like him, you know? You seem like a good guy—so far, at least. John was strong and ambitious, and he took care of my needs, but no matter how close I thought we were becoming, he never softened. He was a true, old school demon, through and through."

I started to say something to assure her there were plenty of things to like about her. But I pulled away, remembering what she really was and how she'd ripped out Hillary's heart and offered it to me like it was a s'more.

Sybil stood up with her coffee in hand.

"You said you woke up in John's body yesterday morning, and you have no idea what happened to him?"

"Not a clue," I said. "Ahriman said he'd heal my body—that I'd live and be able to make more music, more songs. But he never said anything about Ashburn or waking up inside the body of his favorite demon enforcer."

"The basic arrangement for this kind of thing is that a demon, even one as powerful as Ahriman, can't take your soul without offering something in return that the host has to accept. I bet he went back to basics with you and arranged a classic switch. Your soul—your essence—went into John's body, and John's spirit was placed into yours."

I stood up and walked over to the mantel, examining the stacks of small notebooks piled on top of the shelf above it.

"I got his body and he got mine? Doesn't seem like a smart trade on his part, since I was dying of cancer. I wonder how Ahriman tricked him into agreeing to that?"

It was Sybil's turn to shrug.

"I'm not saying Ahriman would have been up-front about everything, but John was savvy. He would have known what he was getting into, and he would have understood the risks. John must have said *yes* to some kind of deal, just like you did."

"But why? It's not like he had a reason for doing me a favor."

"He didn't do favors for anyone," she said, lowering her eyes. "He only did things that benefited him."

"I'm not sure it makes any difference, but Ahriman said I was here to pay John back—that he was the one I owed."

She rubbed her chin and her eyes took on a far-away gaze.

"Maybe John wanted you to owe him. I guess that's possible. Or maybe Ahriman was lying to you about everything, and nothing is at all like it seems. That's more likely, I think."

She tilted her head back and downed the last drops of her coffee.

"We could sit here wondering all day about the deal Ahriman and John struck. But let's worry about you for a moment and how you plan on convincing people that you're still John. Tell me what you've learned so far about what a demon's body can do."

"When you left me with those three guys outside the bar—I jumped into one of them when I touched his chest."

"You possessed him," she said, correcting me.

"As in demonic possession?"

"Of course," she said. "What did you think you were? A fuzzy bunny? All demons can do it to humans, to one degree or another. Even though John was only a minor demon, he was particularly good at possession. By the way, don't ever try that move on me again or with any other demon or supernatural being. It can be done with enough power, but it's dangerous for both parties. Tell me what else you've figured out."

"I can read people's faces and their body language almost perfectly now. John must have been very perceptive, just like he was good at possessions."

She shook her head.

"That's just you seeing the human world through a demon's eyes. For us, all humans are slow, and their intentions are transparent. They don't hide their emotions nearly as well as they think they do. What else?"

"It feels like I'm stronger, sometimes."

She laughed.

"You're a *lot* stronger than you used to be. Much stronger than humans and more powerful than a lot of other demons. You're also weaker than many of them, too, so don't get too cocky. Don't forget that. John was pretty formidable for what he was, but he was still just a small demon with big ambitions."

She went to the kitchen and poured herself another cup of coffee before returning to the couch.

"He was here longer than most of us—for centuries at least," she said. "Way before this place existed as a suburb, when everything around us was wilderness. Even back then, Ahriman used this area to imprison beings with supernatural powers—lesser demons, forgotten gods, fallen angels, and other—creatures. Anything he could steal power from that wasn't strong enough to escape on its own. The stronger he became, the more powerful beings he could imprison."

"He said he put his enemies here," I said. "And creatures that were a danger to the world."

"Sometimes he has a good sense of humor," she said with a scowl. "Most of the supernaturals here didn't even know who Ahriman was before he imprisoned them. Now they all know him."

"What about you?" I asked. "How'd you end up here?"

"I'd heard rumors about Ahriman—the demon who wanted to become a god—but I never met him. I certainly wasn't his enemy," she said, giving a short laugh. "I was in Paris one day, about to dine on some fresh meat, when suddenly he appeared, spoke my true name, and commanded me to follow him back here. I still don't know how the hell he knew my real name, but I had to obey. There were only a few farms in the area when I showed up, and I remember being hungry a lot because the pickings for food were so slim, especially with John enforcing Ahriman's commandments."

"John was Ahriman's enforcer from the beginning?"

She nodded, staring into her coffee.

"He was always Ahriman's guy, as far as I know. But after a while, John started treating Ashburn and all of its inhabitants like they belonged to him. Even though he always did Ahriman's bidding and enforced his rules, John was plotting something big. I didn't know what it was, but he wasn't satisfied playing the lead role in Ahriman's cage. Like I said, he was a minor demon, but he had major league dreams."

Sybil stopped drinking, and I could tell from the glint in her eyes that she was thinking something through.

"Any idea why Ahriman would choose me for this?" I asked. "It's not like I have the best resume for this job."

"Who were you before all this happened? What was your name?" she said.

"I was David Steele," I said. "I still am."

Her eyes opened wide.

"As in, *the* David Steele, the one who sang the *Yeah, Yeah* song?"

I nodded, as I had countless other times when answering the same question throughout my life.

"How poetic," she said as she broke out laughing. "John really hated that song."

"You mentioned that already," I said, my face expressionless.

Sybil laughed even harder.

"You can think of yourself as David Steele if it makes you feel better," she said, wiping tears from her face. "But if I were you, I'd make sure everyone around here keeps thinking you're John."

"That's what Ahriman said."

"He was right," she said as her face darkened. "If they knew what I know, they'd rip you to pieces."

For a moment, neither of us spoke, as her silent threat sunk in. Then she grinned and her body relaxed.

"The truth is, I figured out you were an imposter in less than twenty-four hours," she said. "And others will too if you don't start behaving more like John—more like a real demon."

"I'll work on it," I said. "But I'm still a human inside. It's who I am."

I felt Shadow's hot, wet breath on my calf and reached down to pet him.

"First off, try not being so nice to me and Shadow. That's a good place to start."

I looked at Shadow, and he looked up at me. I wasn't sure I could be mean to that face, but I understood Sybil's point.

"I'll try," I said as I rubbed Shadow between his ears. "But what I really want to know is how John used to leave Ashburn."

"If I knew that, I wouldn't be here," she said. "But I figure the best place to look is back at the bookstore. John spent more time there than he did at home."

We set our empty coffee mugs on the kitchen counter, then walked toward the door to the garage.

I turned around and pointed a finger at Shadow.

"Stay," I said.

Sybil rolled her eyes, but Shadow sat down and looked up at the ceiling, his tongue lolling out of his mouth.

A few seconds later, Sybil and I entered the garage and got in the car, leaving Shadow behind.

"I looked through the store yesterday, but I didn't find anything."

"That's because I wasn't with you," she said as I opened the garage door with the remote, backed out of the garage, and pulled away.

As the house grew smaller in my rear-view mirror, Shadow let out a sharp bark from the back seat that made me jerk the wheel and almost drive off the road.

Once my heartbeat settled down, I thought about asking Sybil how Shadow had ended up in the car with us. I thought about chastising him. I thought about turning the car around and taking him home.

In the end, I shook my head and didn't say a word.

CHAPTER 18

W E PULLED INTO the parking lot in front of Ancient Pages under the noon-day sun, my mind racing with the hope that Sybil might find something I'd overlooked.

Once inside, Shadow settled on the floor, while Sybil and I went through the small office in the back of the store. At one point, I even checked inside the toilet's water tank, because I saw a movie once where a gangster hid his money and his cocaine there.

John must not have seen the same movie.

The only thing we found was a lot of dust. Frustrated, we moved to the front of the store and hit the bookshelves. Sybil opened a book and flipped through its pages, then moved on to the next one. She made it through a whole row before giving up and checking the walls.

After an hour of checking the store and a dozen sneezes, I slouched into one of the comfy reading chairs and picked up the copy of "The Serpent and the Rainbow" I'd set aside earlier. I ran my finger along its spine, wondering if it held any secrets that might help me with my Marie situation.

Meanwhile, Sybil returned to the shelves and slammed one of the books into place so hard, it shook the whole store. Then she turned and glared at me.

"Come over here and close your eyes," she ordered.

"Should I lock the door?"

She laughed, but wasn't amused.

"Normally, I'd welcome sexual advances from you or John or

anyone else for that matter, but right now I want to see if you really have any of John's muscle memory tucked away in your brain. Close your eyes, relax, and picture yourself leaving Ashburn."

"That's all I've been thinking about since I got here," I said as I closed my eyes and focused on the sound of my heart.

It was strong and beating so slowly I was worried it would stop. I ignored my anxiety and focused only on being somewhere else. Anywhere else.

Nothing happened.

I was about to give up when I felt a pull from behind me. I turned around, with my eyes still squeezed shut, and stepped forward, letting my instinct guide the way.

Sybil didn't say a word, but I sensed her following close behind me as Shadow panted at my feet. After a few more steps, I stopped. It felt like I had arrived somewhere familiar.

"John stood here a lot," I said with something close to hope in my voice. I opened my eyes and stared at the wall three inches away from my face.

"Then again, I could be wrong."

Sybil nudged me aside.

"There could be something behind the wall," she said as she ran the palms of her hands over the drywall. Her hands began to glow, giving off a deep red light, but after a few moments, she shook her head in frustration. She kneeled down and knocked on the carpeted floor, checking for a false floor or a tunnel, but there was nothing there either.

"Sorry for the false lead," I said, just as she stood up and punched her hand through the wall.

When she pulled it back out, pieces of drywall and white dust flew everywhere. She stepped forward and looked into the hole she'd created.

"See anything?"

"Just the studs," she said.

I bit my tongue to keep from making the obvious sarcastic comment.

"Looks like you were right the first time," she said, wiping her hands on the legs of her jeans. "There's nothing here."

"We can try some more later," I said. "I skipped breakfast and it's already two, and I'm starving. I think I'm going to try next door, if you're interested."

"I only eat at night," she said. "Enjoy your human food if you wish, but eventually you'll have to give John's body what it needs to sustain itself, and pad thai isn't it."

"I'll get an order of fresh human hearts if I'm not full after the noodles," I said.

"That wouldn't be a bad idea," she said as she turned and walked out the door, with Shadow following behind her.

I stuck my head out the door and watched as Sybil and Shadow walked across the parking lot amid the sounds of screeching tires and honking car horns. I didn't know much about succubi. But they were famous for their ability to seduce humans, and I wondered if her magic was affecting me as well. If the myths were true, she fed on men's souls the way other women ate chicken wings, but even so, I was still disappointed she was leaving.

That didn't surprise me because I'd never made the best decisions about women. Plus, the closest I'd ever come to having a girlfriend as hot as Sybil was when I went on three dates in a row with Susie in ninth grade. She was a total goth, and I was a skinny guy with bad skin who'd just started playing the guitar. I remember thinking she was cute but weird enough that I might have a chance with her.

I was mistaken.

Shaking thoughts of Susie and Sybil from my brain, I turned off the lights in the store, made sure the sign on the door said we were closed, and locked up before heading next door.

CHAPTER 19

T HE SMELL OF the food in Bangrak Thai instantly made my stomach growl as I anticipated a bowl of carbilicous drunken noodles. I didn't know if Sybil had been telling me the truth about what I should be eating now that I was occupying a demon's body, but I was in the mood for Thai food, not blood.

The restaurant wasn't huge, with about twenty booths scattered about and a small bar to my right with a flat screen TV mounted above the cash register. Since it was after the lunch rush, the place was mostly empty, with three servers working to get the room ready for dinner later that day. As soon as they saw me, they stopped what they were doing. One of them nodded to the other two and came closer to greet me with her head bowed.

"Will someone be joining you for lunch?" she said in a sweet but trembling voice that did a poor job of hiding her fear.

"I'm on my own today, but maybe you can let Rose know I'm here," I said.

The server sat me in a booth, handed me a menu, and took my drink order before stepping away.

When I turned back to the table, Rose was sitting across from me, wearing a conservative red dress and a smile that looked perfect on her aged, but pretty face.

"I am pleased to see you again so soon, David," she said. "I hope you do not mind me joining you."

I shook my head and raised one eyebrow.

She'd called me *David* again, but I'd been prepared for it this time, and instead of scaring the shit out of me, hearing my name comforted me.

"I have instructed my cooks to prepare our order immediately," she said.

"Pretty good trick, especially since I haven't told you what I want yet."

She grinned, shaking her head back and forth ever so slightly, as if she were tolerating a young child.

"I am sure you will enjoy your Drunken Noodles."

I wanted to tell her she was wrong, but of course, she wasn't.

"I guess it doesn't make much sense to ask if you're one of—us," I said, leaning closer to her. "That's how you knew my name and what I wanted to eat. And how you ordered for us with your mind."

She laughed lightly.

"I guessed your order correctly, because Drunken Noodles is one of our most popular dishes. And because your menu is open to the page where it is listed…and because I know it is your favorite Thai meal."

"How do you know that?" I said, trying to look nonchalant as I sipped the water that had suddenly appeared in front of me.

"I have watched you for some time now, and I have long admired your gift for music."

Now it was my turn to laugh.

"You're one of the few," I said. "The only song that ever went anywhere was *Yeah, Yeah*. I don't think anyone even listened to the other tracks on the album. And I hope you don't like the songs on my new record. They're not even mine."

"All music has a place and a purpose in this world, even if we do not immediately divine what that may be."

"Enlighten me as to the value of a tune called *Yeah, Yeah, No, No, Maybe*," I said with a flat smile.

"Your song still brings joy to many people, and that is no small blessing."

Maybe she was right about the joy part, but although *Yeah, Yeah* was my biggest success, it was also a constant reminder of my life's failure. But I wasn't there to talk about my ruined music career.

"I'm getting out of here as soon as I can," I said. "Any help you can provide would be appreciated."

"You are not planning on performing your duty as Ahriman's enforcer? It is a position of great importance in Ashburn."

"I don't have much of a choice for now," I said, inadvertently touching my stomach. "When I try to ignore my duties, his spell eats away at me until I give in and get to work. But it only seems to happen when I know about something that needs my attention. If I leave Ashburn, I won't know what I don't know. That's the plan at least. You're a prisoner here, just like me. Don't you want to be free?"

"I am no prisoner. I am here because one of my many destinies lies in Ashburn, with these creatures—perhaps even with you."

"Maybe *your* destiny is here," I said. "But mine isn't. I want to leave and start my new life—the one Ahriman promised me."

"Yes, I understand your desire," she said, her face suddenly stern. "But that is the thing about destiny. You do not get to choose it. Already, your fate is intertwined with this place. Leaving will not change that. If you were to escape somehow, he would find you, and you would not survive his wrath—not yet. You are not ready."

I hated her at that moment, but I realized she was telling me the truth.

"John knew how to leave Ashburn, and he did so a lot, without Ahriman finding out."

"Perhaps he did. Perhaps he did not," she said. "But where is he now?"

I rubbed my forehead. Rose was forcing me to think about things in a reasonable manner, which was giving me a headache.

"If he woke up in my body, he's dead," I mumbled.

Rose's voice and her face softened, and she touched my hand with cool fingers that acted like a sedative. My heart slowed, and my shoulders relaxed.

"My advice is for you to take your time. Embrace the role you have been given—for the time being. If you play your part well, Ahriman will not suspect what you are actually doing."

"And what is that?"

"Planning and waiting for your *real* opportunity. Remember, you are in a demon's body now, and time is something you have in abundance."

"That's great. But if I can't leave Ashburn, what am I planning for?"

"How to destroy him, of course," she said in a whisper. "Doing so is the only way you will ever be free. And so, although you possess the heart of a true artist, kindness and understanding will not help you defeat Ahriman or rule this place. You must be ruthless when called for."

When I looked into Rose's eyes, I saw the star-riddled night sky where her irises should have been. The sight slowed my breathing, calmed my soul, and made my problems seem small and insignificant.

We sat in silence until the server arrived, holding a tray with our food on it. Before she could do anything, Rose reached out, first with her two arms and then with two additional arms, grabbing our food and arranging our dishes in front of us at lightning speed.

In the time it took to blink, Rose had only two arms again and was sitting across from me suppressing a grin.

"What are you?" I asked.

"A god, or a goddess if you prefer," she said as she ate her tofu and dumplings. "One of many, but a deity, nonetheless."

I looked at her, at a loss for what to say. I'd been an atheist all my life, and even in the depths of fighting my cancer, I'd never once prayed to any god in any way. It just wasn't in my DNA. But sitting across from a self-proclaimed goddess who'd just used her four arms to serve our food was pretty convincing proof that divine beings actually existed.

"What are you doing running a Thai place in Ashburn? Can you leave any time you want, and could you take me with you? Theoretically speaking, of course."

She smiled and shook her head as I shoveled noodles into my mouth.

"I enjoy Thai food. The spice is a critical part of the food's flavoring and does not make the experience of eating unbearable. And yes, I can leave here at any time, in my own way. But no, I could not take you with me. Now stop talking and finish your noodles."

"Why not, if you're really a god?"

"Are you familiar with the term *omnipresence*?" she said. "You are witnessing it right now. The part of me speaking to you is only one of my many manifestations that exist across multiple dimensions. All of them are me, just as none of them are me. I am in thousands of places, having countless thoughts and engaging in conversations with all sorts of people and creatures, of which you are only one. It is not that I would not take you with me, but I do not travel and move through time and space in ways you can understand or replicate."

I thought while I chewed more noodles.

"Are you telling me that it's a *goddess* thing, and I wouldn't understand?"

She smiled.

"Essentially, yes."

I nodded and went back to my food.

Two bites later and I'd cleared my plate. As Rose started in on her last dumpling, I was silently pleased that the human lunch I'd just eaten had filled my stomach and eliminated my appetite.

"Would you like dessert or coffee?" she said.

"Do you know how I'm going to respond, or are you just being polite?"

"Manners are next to godliness," she said as the server arrived, holding a tray with two orders of mango sticky rice and two jet black Thai coffees.

"I think you mean *cleanliness*," I said.

Rose laughed briefly.

"I am quite sure of what I meant."

I nodded slowly and took a sip of the strong but sweet brew. Who was I to argue with a god?

For the next hour, Rose steered the conversation back to my music again. But this time, I humored her and answered all of her questions.

Soon, I was recounting what had been on my mind when I came up with the title for *Yeah, Yeah, No, No, Maybe* in the first place, and what it felt like to be a star. I didn't usually talk about that time in my life, not because it wasn't great, but because it was so short-lived. Maybe it was her godliness or the maternal vibe she seemed to emanate, but I felt comfortable telling her whatever she wanted to know.

It seemed like I'd only been there a short time, but as people began trickling into the restaurant for happy hour, I had a feeling the work day was over for most normal people and that Rose and her crew would be serving up dinner soon.

Even so, at Rose's urging, I was about to go into my story about opening for David Bowie when I was interrupted by someone bursting into the restaurant. When I looked up, I saw it was Oizys, frozen in mid-step, with one foot hovering over the threshold to the restaurant.

Rose still looked like a sweet old lady, but when she addressed Oizys, her voice made the silverware rattle on the tabletops.

"You are not welcome here, demon whore."

I involuntarily cringed at the insult, but then I remembered Oizys actually *was* a demon, and for all I knew, she may have also been—well, you know…

Oizys ignored Rose and addressed me directly.

"She's gone. Just like I told you would happen."

Rose cocked her head—bewildered. But I knew exactly who Oizys was talking about.

Marie had escaped.

CHAPTER 20

I SQUEEZED MY way past Oizys, hoping she'd remain stuck in Rose's entryway. But as soon as I opened the door to Ancient Pages, there she was, right behind me again.

"It won't be long before Ahriman discovers the Voodoo priestess is missing," she said as I blocked her from entering the store.

The worst part was that she was right. I had until Monday before Ahriman returned. I didn't know what the punishment would be for losing one of his pets, but it wasn't going to be pretty.

"I can help you," she said with a wicked grin. "You don't have to take the blame for this. We'll tell him Sybil helped her. If we're lucky, he might even reward us for turning your girlfriend in."

I wasn't surprised by how easily Oizys was willing to throw Sybil under the bus for something she hadn't done, but I still shut the door in her face.

Instead of leaving, she stood on the sidewalk and glared at me through the window. I made a mental note to install blinds and walked away.

Left alone with my dusty books, I thought about Marie escaping on my second day on the job. I chided myself for being a sucker and for believing her lies. Maybe she'd used magic on me to keep me from seeing her true intentions. Or maybe I'd ignored the obvious truth, because I'd never been able to read women. Either way, I was going to have to pay for my poor judgement.

I plopped down in one of the comfy reading chairs, practicing in my head how I was going to break the news to Ahriman. I picked up the book on Voodoo then set it back down since there was no real reason to read it anymore.

I slouched in the chair for half an hour with my chin resting on my chest, mulling over everything and nothing at all. I looked up when I saw movement outside the shop then stood as the lock turned over and half-a-dozen men spilled into the store.

A lean Latino with an almost-bald buzz cut, obsidian plugs in his ear lobes, and a permanent look of contempt on his face led the group. His arms were inked with tribal tattoos, and he wore a circular silver pendant identical to Miguel's.

I wasn't surprised when Miguel stepped out from behind him. He was still bruised badly and missing a few teeth, but he looked more embarrassed and angry than hurt.

As far as I knew, being psychic wasn't one of my demonic powers, but I had a feeling the leader was the infamous Marco.

"You hurt one of my people," Marco said in a calm and even tone.

"Miguel and two of his little buddies jumped me," I said. "I was defending myself."

Marco laughed.

"My boys don't do anything I don't tell them to do, especially when it comes to customers. Miguel says he woke up with some big guy he'd never seen before beating the crap out him. Says he saw you out cold on the ground and that he was worried about you, amigo. Until he figured out it was you inside the guy beating him up, pulling that possession crap again."

Marco cracked his neck and took a deep breath. I took a whiff of the air. He smelled like a human, but there was something different about him. He wasn't afraid.

"What made you think it'd be a good idea to mess up my boy?" he said.

Being in a face-off with six gang members mostly made me want to run away, but that was the human in me talking. For whatever reason, Marco and his boys seemed to know all about John being a demon, even though that clearly broke Ahriman's last commandment.

As far as Marco knew, I was a badass monster named John. And that meant it was time for me to start playing the part.

"I'm sorry to hear about your boy, but I'm not in the mood for this right now," I said, channeling everything I'd learned in the three acting classes I took back in the '90s.

"It's not personal," Marco said, shaking his head and taking a step closer. "But I can't let you do that kind of thing to one of my own, no matter how stupid he is. You have to make restitution for your actions. I know that you, more than most people, understand what I'm talking about."

The fact that Marco knew what I was and was still in my face was starting to concern me. But I forced myself to stand my ground as one of his crew handed him a wooden sword studded with razor sharp pieces of obsidian.

I cursed myself for not bringing the broken guitar neck into the shop with me as I checked the room for anything I could use as a weapon.

Unfortunately, I was screwed unless Marco was really allergic to dust mites.

With nothing to lose, I did what I'd always done when I got into trouble. I talked.

"You're making a mistake," I said. "Why would I beat up one of your crew and mess with our business relationship?"

Marco grinned as he turned to Miguel, but it was a cruel, humorless expression.

"Did you attack John?"

Miguel crossed his arms in front of his chest and shook his head.

"I know you like stirring things up," Marco said. "Maybe you were testing me. Maybe you wanted to see if I'd hit back. Well, you're about to find out."

Marco was only human, but he looked like a badass who could kick some serious butt. I, on the other hand, was a demon that didn't know how to use most of my powers. So I kept talking.

"You know that's bullshit," I said, sticking my chest out and trying to look intimidating. "Miguel said you were tired of working with me and that my services were no longer needed. As far as I see it, you're the one who started this."

Marco held up a finger, and one of his men locked the door to the store. Then Marco raised his wooden sword like he was getting ready to take a swing at my head.

"Like I said—it's nothing personal, but I gotta look out for my own. And you know, I have to stick up for us humans once in a while, too. You'll be fine though. I know you heal fast."

I flexed my body, waiting for him to attack. Instead, he slowly lowered his sword, and three of his guys, led by Miguel, rushed me.

The first of them was tall and wiry, and he threw a sloppy punch straight out of a bad cowboy movie. I'd seen it in dozens of drunken bar fights, and with my new set of reflexes, I stepped out of the way with plenty of time to spare.

Thug number two was muscly and knew how to throw a punch. When it landed square on my chin, my face went numb and my body spun around like I was practicing ballet.

I cursed as I shook my head and tried to get to my feet. He was a human, and he wasn't supposed to be able to hurt me. But he did.

I turned around just as Miguel tried to kick my head. Dumb move. Faster than I could think about it, my new body reacted. My leg shot out, and my foot connected with his groin, sending Miguel to the ground writhing in pain.

Meanwhile, the muscly guy jumped over Miguel and started grunting and flexing and making a lot of noise. I backed up into the narrow hallway that led to the back office so he and the wiry guy couldn't come at me at the same time.

Mr. Muscles rushed me first, and before I could react, he tackled me and sent me sprawling onto my back. I landed with all 250 pounds of him pressing down on my chest as he pulled his fist back, ready to pummel me. When he did, I saw the silver pendant with the stylized demon face dangling from his neck, and with nothing better to try, I reached up and ripped it off. As soon as I did, his eyes went wide, and he scrambled backward, trying to get away from me as fast as he could.

Grinning, I tossed the pendant to the back of the store and grabbed his ankle before he made it too far.

I didn't know what my new body was capable of yet, but I knew one trick, and it was a pretty good one. With his ankle in my hand, I closed my eyes and jumped into his body.

As soon as I took over, I knew everything he knew. His name was Julio, and Julio was good at fighting and not much else.

Luckily for me, I didn't want him for his brains.

I stood up in Julio's body and made sure I was blocking access to John's empty shell on the floor behind me. Marco and most of his gang were hanging back, except for the wiry guy whose name was Santos, and Miguel, who, to his credit, was up again and ready for more.

Miguel and Santos glanced back and forth between me and John's body, sizing up their chances of making it past me. Meanwhile, Julio's spirit cowered in the corner of his mind. He really didn't enjoy being possessed, and I could not have cared less. In fact, I was in a bad mood and decided I was going to be as brutal and efficient as I had to be to protect John's body, even if it meant sacrificing Julio in the process.

Sybil and Rose would have been proud of me.

I tore into Miguel first, since he'd started this whole thing. I put him in an arm lock that must have been one of Julio's favorite moves, then lifted him up and slammed Miguel, neck-first into the floor. I dragged him to his knees and put his arm in the same lock again, and when I spun around to face Santos, I heard the delicious snap of his arm.

I'd been in plenty of bar fights, and I'd lived through mosh pits that would have killed a normal man, but I'd never enjoyed inflicting pain—not even on my enemies. But when Miguel cried out, a shiver of pleasure flowed through my darkening spirit, and I smiled—feeling happy and disturbed at the same time.

I glanced back at John's body behind me and weighed the risks of moving farther away to take the fight to Santos.

I was doing the best I could, but I was still new to using someone else's body like a battle bot, and while I was deciding on my next move, Santos pulled a knife and shoved its blade into my bicep. Julio screamed inside my head even though I couldn't feel a thing. I pushed the knife in deeper to make sure Santos couldn't take it back and use it on me again.

That freaked Santos out a little, I think. His eyes went wide, and he started backing away, but I reached out, grabbed him by the front of his shirt, and pulled him to me. He opened his mouth to say something, but I tossed him to the left, slamming his head into a fold-up metal chair leaning against the wall. I had to give it to him—for such a skinny guy, his skull was pretty damn hard. It left a good-sized dent in the chair, but the chair won, and Santos slid to the floor, unconscious.

With Miguel and Santos out of the picture, I turned to Marco and the rest of his gang, ready to fight until Julio's body had nothing left to give. Instead, Marco looked at me with a genuine smile on his face and started clapping.

"I knew it was still you," he said, handing his wooden sword back to one of his guys as he approached me.

Part of me wanted to kill him just for ruining my afternoon, but the other half of me was too stunned to act.

"You can go back to your own body now," he said. "You and me are totally cool."

"You don't need to teach me a lesson anymore?"

He waved a hand in the air, like he pushed aside the notion.

"I was just talking shit," he said, motioning to Miguel and Santos on the floor. "I heard you've been acting pretty strange lately, amigo. And I gotta admit, when I walked in here, I didn't think that was really you. You looked like John, but something was off. I thought maybe someone was possessing you! But after watching you in action, I'm convinced. You're as mean as ever—just the way I like you."

I nodded and wiped some blood from Julio's mouth before stumbling back to John's motionless body. Before leaving Julio, I twisted the knife in his bicep one more time to make sure it really hurt. As soon as I was back in John's body, the first sound I heard was Julio screaming his bloody head off.

Before I could tell him to keep the noise down, Marco delivered a solid blow to the back of Julio's head and knocked him out.

Back inside John's body, my mind recalled Julio's pendant. I wasn't about to touch that thing while Marco was still around, but it was too powerful to let them have it back. With a casual kick, I sent papers flying into the air behind me so they covered the magical piece of jewelry when they landed.

Marco looked me over.

"What's going on with you, man?" he said with a laugh that showed off his gold-capped front tooth. "Not getting enough sleep? I have some pills that will help with that if you need something."

His crew—besides the three he'd sent after me—started laughing, and I did too. Not because anything was funny, but because it seemed like the kind of thing John would have done.

"Seriously," Marco said, with eyes that were suddenly cold. "What is going on with you? Miguel said you were acting like you didn't know him *or me* last night."

I nodded toward Miguel who was weeping quietly on the floor.

"How could I ever forget you? Like I said before, Miguel's the problem. He's the one who didn't know what was going on and the one who attacked me. He's lucky he's still alive."

Marco shook his head with a frown and glanced down at Miguel.

"I'll have a talk with him later. In the meantime, I'm glad we're good again. I heard you had a falling out with the big guy—that you were gone, or dead, or whatever the hell happens when things like you get disappeared."

"I don't know what to tell you," I said, shrugging. "Ahriman and I are still tight. He's stopping by on Monday, as a matter of fact."

Marco smiled then clapped me on the shoulder.

"That's what I wanted to hear," he said. "Now that I know everything's cool, I'll be back tomorrow with the delivery. Same time as always."

"I'll be waiting," I said with as much confidence as I could muster, even though I had no idea what he was talking about.

Marco raised his left eyebrow.

"You do that. And be ready with my payment. I've been waiting all week for Friday, and I'll be ready to party."

I nodded and reminded myself to talk with Sybil about finding some money. I may have been a demon, but Marco was a scary guy, and despite being human, he knew more about this place and how it worked than I did. And even though I'd just beaten three of his thugs, that was only because of dumb luck.

Next time, I was certain Marco and his people wouldn't be so careless.

I watched as they picked up their wounded and left the store.

They were out of sight before I walked over and picked up Julio's silver pendant and examined it more closely. It was circular with a stylized face in the middle of it that was sticking its tongue out—a monster as best I could tell—maybe even a demon. As I held it, I felt suddenly weak and sick to my stomach.

I set the pendant down at the far corner of my desk and stepped away, taking a deep breath as my strength returned. Returning to the main part of the store, I was amazed it hadn't been completely destroyed. The only damage was to the metal chair that still bore the imprint of Santos's head and to the floor that was smeared with blood in several areas.

I sighed and went to find a mop.

When I returned, the blood stains were gone, and Shadow sat in the middle of the floor, licking his jowls.

I looked at the closed door to the store, then behind me, expecting Sybil to be with him. But the dog had come alone.

"You came back," I said, looking out the window again for Sybil, who was still nowhere to be seen. "But how'd you get in here?"

I plopped down in the comfy chair again and looked at Shadow and his deceptively cute, eye-patched face.

"If you and I could only talk for a minute, I bet you could tell me a thing or two about this place, couldn't you?"

Shadow pranced up to me, wagging his tail, and I patted the top of his rock-hard head. Then he barked once and ran to the back of the store.

CHAPTER 21

A MINUTE LATER, Shadow returned with a pair of dark-lensed, black goggles in his jaws.

After cleaning them on the leg of my jeans, I put them on, and when I did, I almost lost my shit. Literally.

Shadow, the cute dog with a penchant for blood was no longer there. In his place stood a huge beast covered in mottled black fur, towering above me by a foot. His eyes glowed a deep red, and his teeth were as deadly as ice picks.

Ripping the goggles from my face, I backed away and stumbled over the arm of the chair. When I looked again, the Shadow I'd grown used to was back.

I tried to clear my head before putting the goggles on again. This time I was prepared for the giant devil dog that reappeared as soon as I had them on.

I calmed my breathing and eased back into the chair.

The monstrous Shadow lowered his massive head and nudged my hand, asking for me to pet him. I reached out with a shaky hand and rubbed the fur on his chest.

I couldn't tell for sure, but I thought he grinned as I worked my fingers through his thick coat of hair.

My mouth dropped open when I looked at my hand and saw its deep red and purple-black skin and black, claw-like fingernails.

A chill ran through my spine as I flashed back to Sybil's true face and wondered if mine was as horrific.

I eased myself around Shadow and walked up to the store window. It wasn't going to be the same as seeing myself in a mirror, but that's why I chose it—so I could view myself the way a child looks at his first horror film through spread fingers covering his eyes.

When I stared into the window's reflection, I saw John's more-or-less human face staring back. My hair was thick and black, and I was handsome in a dark, diabolical way. I even had a few scars on my face that made me wonder how John had earned them. My forearms were veined and muscular, and even though I wore a shirt, I could tell that my chest was huge. What surprised me the most were the two black, bone-like protrusions sprouting out from my forehead. My horns weren't as large as Ahriman's, but they left no doubt that I was a proper demon.

I wondered how many times in my former life I'd walked past a demon or spoken to one without knowing. I took a deep breath and stepped outside into the Ashburn twilight to take a real look at my surroundings for the first time.

What I saw through the dark lenses of the goggles made me catch my breath.

Most of the people in the parking lot were clearly human, but there were also a lot of other creatures walking around that were anything but. Some had skin the same coloration as mine, whereas others were black with green highlights, and one had skin of the darkest blue. Most had horns jutting from their heads, but others had bony protrusions sticking out from their shoulders, backs, and legs. One even dragged a reptilian tail behind it.

The fact that there were demons everywhere wasn't what fascinated me the most. It was the town of Ashburn itself that was the most stunning. The boring suburb shimmered and glowed in bright reds, greens, yellows, and blues. Energy trailed from or surrounded the demons themselves, but many of the brightest concentrations of energy were located at the entrances to stores, around various cars, and attached to pieces of nature, like the trees, the rocks, and even some patches of grass.

I turned to check out the door to Bangrak Thai and saw it was bathed in intense, pulsing white energy. I looked at the doorknob to my store, Ancient Pages, and saw that it was glowing red.

Across Claiborne Parkway, the paved walking path that stretched alongside the road was protected by a canopy of white energy that covered the trail for as far as I could see in both directions.

When I held my hand out in front of me, it crackled with red and orange energy, and when I looked past my hand to the sky above, I saw Ashburn for the prison it was.

"Ahriman, you piece of shit," I said out loud in a whisper. Far above me, the sky shimmered with black energy that formed an enormous dome around the town—the same wall of magic that had kept me from leaving the day before.

At least I could see the bars of my cage. But given the fact I had to wear my goggles to do so, I wondered how many of Ashburn's supernatural beings could say the same.

Finally, I understood why John wore his goggles all the time. Knowing immediately whether something was a human, a demon, or a god would provide a clear advantage in almost any situation.

Forcing myself to turn away from the magical world of Ashburn, I went back inside, took off the goggles, and sat down, trying to process what I'd just seen. I looked at my arm, pale and white, with normal fingers and fingernails. Shadow sat down at my feet, once more a sweet, cuddly dog with a black eyepatch of fur.

"What the hell have I gotten myself into?" I said, looking down at him. He cocked his head and raised his ears. He might have been a demonic hellhound that could travel across town in an instant, but he was also becoming the closest thing I had to a friend in Ashburn, and I rubbed his head warmly.

"Thanks for the present," I said. "At least I can see what's going on now."

I gave his thick chest fur another vigorous rub. He sat up straighter and made a comforting noise of bliss. We were having a real moment before he curled his body inward and started licking his private parts.

"Good boy," was all I could think to say, but as I watched him behaving like a normal dog, his true form flashed through my mind again. He stopped his licking and stared up at me as if he could read my thoughts. I stared into his eyes, and somehow I could tell he was comfortable with what he was—both a loyal pet and a vicious, demonic beast.

I decided it was time to follow his lead—to embrace who and what I had become—to accept my new life and to play the long game Rose had suggested.

When I reached down to pet him again, his hackles stood on end, and a second later, one of the runners who'd flipped me off the day before rushed into the store.

The stranger bent over with his hands on his thighs, trying to gulp down enough air to catch his breath. He held up his hand palm toward me while he composed himself. Shadow started into a low growl, and I slowly slipped my goggles back on to assess my new visitor.

What I saw was—unexpected.

He was surrounded by magic—not as white as the energy that spilled out of Rose's restaurant, but close. He was good looking enough to be unsettling with white hair to his shoulders and a face that was too perfect and which lacked the normal lines and creases of age. Two ashy-gray wings protruded from his shoulder blades, ruining his otherwise pristine appearance. They might have once been as white as his hair, but they were covered in gray dust and seemed old and unused now.

I couldn't be sure, but as best as I could tell, a fallen angel had just entered my store.

CHAPTER 22

A NGEL GUY WATCHED me as I pretended to be unfazed by his presence.

I'd spent the last two days dealing with demons and a goddess who ran a Thai joint, and I had no problem accepting their existence. But for some reason, learning that angels were real disturbed me.

"Looking for a book about running?" I asked, clearing my throat. "Or maybe a copy of 'Dante's Inferno' would be more up your alley."

"You're funnier than usual," the angel said, still breathing heavily. "I don't like being here any more than you do, Hell spawn. But there's been an accident involving one of the humans at the corner of Claiborne and Waxpool. You need to get there right away."

The runner turned away and left the store. He stood on the sidewalk, stretching.

I looked down at Shadow and he looked up at me. I could tell we were both thinking the same thing—if angel guy expected us to break into a run and follow him, he was crazy.

For a moment, I considered ignoring him altogether. But I was pretty sure angels weren't known for being big liars. So I locked up the store—again—and headed for my car with Shadow following at my heel.

When I turned to ask the angel if he wanted a ride, he was already running across the parking lot toward Claiborne, his useless wings flapping behind him like two kites struggling to get airborne. He may have been a glorious, heavenly solider at one point in his existence, but from what I could see, that was a long time ago.

As the sky started to turn to evening, Shadow and I hopped in the car, and within seconds, we were on Claiborne Parkway, passing the angel who was running on the asphalt walking path that snaked alongside the road.

I looked up and saw him flip me off in my rear-view mirror as he passed under one of the lamps that had just turned on and was illuminating the trail. Maybe he was pissed off at John for some reason. Or maybe his anger management issues were the reason he'd fallen from grace in the first place. I didn't know and didn't care.

As I hit the gas, I braced myself for whatever was coming next.

The flashing red and blue lights of three police cars and the ambulance blocked the intersection at the next light while one officer directed traffic around the wreck. I didn't feel like I belonged there, but I pulled over behind one of the police cars and stepped out.

I looked back and pointed at Shadow.

"Stay here, boy."

He looked at me briefly then jumped out and followed me. If dogs could laugh, I had a feeling he would have been holding his belly. I shook my head and headed for the group of police officers. A few feet from where they stood, EMTs worked on a lone figure sprawled in the middle of the road.

One of the cops walked toward me, holding a flashlight, and nodded.

"Thanks for coming so quickly," he said. His words were welcoming, but the micro expressions of disgust and contempt on his face told me he wasn't happy about seeing me at all. It was a sentiment I'd encountered more than once when I worked as a private investigator for a few years in the '90s. More often than not, I was just a glorified peeping Tom, following cheating spouses and taking photos through half-open blinds.

"What's going on?" I said, noting the name on his badge read *Boreman*.

He motioned for me to follow him. The EMTs had stopped their work and covered the body with a white blanket to shield the sight from passersby. One of the EMTs paused as he packed up his bag. He looked up at the Sheriff and shook his head.

"We have a problem," the Sheriff said to me as he squatted next to the body. With the beam of his flashlight pointed at the body, he pulled the blanket back enough to reveal the face of a middle-aged woman whose only obvious sin was that she'd spent too much time in the sun.

"Was she hit by a car?" I said.

"I don't think so," he said, pulling back the sheet farther so I could see the woman's undamaged torso. Her tee-shirt wasn't torn, and her makeup looked as if it had just been applied.

Behind me, Shadow let out a deep growl, and I felt a breeze on my back as the angel stepped up beside me.

"Thanks for fetching him, Raziel," the Sheriff said.

"Other than being dead, she looks pretty good," I said. "I'm not sure how I can help her."

"I grew up in Alaska in a small town called Whittier," the Sheriff said. "I saw a lot of strange things there, believe me. And this here— it just feels wrong. Maybe she had a heart attack, but my gut says something else is going on—something that falls under your area of expertise."

"Why is that?" I asked, not wanting to know the answer.

"We have a witness who saw it happen," the Sheriff said, leaning in to me, like he was afraid someone else would hear him. "He saw her crossing the street the same time a car turned onto Claiborne and cut her off."

"Sounds like a hit and run," I said, but the Sheriff and Raziel both shook their heads.

"The witness is on record as saying, quote—*an invisible force*—end quote, picked her up, held her three feet in the air and then dropped her. And *that* is why you are here, John."

Both the Sheriff and Raziel stared at me, waiting for me to say something about the crime scene. The problem was, I wasn't John, and none of what I was thinking made any sense.

"I'll look into it right away," I said slowly, figuring the best I could do was to stall and add this to the list of things to ask Sybil about. "But it might take me a while to figure out who or what did this."

The Sheriff took a deep breath then exhaled before speaking.

"I don't mean any disrespect," he said. "But our humans are supposed to be off limits to your kind. Up until now, I haven't had to deal with anything that couldn't be explained away with some creative paperwork. But this was done out in the open, in the daytime for everyone to see. I can't have that sort of thing happening around here, especially since neither one of us wants to draw extra attention to— our situation."

"We do not wish to cause you any problems," Raziel said, his voice taking on a soothing tenor that my ears immediately detected. I didn't know what Raziel was up to, but the Sheriff calmed down.

"John will determine which creature committed this atrocity, and I assure you, he will punish the guilty party appropriately. That is one thing he does very well."

I turned and looked at Raziel. I felt horrible about the dead woman, but I didn't like some random angel making promises I might not be able to keep.

"I'll do what I can," I said with a tight smile aimed at the Sheriff. "That's all I can promise."

"You've always been good to your word," the Sheriff said. "But whatever you're going to do on your end, do it before this happens again."

I nodded and took another look at the dead woman's face.

She'd been attractive, with prominent cheek bones and short, jet-black hair. Anyone could have told you that. But there were even more details I could see that no human would have noticed—namely the few grains of yellow-orange powder on the inside edges of her nostrils.

I closed my eyes and cursed under my breath because I'd seen the same powder before in the soul jars at Marie's house.

"When did this happen?" I said to the Sheriff.

"About an hour ago."

I nodded. Oizys said that Marie had escaped from Ashburn earlier in the day, so something wasn't adding up. It was possible she'd returned to kill this woman for some reason, but it didn't seem likely. Once again, I wondered if Oizys had lied to me. Maybe Marie hadn't gone anywhere at all. Regardless of whether Marie had really escaped or not, she was connected to this woman's death somehow. I would rather have left things up to the Sheriff and his people, but I could feel the gnawing of Ahriman's magic alive in my stomach, compelling me to get to work.

"I'll figure it out," I said again. But this time I meant it. "What was her name?"

"The credit card in her pocket said *Laura Henders.*"

I stood up and stretched my back even though I didn't need to. Some habits die hard.

"Where will you start?" Raziel asked.

"Don't worry about that," I said, trying to be a little more of the asshole I was supposed to be. I ignored Raziel, walking past him and signaling for Shadow to follow me to the car.

By the time I left the murder scene, it was getting late. I needed to find out what had happened to Marie and how she was connected to Laura Henders' death, but I wanted to talk with Sybil first, and I needed some sleep. So I headed home, hoping to catch her before she left for the night.

After a short drive, I pulled into John's garage and let Shadow into the house. Before I went inside, I opened the trunk and pulled out the guitar neck that had saved my ass the night before. Destroying such a beautiful musical instrument had been a sin, and holding the walnut neck in my hand felt like I was carrying the physical remains of a dead person. But I couldn't change what had happened. Based on what Chaz told me about the strings, I carefully unwound them from the headstock, rolled them up, and left them in the car.

"You need a better name than Guitar Neck," I said. "Maybe something fierce like *Demon Killer.*"

Seeking inspiration, I took a look at the guitar neck using my goggles, but I ripped them off immediately as intense white energy stabbed at my optical nerves. I wasn't sure exactly what Chaz was— maybe an angel or even a god—but whatever he was, he put a lot more than love into his instruments.

"No wonder you did so much damage to those assholes," I said. "I should call you God Stick."

I shook my head.

"That's not much better than Guitar Neck. How about I call you Gus?"

Gus was a guy who used to drive my bus all over the country, right after *Yeah, Yeah* became a hit. To me and the rest of the band, he was the nicest person ever, and we all liked him. But he also used to box, and no one ever messed with him either.

"*Gus* it is," I said with a wry grin.

I thought about carrying the weapon inside with me, but I didn't think Sybil would like it. I hadn't looked at the color of her magic yet, but I was pretty sure it wasn't white.

Instead, I returned Gus to the trunk, then stepped inside and called Sybil's name. I hollered again before going upstairs to check for her, but she wasn't home.

Alone in the house, I plopped down on the leather couch in the living room and waited for Sybil. Shadow jumped up next to me and licked my hand. I couldn't help but grin as I reached over and gave his chest a good rubbing.

I mindlessly turned on the TV and surfed the channels until I came across an old Scooby Doo episode. I chuckled when I realized it was one of my favorites—*Mamba Wamba and the Voodoo Hoodoo*. In it, a music group performs a song based on an ancient Voodoo chant and accidentally summons a long-dead witch doctor who wants to turn them all into zombies.

Those crazy kids.

As I watched Scooby and his friends chase and be chased, I reviewed everything I needed to ask Sybil and what I had to do the next day, but I lasted only five minutes before my eyes were too heavy to stay open.

When I woke up, it was one in the morning. I shut off the TV, peeled myself from the leather couch, and let Shadow out one last time before turning off the lights and heading upstairs. Once in the bedroom, I settled my head into the stack of comfy pillows and was asleep again in seconds.

CHAPTER 23

T HE NEXT MORNING, I slept in, relishing the peaceful darkness of the curtained bedroom. I wanted to stay where I was and let everything in Ashburn happen without me, but my stomach pangs started up the second I thought about it.

I placed my hand on the cold sheets next to me, but Sybil wasn't there. To my surprise, I felt something close to jealousy and concern mixed together in a single emotion.

After I got dressed and fed Shadow, I sipped some coffee that was strong but still without much flavor as my little hellhound dropped another foul load in the back yard, right next to the one he'd deposited the day before.

I still didn't know who was on poop detail, but it wasn't going to be me.

As I drained the last drops of java and brought Shadow inside, I thought about how I was going to figure out who had killed Laura Henders and what had really happened to Marie.

Since Sybil still wasn't home, I decided to return to the store and hit up Rose with some of my questions. A minute later, Shadow and I were headed for the bookstore again. On the way there, I thought about snooping around Marie's house for some clues and to see if I could learn more about the yellow-orange powder in her soul jars, but I thought someone might notice me breaking into her house in the middle of the day.

When I parked in front of Ancient Pages, Ashburn was already in motion. Securing my goggles to my face, I checked out the parking lot and watched the soccer moms, business dads, self-entitled kids, weekend warriors, and more than a few demons and angels intermingled with the humans, going about their day.

With Marie still on my mind, I unlocked the door to the bookstore and stepped inside.

I was greeted by Marco sitting in my favorite reading chair.

"You're late," he said, trying unsuccessfully to conceal his anger, but I wasn't in the mood to be bullied around, especially in my own store.

"You're in my chair," I said with a sneer.

Marco raised his eyebrows.

"I've been here for an hour, amigo," he said. "And you know I don't like to wait. We can talk about your manners later, but right now I got your stuff out back in the truck, and I seriously need to get paid."

Marco moved toward me with purpose, wearing the same silver pendant around his neck that I knew about all too well. My body tensed, preparing for another fight, and I suddenly felt weak and drained.

Shadow growled and barked, causing Marco to stop a few feet away from me.

Good dog, I thought.

"It's not cool to make me wait a whole hour," Marco said.

"I had other things I was taking care of," I said, lying.

He narrowed his eyes and glared at me.

"I'll tell the boys to start unloading the truck, unless you have somewhere else you need to be."

He opened the back door to the store, revealing the back end of a box truck that was flush with the loading dock. Miguel, Santos, and another gang member—a short, stocky guy with thick arms—started unloading and stacking Styrofoam and cardboard boxes against the hallway wall. They moved efficiently, maneuvering around each other like they'd done this a hundred times before.

"Where's my buddy Julio?" I said, trying to make small talk.

Marco looked at me and smiled an evil smile. But he didn't say a word.

Within ten minutes, the wall was almost completely hidden by the boxes stacked in front of it. When the gang members put the last package in place, they stood next to Marco, breathing hard and covered in sweat.

Marco raised his eyebrows expectantly.

"I found everything you wanted," he said. "I hope you appreciate how hard that was. Now you owe me something in return."

I could tell that Marco wasn't the kind of guy who was very understanding when people couldn't pay him. But I noticed a crack in his tough guy exterior. As he waited for me to say something, he tapped his foot on the floor as fast as a woodpecker at work, and he rubbed his forearm, like he was suddenly cold. He was turning into an unstable cocktail of emotions—a mix of desperation, fear, longing, and anger. But what I mostly saw was panic.

He had the look of a junkie who was terrified of not getting his next fix. And in that instant, I understood all I needed to know about him.

I cleared my throat.

"You don't mind if I take a look at the boxes, do you?"

Marco cocked his head, maybe because John had never asked to look at the merchandise before, but probably because it meant he had to wait longer to get paid. I didn't know, and I didn't care. He let out an irritated breath, then motioned toward the hallway with his hand.

I moved over to a Styrofoam box the size of a cooler and ran my fingers along the tape that sealed it.

The next noise I heard was a loud click near my ear as a shiny blade appeared in front of my face. My heart skipped a beat as Santos drew the razor-sharp knife across the tape, slicing it in two.

I removed the lid and lifted up a large plastic bottle packed in dry ice and filled with human organs suspended in a cloudy liquid. I turned to Marco and tried not to curl my lip in disgust.

"Looks good," I said.

"You can taste it if you want," he said. "I ain't in any hurry."

"I have a question for you," I said, drawing things out as long as possible—making him wait. "Any chance you or one of your boys know anything about the woman they found dead yesterday on Claiborne?"

Marco shook his head and snarled.

"I think you have things backwards," he said. "I deliver your shit, and you pay me. I don't tell you anything without getting paid."

I reached into my pocket, pretending to look for some cash, then pulled my empty hand out with a dramatic flourish.

"Looks like I left my checkbook at home."

Marco's forehead beaded up with sweat and his top lip curled.

I didn't know how I did what I did next, but on instinct, I dropped my human disguise just enough for him to see my fiery red eyes and my horns. Miguel, Santos, and the new guy crossed themselves and touched their silver pendants.

"That's not funny," Marco said with a dour face.

Marco didn't move any closer, but Shadow started growling again anyway.

"I thought you had a better sense of humor," I said as Marco struggled to keep his anger and frustration under control.

Just when things were about to erupt, I heard someone clearing their throat behind me, and Marco and his three homies took a collective step backward.

I turned around and saw Sybil standing behind me.

I started to say something, but she moved quickly, and before I knew what was happening, she'd pulled the blade of an iron knife across my forearm, making my head spin and my vision dim.

She held my gaze the whole time as she moved a silver vial to my open wound and filled it with my thick black blood that drained from me with the consistency of syrup.

Marco stared at my arm, a drop of drool running down the edge of his chin.

The wound started to close on its own as Sybil put a stopper in the vial and handed it to Marco.

While Marco stared at his payment, Sybil lowered her head and sucked at my quickly disappearing wound. When she was done, she cleaned my arm with her tongue and wiped her mouth with the back of her arm.

What a lady.

"Thanks for the snack," she said with a dreamy look in her eyes. I gave her my best pretend smile, which was about all I could muster.

"Consider yourself paid in full," she said to Marco. "Now get out."

Marco frowned but nodded as he placed the vial in a padded container that resembled a fancy cigar case.

Now that he had what he wanted, he was as eager to leave as I was to have him gone. Without another word, he and his three hoodlums left through the back door and drove away in the box truck.

I stared down at my arm. Marco wasn't a normal junkie. He was addicted to demon's blood—in particular, he was addicted to John's.

"What was that all about?" I said. "Did you see all this shit he left here?"

"This happens every week," she said. "Marco finds and delivers specialty items the supernatural population can't get in Ashburn or through the Internet. You pay for the items with a vial of your blood, half of which probably goes directly into Marco."

"And the rest?" I asked.

"He sells it outside of town at an insane price, I imagine. And by the way, from what I just tasted, he got the better part of the deal today."

"My blood tastes different from John's?"

Sybil placed a light hand on my chest, rubbing me and looking deep into my eyes.

"It's stronger and sweeter—like it's cut with honey. I might need some more of that tonight after I get home."

I gently pulled her hand from my chest and led her to the reading chairs in the front of the store.

"Do you know anything about the woman who was killed yesterday?"

Before Sybil could answer, a young girl in bedazzled jeans and pigtails bounced in through the door. At first glance, she looked like a little kid. Because of the way Sybil's face soured when she saw her, I put my goggles on. With them, the illusion gave way, and I could see the girl was actually a short, red, impish, male demon.

I opened my mouth to ask the imp what he wanted, but a crowd of supernatural beings stepped on top of and over one another as they entered the store.

"They're not here to buy books, are they?" I said to Sybil.

"Not likely," she said with a sneer. "They're here to pick up their packages."

CHAPTER 24

F OR A HORDE of demons, they were well behaved, forming a
single file line and whispering amongst themselves while they
waited.

The imp was first, his red skin taking on an orangish sheen under
the store's fluorescent lighting. The next demon in line waited a
respectful distance behind him, his arms crossed as he avoided eye
contact with me.

"Did you get it?" the imp said.

"Of course," I said, taking Marco at his word that he'd found
everything John had ordered from the previous week.

I turned to the stacks of boxes but had no idea which one belonged
to the imp. Sybil picked up a package the size of a lipstick container
and held it up for the little demon to see.

The imp smiled and reached for it.

"First, you pay," Sybil said, pulling it back.

The imp sighed, then whispered three words of abrasive, brittle
magic and held out his hand. A small piece of parchment paper, the
size of a playing card, appeared in his palm.

I plucked the piece of paper from his hand and studied it. Hand-
written arcane symbols were scrawled across it, and its edges were
uneven, like it had been cut from a larger sheet. The symbols might
have formed a word, but if they did, I didn't recognize it or the
alphabet in which it was written.

The imp looked to his left, then his right, before leaning toward me.

"I did what you told me," he said in a low voice. "I kept it safe and didn't let anyone see it."

"Are you saying I gave this to you to give to me?" I said, with irritation more than menace in my voice.

The imp's face swelled into a grin.

"I see what you're doing. You're testing old Abby, aren't you? I'm giving it back to you because that's what you told me to do. And that's all I need to know! Now, you have what you want. And I want what is mine."

"After we discuss next week's delivery," Sybil said.

Abby rubbed his chin and looked up at me with a coy grin.

"I…seek a copy of…Home Alone 3 *and* 4. On DVD. They are both rumored to be superior to the original."

I narrowed my eyes and stared at him.

"You want two movies about a little kid playing tricks on adults?"

Abby crossed his arms and raised his bony eyebrows.

"He likes to play tricks, so it's like an educational video for him," Sybil said, jotting down what the imp wanted on her smart phone. "What do you require in return for this treasure, John?"

I contemplated asking Abby to find out what he could about Marie, but I couldn't afford to wait until next week for that information.

With a shrug, I decided to punt and to start making the job my own.

"Consider this one on me," I said.

Sybil elbowed me hard, but Abby let his arms fall to his side, happy but stunned.

"Is this a trick?" he said as others behind him stirred, having overheard my promise of free stuff.

"All orders are free next week," I said louder as I took the tiny box from Sybil and handed it to the imp. "But only this once. This is a special deal for existing customers only."

It wasn't much, but giving away a bunch of odds and ends in exchange for a little blood didn't seem like such a bad deal to me, and I thought it might earn me some trust with the supernatural community instead of only their abject fear and hatred. Rose was right about me having to be Ahriman's enforcer, but that didn't mean I couldn't do things my own way.

With a wide smile, Abby skipped out of the store, clutching his tiny package to his chest. The next demon stepped up, and the ritual began again.

One at a time, they made their way to the front of the line. Each asked for their package, Sybil found it and handed it to me, and I took their order for the next week.

Several of the boxes were filled with internal organs and other body parts—which I assumed were seen as fine dining by some of my customers and quite hard to come by, since eating humans in Ashburn was forbidden. Every once in a while, I saw something really unexpected, like a jar of thimbles or a stuffed animal. I didn't bother asking about any of it.

While I was waiting for one of the larger demons to pick up his package, I glanced at Sybil through the lenses of my goggles. There she was in her full demonic form, but this time, I saw more beauty than horror. Her skin was a dark red that bordered on black, but her body was athletic, shapely, and feminine. Behind all of that, her eyes, although red like most of Ashburn's demons, had a depth that hinted at hidden substance behind them.

I had to stop myself from staring at her because the next customer stepped up, demanding my attention.

"Do I have to do this every week?" I asked.

"This is how you keep your fingers on the pulse of the town," Sybil said. "You get them what they can't find on their own or through the Internet, and they give you information and secrets—and other things you want. This is how you learn things, although next week you won't be learning anything because you're giving away everything—for free."

As the afternoon wore on, some of the demons didn't have what John had asked for, but to their credit, they didn't try to bullshit me. Instead, they handed over ancient coins or other baubles infused with different types of supernatural energy or magic and begged me to accept them. I took whatever they offered, once again trying to improve John's reputation.

When I looked up, expecting the next demon in line, a bright white light directly in front of me stabbed into my eyes like hot needles of pain.

I ripped my goggles from my head and blinked. It was my old friend, Chaz, the guitar maker.

"I have procured the information you sought," he said, his demeanor restrained and respectful.

Images of his broken guitar flashed through my mind.

"Whatever I wanted to know last week, I don't want to know it anymore," I said. "You can have your stuff for free this week and next week, too."

"That is very kind of you," he said with a grin. "But I will pay for my package on this day. I have more important plans for what you owe me."

"You don't understand," I said. "I'll still be in your debt. I'll still owe you for the guitar. But in return—when you get a chance…I was wondering if you could maybe make another one just for me?"

He paused for a moment, thinking.

"What happened to the instrument I gave you?" he said, his lips sagging into a frown. "I made that ax with my own hands. It carried a piece of my soul."

"It was the perfect guitar," I said. "It was so perfect that it saved my life. Although it did receive a little damage in the process…"

In an instant, his face changed from upset to skeptical and then to angry.

"And how did it save your life?"

I grimaced as I remembered smashing his guitar to pieces on Miguel's head.

"Some very dangerous people—professional assassins probably— jumped me outside the pub. I had nothing else to use as a weapon."

"So it is only broken," he said, exhaling loudly. "I am certain I can repair it. I am very good at fixing things."

I shook my head and gave him a tight-lipped smile.

"There's not really that much left of it to fix," I said. "But it really saved my butt—"

"You already said that."

"I feel horrible about destroying such a piece of art," I said. "I've played a lot of great guitars in my lifetime, but nothing came close to yours."

"That is kind of you to say," Chaz responded as he calmed down. "And I am—glad it helped protect you."

I placed my hand on his shoulder, and he tensed at my touch.

"So, what do you say?" I asked. "I promise to take better care of the next one. Please."

"And—" he said.

"And if you make me a new guitar, your packages will be free for the next year."

"And—" he said again.

"And, I'll still owe you the original favor."

He pretended to think for a few moments before answering.

"I will begin forging your new instrument tonight. But such an artifact is not created in one evening. The work will be done when it is done. I will bring it to you when I am finished."

I nodded and handed his box to him, which he opened to check. I caught a quick glimpse of a thick plastic bag filled with something pink and fleshy.

"Pig entrails," he said with a smile. "Exactly what I was looking for."

"Glad you like them," I said, even though I had no idea why he wanted them. Maybe they were a delicacy in his home country.

"What information do you have for me?" I asked.

Chaz handed me a small envelope made from animal skin.

"This took me longer to find than expected. I was almost discovered several times, which would have meant horrible pain and suffering for me. I want you to know how hard I worked for you."

I thanked him again, and he walked away, cradling his package of pig guts.

"What the hell *is* he?" I said. "Some ancient god of music or the arts?"

"At one time in history, he was the premier Sumerian god of pig farmers," she said with a laugh. "But it turns out there aren't many pig farms in Ashburn, so he opened a music shop to keep himself occupied. He's still an industrious deity, and he uses pig guts for his strings. The word is that he talks to them, and they agree to never break or go out of tune. The angels even buy their harp strings from him."

I looked at her and stifled a laugh.

"Angels really play harps?"

"In every myth, there's an ounce of truth," she said, shrugging.

"They like playing harps. It reminds them of home."

I was ready to tear open the envelope from Chaz and see what had been so hard to find. But something felt wrong, and the store had gone quiet except for the sound of Shadow's panting. When I looked up, I saw a single creature, standing alone with a hoodie pulled up over his head.

When he revealed his face, a faint white glow emanated from it. I recognized his smooth, too-perfect countenance and white hair at once.

"Nice to see you again, Raz," I said, lying. "Are you here as a customer or to tell me about more dead humans?"

The angel glided toward me, doing his best to stare me down.

"My name is *Raziel*, not Raz, and you know why I'm here."

"I thought you didn't like dealing with my kind," I said as I crossed my arms in front of my chest, enjoying myself for the first time that day.

"I believe you have a package for me—" he said in a quiet but dangerous voice.

"You don't have to whisper," I said. "You're the only one here."

I looked behind me and saw there were only two boxes left. Both were small and had the word *FRAGILE* stamped on them.

"Which one is it?" I said.

He pointed to the smaller of the two, which I picked up and held in front of me.

He reached for it, but I pulled it away, and Shadow growled, warning him to stay where he was. Raziel struggled to stay still as I opened his care package in front of him. I didn't care what was in the box, and I wasn't interested in his personal business, but I was enjoying the hell out of making him uncomfortable.

Inside the box, encased in molded Styrofoam, was a small glass globe filled with something white and fluffy that swirled like a captured cloud.

Its lightness stood in stark contrast to the rest of the packages I'd given out that morning. I handed it to him, and he took it without saying a word.

"What is that?" I said as he tucked the container under his arm like he was afraid it would spontaneously shatter.

"You know very well what this is," he said. "It's a human soul—

something you will never truly possess."

"He collects and keeps them like pets," Sybil said. "Pretty twisted, if you ask me."

"No one is asking you, hellion," Raziel said with a curled lip. "And this is not just any soul. This is a pure soul."

"Whatever gets you off is your business," she said, and Raziel's face turned even redder.

"A pure human soul does not *get me off*. Being trapped in this place has stolen so much from me, but being cut off from the purity of souls on their way to Heaven is unbearable. One day, when I leave, I will take the ones under my care into the heavens with me, and I will set them free to be with the Divine One."

I wanted to say a lot of things, but I remained quiet. If Raz wanted to collect souls, that was his choice, but I agreed with Sybil that keeping human spirits from moving on so he could collect them like action figures was pretty damn twisted. It was also something he probably didn't want his fellow angels to know about.

"Where's my payment?" I said.

He reached out and placed half of an ancient gold coin in the palm of my hand. It was tough to make out the image on the front side of the coin, but it looked like half of an eye with sun lines radiating out from it. On the other side of the coin was half of a simple, stylized heart.

I looked over at Sybil. She shrugged, but she also cleared her throat and fidgeted.

"Half a coin seems a pretty cheap price for a soul," I said.

"This is what I found where you told me to look. The coin is in your hands now, and I consider our transaction complete."

I stood in silence, looking at the partial coin in my hand. I didn't know what John had been looking for or where he'd told Raziel to look, but I didn't want to ask too many questions or he'd know something was different about his friendly neighborhood, demonic enforcer.

"Do you have an order for next week?" I said as I pocketed the half-coin. "Maybe a kitten?"

"I will contact you if I am ever in need of your services again," he said before pulling up his hoodie and storming out the front door.

With the angel's business concluded, the place was empty at last, except for Sybil, Shadow, and me. But there was still one package sitting on the floor.

"Is anyone ever this late on delivery day?" I asked Sybil.

"Never."

I picked up the last box and opened it carefully. Inside was a porcelain figurine of a little girl holding an umbrella. I turned it over and saw the word *Hummel* written on the bottom.

It wasn't what I was expecting to find. I shrugged and closed the box, thinking it might belong to one of the angels who'd been too shy or embarrassed to pick it up in person.

"Any of the regulars not show up today?"

"Only one," Sybil said with a frown. "A man named Blaire."

"What's so bad about Blaire?" I asked. "Other than his name."

"It's not him. It's his job. He works for Oizys. Picking up her packages is only one of his many responsibilities as her assistant."

"Poor slob," I said as I placed the figurine back in its box and picked up the envelope from Chaz. I broke its seal and removed a single sheet of handmade paper.

"What does it say?" Sybil asked.

Confused, I stared at the name that was hand-written on the paper. I handed it to Sybil who read the name out loud.

"Rose," she said.

"Any idea what this is about?" I said.

"John didn't tell me why he asked for half the things he did," she said, shaking her head. "But he never did anything without a reason."

CHAPTER 25

I SET THE package for Oizys in the car seat with Shadow and headed for Marie's. As I waited in line with the rest of the Beamers, Audis, and Mercedes at a stoplight, I wondered about the piece of paper with Rose's name on it. I considered asking Chaz for more information, but if I did, he'd figure out I wasn't the real John in a heartbeat.

When I pulled up to the curb in front of Marie's house, her zombie gardeners were still on the clock, pretending to care for her yard as always.

I stepped out of the car, and the clouds darkened overhead, blocking out the sun. Before making my way to the front door, I scanned the yard using my goggles, and things looked a lot different from the way they had before.

The workers showed up as human—no magical energy around them at all—nothing. But their skin was gray, and they looked like what they really were—animated corpses without their ti bon anges, their souls.

The charms and the other objects hanging from the trees glowed with shimmering purple and black magic and were connected with lines of black energy that formed a magical net around the house. Some of the black lines crossed the path leading up to Marie's front door—trip wires to protect her from unwanted visitors. I must have broken them the first time I'd visited her even though I'd been allowed to pass through without incident.

I took a deep breath and walked through the lines of invisible energy, hoping I'd make it through the house's defenses again.

The gardener with the dark ebony skin turned to look at me, the same way he had the last time, with lifeless white eyes and a face without expression. Just as before, he didn't try to stop me before turning back to his work.

Standing in front of Marie's front door, I wondered why the police hadn't taped it off, but then I realized the authorities wouldn't be interested in someone just because they'd left Ashburn. Normal people did that all the time.

I was the only one who cared about that. And Ahriman, of course.

Even though I didn't expect Marie to be home, I rang the doorbell and knocked before trying the doorknob.

It was locked, but with the slightest push, the deadbolt snapped, and the door swung inward.

I stepped inside, closed the door behind me, then scanned the foyer and the library before moving into the living room. With each step, it felt like someone was watching me. I looked up, but all I saw was the drawing of Marie's ancestor—the Baron—hanging on the wall above the fireplace mantel. It was a good drawing—so much so that it felt like he was following me with his eyes—a living skeleton keeping track of the living.

I picked up one of the six soul jars on the mantel and brought it closer to my face. Inside was a torn piece of clothing, several strands of hair, a couple of teeth, and a small, roughly shaped figure made of black wax. And just like I'd remembered, everything in the jar was covered in a dusting of yellowish-orange powder—the same substance I'd seen inside Laura Henders' nostrils.

It was enough proof for me that there was a connection between Laura and Marie, but exactly what that connection was, I could only guess. According to Oizys, Marie had disappeared and left town before Laura's death. And even if she'd been in Ashburn at the time of the killing, I couldn't picture Marie murdering Laura.

I placed the jar back on the shelf and backed away, sobered by the thought that I'd held one of the gardeners' souls in my hands.

A part of me wanted to get the hell out of there after seeing the powder, but my gut disagreed, and the pain from Ahriman's spell convinced me to look around a little more.

I checked upstairs and stuck my head into her bedroom to make sure she wasn't there before heading back downstairs to investigate the kitchen.

Everything was the same, except the giant wooden cutting board—it was stained with blood that hadn't been there the last time I'd seen it. On the floor, Shadow was sniffing a small white feather, probably left over from one of the chickens unfortunate enough to have been purchased by Marie.

I picked up the feather and rolled it between two of my fingers. Seeing the remnant from the slaughtered animal reminded me that Marie was capable of doing unpleasant things in the name of her faith. It also triggered an idea about where I could go next.

Letting the feather drop to the floor, I left her house and did my best to pull the door with the broken lock shut on the way out.

The clouds were heavier outside than when I'd arrived, and the sun was nowhere to be found as the first drops of rain pelted my face. I dashed to the car as the rain came down in hard sheets. Shadow disappeared in front of me and reappeared in the Audi's passenger seat, dry and wagging his tail.

As I slid into the driver's seat and pulled my tee-shirt up to wipe my damp face, Marie's gardeners continued their facade of work in the downpour.

I had a thought about where I could discover more about Marie and maybe how she'd escaped, but I needed some information first. I pulled out the card Oizys had given me, then looked at her forgotten package. She'd know the answer to my question, but I didn't trust her. She might even offer to help me, but not without first trying to extract another favor from me—something I wanted to avoid.

But her assistant Blaire—the one who'd forgotten to pick up the box—I was pretty sure he'd be a lot more willing to tell me what I needed to know.

CHAPTER 26

T HE RAIN BEAT down as I pulled into the parking lot for the Broadlands Nature Center—home to the infamous homeowner's association. I'd never heard of an HOA before, but from what Sybil told me, it was the closest thing most suburbanites would ever come to experiencing Hell on Earth.

Seen through my goggles, Ashburn's trees and its walking paths glowed like sparklers. But even amongst the din of supernatural energy, the Nature Center stood out. The building pulsed with angry dark red magic, and ancient runes floated in the air above it, written in fire that was normally hidden to the eyes of humans.

After checking to make sure the pink VW Beetle that belonged to Oizys was nowhere to be seen, I parked and told Shadow to wait. Then I got out of the car and ran through the rain to the overhang in front of the entrance. I wasn't surprised at all when Shadow was waiting for me at the door. Unlike me, he was completely dry.

I wiped water from my goggles and craned my neck so I could see the fiery sigils floating above. They looked ominous up close as the rain passed through them, and I could only guess what type of magic they were invoking to protect Oizys and her HOA lair.

The wind shifted, lashing Shadow and me with rain, and prompting me to get inside. I opened the door, and we both stepped into the unnaturally cold, air-conditioned climate of the Nature Center.

The lobby was decorated with plants and a few small trees in an attempt to create the illusion of the outdoors. Adding the educational element, a children's reading room was set off to one side. Cheesy displays and kiosks were scattered everywhere, telling visitors about the local wildlife that used to thrive in Ashburn before Ashburn had become Ashburn.

From behind the front desk, a thin man with perfectly quaffed black hair, wearing a bespoke blue suit with shiny brown shoes, stepped into the lobby. He approached me with a clenched smile and a gait that was a little *off*, as he tilted slightly to the right with each step.

My goggles told me he was a human.

So much for Ahriman's third commandment, I thought, as I remembered Marco and his gang also knowing about Ashburn's supernatural community. Either the boss demon allowed some exceptions to his rules or he somehow didn't know about Oizys's helper and the Olmecs. Either way, it meant his commandments weren't as insurmountable as they seemed, which gave me hope.

I removed my goggles and accepted his hand when he reached out to shake.

"How may I assist you today, John?" he said. "And before you respond, you know very well that Mistress Oizys does not allow dogs inside the Nature Center. That especially includes hellhounds."

"Feel free to make him leave, if you want," I said with a shrug. "Maybe he'll listen to you more than he does to me."

I wasn't one hundred percent certain, but my guess was I was talking to the infamous Blaire. Before he could say anything else, I pulled out the small box meant for Oizys and held it out to him.

Blaire tried to hide his surprise. He wasn't successful.

"I believe this belongs to your boss," I said. "It seems someone failed to pick it up this morning. I stopped by to give it to her in person—if she's in."

His eyes opened wide and his face flushed pink with embarrassment.

"Perhaps you should come with me," he said, clearing his throat and motioning for me to follow him.

Remembering Sybil's advice to be more of an asshole, I stayed where I was.

Blaire turned around when he noticed I wasn't coming along.

"Forgive my manners," he said. "Would you *please* come with me?

It would be best if we did not have this conversation where others could hear us. It is safer if we speak in one of the offices."

I still didn't move.

"Safer for whom?" I said. "I feel fine right here, so we can either chat now or I can come back later and tell Oizys how *not* helpful you were."

"Oh," he said, looking around as if by speaking her name, I might have summoned her. "That will not be necessary."

"Does this or does this not belong to her?" I said, holding the box up again.

He nodded and stared at the floor.

"And is she in?"

"She is not," he said.

"And are you her assistant?" I said.

He raised his head at my question, and I cursed myself for being so loose with my words again. I'd just asked something John would have already known. Instead of fumbling for an excuse, I doubled down.

"I asked you a question," I said. "Are you her assistant or not?"

"You know very well that I am," he said, still looking wary.

"Then why didn't you show up today and do your job?"

"It will not happen again," he said. "Something—came up—that precluded me from procuring her package. Is there any way we could keep this between the two of us? I would be, of course, in your debt."

It felt good to hear someone else say that for once, so I smiled and handed him the box.

He held onto it in much the same way Raz had clutched his black-market soul. Even though I wanted to know why Oizys would order something as sweet and innocent as a Hummel figurine, that wasn't why I was there.

"I believe payment for the package is due," I said.

His body shook and a micro tremor ran across his face. But even with my demonic senses, I couldn't tell whether he was excited, scared to death, or both.

"As I said, the mistress is not here at present," he said as his upper lip twitched. "As such, I am unable to—"

"Then I'll have to tell her you screwed up twice."

As soon as he heard my renewed threat, he squirmed and discreetly adjusted the front of his pants.

I didn't know much about magic or things supernatural, but as a once-famous musician, I'd been around plenty of kink, and I recognized the signs at once.

"What's the real reason you didn't pick up the package this morning?" I said, with a grin. "You knew it would make Oizys angry—that it would make *me* mad."

Blaire nodded and bent slightly forward at the waist.

"I am very sorry if I have angered you," he said.

"Why'd you do it then?" I repeated, using my deep, demonic voice that rattled the air in the room.

"She—punishes me when I make a mistake," he said, avoiding my eyes.

I nodded and stifled a laugh. He was a textbook masochist—the perfect administrative assistant for a demon who thrived on the suffering of others.

"Whatever gets you through the night," I said. "It's all right with me. But I still need to be paid."

He nodded.

"I was told that the agreed upon price was that Mistress Oizys would answer a single question—any question—at some point in the future, in exchange for her order."

"That's right, but the bad news is that I have more than one question," I said. "The good news is that I think I'd be willing to let you answer them for me. And if you do a good job, I'll still tell Oizys how bad you've been. How does that sound?"

I watched as a wave of ecstasy crossed the poor guy's face.

"Whatever you think is best, sir," he finally said in a faint voice. "What is it you wish to know?"

"I want to know how Oizys knows Marie Lacroix escaped Ashburn. You were watching her house. Did you see her leave?"

"She didn't come home last night," he said, wrinkling his brow, stressed. "But I did not see her physically leave the boundaries of Ashburn. As far as I know, none of your kind are able to do so, other than you, of course—if one were to believe the stories."

I wanted to press him further, but I could tell he was telling the truth, or at least he thought he was.

"Next question. Where does Marco and his gang hang out? And yes, I know I already know the answer, but I want you to tell me anyway."

"Of course," he said. "I will be happy to write down the address for you. Do you have any more questions? I could also tell you about a spectacular party coming up, if you'd like."

"No thanks," I said. "There's only one last thing I want to know—for now. Where would I go in Ashburn if I wanted to buy a few live chickens?"

CHAPTER 27

I WASN'T SURPRISED Blaire knew where to find Marco, but his knowledge about purchasing live chickens was impressive.

Following his advice and his directions, I decided to visit a place known simply as The Farm—an actual working farm at the western edge of Ashburn. It wasn't a lot to go on, but if Marie really was trapped in the suburbs like the rest of us, either someone gave her the chickens she'd sacrificed or she'd found some place nearby to buy them.

As I moved farther away from the McMansions and the stacked rows of townhouses, the side of the road filled in with colorful wildflowers and trees that were vivid green in the sunshine of the post-rain afternoon. Even though I would have traded all the nature around me for a busy city block and a few screaming cab drivers, I couldn't deny the stunning beauty of the scenery.

After ten minutes of ever-increasing wilderness, a sign pointing to The Farm directed me to turn left. When I did, I was surprised-not-surprised, to find myself entering a hidden development filled with— you guessed it—more houses that all looked the same.

I shook my head and glanced over at Shadow, who was too busy smearing the window with his nose to notice me.

As I slowed down and scanned the neighborhood, I wondered if Blaire had given me the wrong address. For a moment, I pictured him and Oizys having a good laugh at my expense back at the HOA offices.

I drove past a small outdoor store on my right but still didn't see a farm anywhere. When I came to the end of the road, I made a frustrated U-turn and doubled back.

On my way out, I pulled over near the roadside store, hoping someone could tell me where to find the mythical farm I was looking for. I opened the trunk and checked on Gus to make sure the guitar neck was still there, but I decided to leave it in the car. Shadow and I crossed the neighborhood street and walked over to the store. As soon as we passed under a decorative arch that led to the store, I saw that the field in front of it was filled with rows of berries, flowers, lettuce, and other small crops I hadn't been able to see from the road.

If this little place with its vanity crops was the farm Blaire had told me about, I was screwed, because I didn't see a single chicken anywhere.

I stepped under the store's awning and checked out the contents of its outdoor refrigerators and then the produce that was artfully arranged on its tables.

"Something I can help you with?" a sweet voice said from behind me.

I turned around and saw a stunning woman dressed in overalls and a sodden white tee-shirt with sleeves rolled up to her shoulders. She looked at me from under the brim of her tan baseball cap.

"Is there a real farm somewhere around here?" I said in the nicest voice I could muster.

She smiled at me through squinted eyes.

"I don't know about a *real* farm, but there's a trail on either side of the store. They both lead out back to the place with all the dirt. That's where we found all of this stuff we're selling. You're free to go check it out. I won't tell on you."

"I appreciate that," I said. "I'm—John."

"Sue," she said, shaking my hand.

"Strange question for you, but I don't suppose you sell live chickens, do you?"

She cocked her head and grinned.

"We have some of those on the farm, but we need all the ones we have. Hope your dog there doesn't like to eat them, by the way. We try to give our animals a good, safe home."

"Before you kill and sell them?"

"That was totally uncalled for," she said with a laugh. "But, yeah."

"Don't worry. Shadow loves other animals," I said as I tussled the fur on top of his head. "Isn't that right, boy?"

Shadow snorted and licked his lips.

"In that case, have a good time," she said with a smile that was brilliant white against the canvas of her dirt-smudged cheeks.

As I backed away, I put my goggles on to take a quick look at her.

For some reason, I was happy to find out she was a human with no magic anywhere near her.

I took the trail to the right of the store and followed its steep downhill grade for an eighth of a mile before I came to a small bridge that spanned a narrow stream.

The wooden planks creaked as I walked across them. Once I was on the other side, I turned around and looked back up the hill, but I couldn't see a single house or hear a car anywhere. It was as if I'd suddenly been transported to the country. I walked along with Shadow at my heels as the dirt trail turned uphill. Soon, I passed through an opened metal gate and found myself at the outskirts of what had to be The Farm.

There were several fields on my right that looked more like what I'd expected at a farm. Even so, there was something that seemed *off* about them. To my left stood two wooden farmhouses and a four-wheel ATV with mud-caked wheels.

I stepped up to the edge of one of the fields, and my stomach turned at the stench that reached up and invaded my nostrils. The plants—row after row of them—were black, and the field smelled of sewage.

I coughed as I slipped the goggles from my face. Without them on, the field looked like it was filled with bright green plants, flourishing in the sunlight. Even the rank smell was gone.

I cursed under my breath and wondered if anything in Ashburn was as it really seemed.

Gravel crunched beneath my feet as I walked over to what looked to be the main barn. I knew Sue had said they didn't sell their chickens, but I had to check to make sure. The door was locked, so I looked around the side of the building, but saw no one.

When I turned to see if Shadow was sensing anything, he was gone.

I looked out across the farm and saw him sitting just beyond the metal gate, his ears high and at attention, and suddenly, I felt uneasy and exposed.

"Come here, boy," I said, using the same friendly voice I used to call Rocky with when he was afraid of something.

Shadow didn't move.

Then I tried my demon voice.

My command for him to come to me reverberated across the expanse between us, but he still didn't respond.

I hated to do it, but I decided to use the secret weapon that had always worked with Rocky.

"Do you want a treat?" I shouted.

Like a shot, Shadow was at my feet, searching to my left and my right for his savory snack. Unfortunately for him, I didn't have one.

"The treat's inside," I said, feeling only a little guilty.

I seated the goggles back on my face, and as usual, everything around me changed. I walked over and stood in front of the barn's large wooden double doors. A thin stream of thick, black magical energy seeped from under them and formed a dark gray fog that snaked its way to the fields.

"That explains the color of the crops," I said in a whisper to myself.

Almost as if he were responding, Shadow whined and let out a single, piercing bark before switching to a deep growl.

I'd watched enough horror movies to know better, but I decided to enter the creepy barn anyway.

I pulled open the doors just enough to look inside, and the odor that hit my face was powerful, like wet fur and death rolled into one. I froze where I was because I'd smelled something that foul only once before—the first time Ahriman had appeared to me at the foot of my bed.

The only good thing about the stench was that it gave me hope I was on the right track to learn more about what had become of Marie. Using all of my will power, I forced myself forward and stepped into the barn. Shadow followed me, his growl turning back to an intermittent whine.

"Make up your mind," I said.

As my eyes adjusted to the darkness and my nose to the smell, I saw and heard a cow chewing on straw in the middle of the floor. To the right of the cow, a horse beat one of its hoofs into the floor of its stable. Further back in the barn, three goats stood on the open floor, chewing hay and watching me suspiciously. I took a deep breath and walked toward the cow, ready for anything.

What I didn't expect to find was Sue sitting on a short stool with a metal bucket in front of her, milking the cow.

"You surprised me," she said with a laugh. "I almost ripped poor Jessie's teat off."

I lowered my goggles and looked at her. Her face wasn't stressed or worried about anything, but something still wasn't right about her.

"How'd you get here ahead of me?" I said.

"I took the ATV down the other trail," she said. "Figured I'd get a start milking Jessie. Did you find those chickens, yet?"

"Not yet."

"I can show you where they are when I finish here if you can wait."

"I don't need to see them," I said, letting my voice reveal just a touch of my true demonic nature. "I really wanted to know if you sold any of them recently—to an individual."

Unfazed by my voice, Sue wiped her forehead with the back of her hand and looked up at the barn's ceiling, like she was trying to remember something.

"That's an odd question, but my answer's even weirder," she said, getting up from her milking stool and walking toward me. Shadow let out a short bark and tensed up, but Sue reached down and patted him on the top of his head. Within seconds, my blood-thirsty hound from Hell was making contented gurgles and wagging his tail.

"I've worked here a while, and like I said, as a rule, we don't sell our animals."

"What about in special cases?" I said.

"There is this one person. Twice a year, in the middle of the summer, she shows up asking about live chickens. For some reason, Dan—the farm manager—sells her three or four of our best birds every time. The summer's just starting, but she was in here last week *and* yesterday morning."

"Was her name Marie?" I said, my hopes rising.

I thought I saw Sue shake her head, but it was more of a twitch followed by a second one as her face turned dark and her smile twisted into a grimace.

Without a word to me, she stood straight as a board and faced me with a blank look in her eyes. Her shoulders rose and fell dramatically as I waited for her to answer my question about Marie. The horse whinnied, stomping its hooves hard into the straw-covered floor. The three goats paced about the barn floor excitedly, like some unseen presence was disturbing them.

I looked to Sue's left and saw an old, dusty shelf high up on the wall. On it sat several old jars made of thick, cloudy glass that obscured their contents. One jar on the end of the shelf looked newer and was clear enough for me to see what was inside—a tuft of black curly hair and some other small objects. And all of it was covered in a yellowish-orange powder.

I was still a novice in the ways of magic and hardly knew anything about Voodoo, but by now I recognized a soul jar when I saw one. Even though I wasn't sure who it belonged to, I was suddenly more worried about Marie being alive and without her soul than I was about the possibility that she'd escaped Ashburn.

My nape hairs stood on end, and Shadow let out another sharp warning bark. His tail beat frantically as he stood with his nose hovering over Sue's milking bucket. When I stepped over and looked inside, I recoiled from the putrid steam rising up from the thick black liquid at the bottom of the pail.

When I turned back to Sue, she was engulfed in an aura of crackling black energy.

"You are not welcome here," she said, but her regular voice had been replaced with a gravelly one that filled the barn and rattled my guts.

"I'm looking for a woman named Marie," I said. "I think she was here yesterday."

"The priestess came seeking a special offering for her loa. The price I asked was high, but she paid in full."

Sue's body rose into the air, her feet hovering six inches above the hay-covered floor. As she hung there motionless, an impossibly large black goat stepped from the shadows at the back of the barn and into the dim light. The animal's eyes glowed deep yellow as it glared at me from across the barn, but it came no closer.

"You and I swore an oath, demon whelp," the voice coming from Sue's mouth said. "A profane agreement you have broken by your presence here today."

Sue's body moved slowly toward me—her eyes now wide open and crazed.

The goat remained still as a statue at the back of the barn, but I could tell it was the one controlling Sue's body. The creature's mere presence filled me with awe and dread just like Ahriman had when I'd first met him, but its power felt more ancient, as if emanating from an arcane source I had no hope of understanding or overcoming.

I stepped back from Sue, thinking I was lucky to have my trusted hellhound by my side. Then I heard Shadow's whining from behind me, and I glanced back to see him standing outside, looking in at me through the open barn doors.

I didn't take that as a good sign, and with Sue getting even closer, I backed away quickly, wishing I'd brought Gus with me.

With a loud bang, the barn doors slammed shut behind me, cutting me off from my only avenue of escape and separating me from Shadow.

Neither fighting a seven-foot-tall goat nor tangling with a beautiful floating farmer seemed like a good idea at the time. So I ran at the barn doors and hit them with my shoulder as hard as I could. The doors burst open, and I stumbled into the brightly lit world outside.

I'm sure John would have stayed and done something demonic and bold, but I decided to run away.

I sprinted past Shadow, across the gravel, alongside the fields of blackened crops, out through the gate to the farm, and up to the small wooden bridge, which was also now pulsing with black energy. I looked back for Shadow, but again, he wasn't there.

Then I heard his piercing bark and looked up to see he was already on the other side of the stream, half-way up the trail that led back to the store.

A deep rumbling erupted from the farm behind me, and I took off running across the bridge. With each step, the bridge's dark magic sapped my strength, trying to weigh me down and prevent me from leaving.

My heart pounded in my chest, but I made it to the other side and took a moment to catch my breath and regain my strength before I started up the hill.

Once I caught up with Shadow, we both headed for the car, speeding past several groups of suburbanites calmly picking berries. Shadow passed me as we crossed the neighborhood street in front of the farm stand. He took a running leap directly at the Audi from six feet away.

I grimaced, waiting to hear the painful thud of dog hitting car. Instead, he passed through the passenger door like it wasn't even there and appeared on the inside of the vehicle, looking at me expectantly with his tongue hanging from his mouth.

Within seconds, I was in the driver's seat, hitting the ignition button, and punching the accelerator in first gear. The car kicked up gravel that formed a gray cloud behind me as I pushed it into second and took off down the otherwise quiet suburban street. Even though we were moving farther away from the barn with every second, I could still feel the black goat's presence all over me, like sticky, evil pollen.

Once I was back on the main road, I sped up to sixty-five as quickly as possible. I didn't even think about relaxing until I saw a strip mall.

My breathing slowly returned to normal, and Shadow relaxed and curled himself into a comfortable ball of fur in the passenger seat, exhausted.

As I drove along, heading for home, I realized I'd only been in Ashburn for a few days, but coming home to John and Sybil's house was already starting to feel normal. My shoulders relaxed at the thought of plopping down on the living room's leather couch.

My moment of peace was shattered, however, when I pulled into the driveway and saw the front door to the house partially open.

CHAPTER 28

S HADOW GAVE A menacing growl as he glared at the house.
"I don't want to hear anything from you," I said, still annoyed
that my own personal hellhound hadn't tried to help me when the evil
goat demon was after me. "Stay here while I make sure the house is
safe."

I got out of the car, waiting for Shadow to disobey me, like usual.
But this time he stayed in the passenger seat, unmoving.

"Now you decide to listen to me?" I said as I snapped my fingers
and pointed to the driveway. "Get out here, right now."

With a huff, Shadow placed a tentative paw into the driver's seat
before jumping down to the ground.

I closed the car door then walked around to the trunk to pick up
Gus before approaching the front door. When I stepped inside, it was
clear someone had taken the flat screen TV and the receiver. I made
sure my goggles were in place and held Gus out in front of me like a
club, ready for anything.

I moved as quietly as I could and opened the door to the coat
closet. Turns out, it was the door to the basement stairs.

The basement—every house had one, and there was no telling
what kind of stuff an asshole like John used to keep in his. I inched
down the stairs, pausing to listen at every step, but I saw and heard
nothing. At the bottom of the staircase, I flicked on the lights, ready

for anything. But all I saw was a large, empty room with new carpet and a few cardboard boxes stacked up against one of the walls.

With a shrug, I went back up the stairs and made my way into the kitchen. The microwave was gone—ripped from the wall—and for a moment, I started to think my house had been robbed by some good, old fashioned human thieves.

Then I decided to check upstairs.

I made my way up the stairway, making as little noise as possible, with Shadow trailing right behind me, his tail wagging peacefully.

Once on the top floor, I inched closer to the master bedroom's double doors, doing a horrible imitation of a police officer getting ready to storm into a suspect's apartment. I turned, with Gus in hand, and shoulder-slammed the door.

The instant I burst into the room, Sybil was on me, letting her demon flag fly as her black talons wrapped around my throat, poised to pop my head like a cork.

"Hi honey, I'm home," I said in a strained voice.

She blinked twice before releasing my neck.

"I was having a bad dream, and you surprised me," she said, plopping down on the edge of the bed.

"Did you know the house has been robbed? They stole the TV and the stereo. They even took the microwave."

"They broke in while I was out," she said, nodding. "We can always get new things, but they took something that's harder to replace."

"What else did they get?"

She smiled lazily, her face once again that of a beautiful temptress.

"Let's just say I'm pretty sure Marco and his gang were the ones who did this."

"I still don't understand," I said, suddenly worried.

"They took your blood," she said with a frown. "All of it."

I scrunched up my face, confused.

"The wine bottles in the refrigerator," she said. "They were filled with John's blood. He always kept a fresh supply on hand in case of emergencies. Even worse, they took the bathroom trash and one of your polo shirts, I think."

I was glad to be rid of the shirt, but I didn't understand why anyone would want my trash or why I should care. I flashed back to the Kanari on the shelf above Marie's mantel and the one at the barn and remembered how they contained pieces of hair and other personal items from the people whose souls they contained.

My stomach turned cold.

I sat on the edge of the bed, next to Sybil, and placed Gus across my lap, thinking. The walnut fret board felt cool and smooth beneath my fingers.

It reminded me of how lucky I'd been to have Chaz give me one of his handmade guitars from his own private collection.

And that's when it hit me.

"I'm going back to the bookstore—maybe try to sell someone a book or two—maybe read one myself."

"What about Marco?" Sybil said.

"I'll talk to him on my way home."

"I should go with you. Shadow, too. I can show you where the Olmecs hang out and be there for backup."

She was right. I needed to find Marco and confront him about robbing the house. John never would have let him get away with that. But speaking with Marco would have to wait until I went back to the bookstore. And I needed to do that by myself.

"What would John have done? Would he have taken you and Shadow with him?"

She shook her head.

"He would have gone alone."

"Then, that's what I'm going to do. Marco already suspects something's wrong, so I need to act as normal as possible. Speaking of which, do you have the wish list for next week?"

She pulled out her phone and started tapping the screen.

"Check the printer in the kitchen on your way out. If you had a phone, I could just send it to you, you know?"

"I'll get right on that," I said, sarcasm soaking my words more than necessary. Sybil didn't deserve my attitude, but I was busy trying to be Ahriman's enforcer and figure out what was going on, and finding John's phone or getting my own would have to wait. Before I did anything else, I had to check the bookstore again, this time using my goggles.

Because if Chaz had a secret room in the back of his shop, I was pretty sure John had one, too.

CHAPTER 29

T EN MINUTES LATER, I stood inside Ancient Pages, with Gus hanging from my belt on a loop I'd made from a leather shoestring.

I slipped my goggles on and examined every inch of the walls in the main room of the store, then I started walking toward the little office in the back of the shop. I checked each wall for signs of magic and spotted a faint line of glowing red energy at the foot of the wall Sybil had punched through.

Sybil had checked behind the wall, but there had to be something hidden there that she'd missed.

If I needed a code word or the right magical incantation to find the hidden door, I was out of luck. The closest I came to knowing magical words were a few phrases in Latin I'd used once in a song I wrote a long time ago. The words had sounded dark and ominous at the time, but after the single was released, I discovered they translated as something close to *My Chicken Eats Corn with Peasants*—not at all the vibe or the message I'd been going for.

I thought about kicking through the drywall, but John wouldn't have created a secret room without including an easy way to enter and leave.

I moved the framed newspaper page to one side and looked through the hole Sybil had made with her fist. There was nothing there other than the metal studs that made up the store's infrastructure.

Desperate, I placed my hand on the wall and tried to envision my arm passing through to another dimension.

That didn't work either.

I slumped against the opposite wall and tried to figure out what I was missing.

Chaz had used an actual key, so maybe I needed one as well. I searched my pockets and pulled out the Audi's key fob—a thick rectangle of hard plastic with three inlaid buttons.

By all accounts, it was a normal key fob, but when I looked at it with my goggles, I could see that it crackled with angry red magic. I flipped over the fob and pressed down on a small button that was sunk into the plastic. A flat metal key popped out, and when I touched it to the wall, a door appeared.

"Son of a bitch."

I took a deep breath, turned the door knob, and stepped into a space that was so large, there was no logical way it could have existed within the physical dimensions of the store.

In fact, it was hard to tell how big the room was at all, partly because it was dimly lit, but also because it was filled with rows and rows of shelves stuffed to capacity with old books and piles of oversized parchment sheets stacked taller than my height.

I watched where I stepped, trying not to upset anything and let out a low whistle. There were more books in John's hidden room than in the rest of the store and probably more than owned by most local libraries.

On the dusty floor in front of me, dog prints led off to the left. I followed them to a small side table with a clear spot where the dust had not gathered. I took off my goggles and set them down. They fit the dust imprint perfectly.

Maybe Sybil didn't know about John's secret place, but Shadow did, and he'd entered it earlier to fetch my goggles. Ahead of me, I saw more paw prints, and I followed them deeper into the mysterious room.

My fingers glided along the ragged edges of a large dusty book as I walked past it. The page I touched separated from the spine and jutted out from the volume.

Before I could take the oversized book down from its stack to examine it more closely, I heard a distant scratching coming from deeper inside the room.

"Who's there?" I said, my voice muted by the density of the room's clutter.

No one responded, so I followed the scratching sound, turning again and again through the maze of stacked paper and bookshelves. With every step, the noise grew louder. Whatever it was had a rhythm and a familiarity that was somehow comforting.

After passing a set of shelves that were as tall as the ceiling and crammed with oversized books, a small clearing opened up on my right. In it, an old man sat naked and hunched over in front of an enormous wooden desk.

The man had long, white, tangled hair and was writing with an old feather pen on a large piece of paper four times the size of a regular sheet. Next to his left hand—the one with which he wrote—was an ink well the size of a bowling ball.

I moved closer until I was five feet away.

His hands were long and gnarled with bulbous knuckles, but his writing was fluid. I looked to where he sat, and I curled my lips. The flesh of his buttocks had grafted itself to the wood of the chair, and he was chained to his station by an iron manacle anchored to a concrete plug in the floor.

"Why are you a prisoner here? Who did this to you?" I asked.

The old man didn't react or respond, but I thought I saw him cringe slightly.

I circled around the desk so he could see me, but he didn't look up or pause in any way.

"Is there anybody in there?" I asked, but once again, he remained silent. I reached out my hand, ready to tap him on the shoulder.

As my finger neared him, he lifted the page with a mechanical flourish and dropped it to the floor, so that it landed on top of an existing stack of paper. When he turned, I could see his face clearly for the first time. Although he wrote with perfect penmanship, his eyes were dull white orbs in his head—those of a blind man. And even though his body showed his age, his face was smooth like that of an innocent boy.

"Do you know where the keys to your chains are? I'll get them and set you free."

When he still didn't answer, I searched the nearby tables, until I looked up at one point and noticed there was no key hole in his ankle cuff.

I stood and watched him some more. His hand traveled sometimes from left to right and other times from right to left as he filled the fresh piece of paper in front of him with words and symbols.

I leaned against the side of his desk, wondering what, if anything, I could or should do. I didn't understand how he was still alive, how he ate, or even how he went to the bathroom. But mainly, I wondered why John had imprisoned him in his secret room in the first place.

The pen's path across the paper was mesmerizing, and after twenty minutes, he'd almost filled up the sheet of paper. Just as before, when he finished, he lifted the giant leaf of paper from his desk and dropped it on top of the stack of paper on the floor next to him.

I bent over, picked up the page and placed it on an empty table to take a closer look.

The paper was filled with rows of words in several languages, the majority of which I didn't recognize. I did, however, see a piece of a song lyric from a tune I knew about a future where music was forbidden and the ultimate act of rebellion was playing the guitar. More than the lyrics, I also recognized the color and weave of the paper. When I pulled out the scrap of paper Abby the imp had given me, it was an exact match, although the words and symbols were different.

I set the paper down and placed the scrap from Abby back in my pocket.

"I want to help you, if you'll let me," I said to the writer, letting out a heavy sigh as I bent down to examine the manacle that held his ankle.

When I touched it, he kicked frantically, grunting, and choking. His reaction startled me, and I fell backward onto my butt. As soon as I wasn't touching him, he calmed down. The whole time, he never stopped writing—never even paused.

"Do you at least have a name?" I said.

As expected, he didn't answer.

"I've got to call you something—maybe just The Writer for now," I said, looking at the stacks and stacks of pages he'd penned. "Or maybe Writer of All Things? That sounds much cooler and a lot more accurate."

I paused, giving the old man a chance to comment.

"Yeah, I see your point," I said, pretending he'd answered me. "Writer of All Things is more of a job description than an actual name. How about I call you Walt? It's a name and an acronym, all in one."

Walt paused for a second and turned his head slightly toward me before he went back to his paper to write some more.

I shrugged and left my newfound tenant to his scrawling as I stepped into the hallway to check out more of the room.

After a few minutes of exploring, I reached a wall lit with a row of fluorescent lights that illuminated an antique wooden desk similar to Walt's.

The desk was overflowing with random items—bottles of glue, empty glass jars, and pairs of scissors. Much of the desk was covered with scraps of paper that looked like they'd been cut from some of Walt's sheets.

I rifled through the items on the desk, hoping to find something useful or at least understandable I could use.

After a minute of searching through scraps of paper filled with words from unintelligible languages, I uncovered an iron dagger with an ornamental, rippled blade hidden under an old notebook.

It didn't have as much gravitas as Miguel's wooden sword, but it glowed crimson when I held it, and I could feel its power. Nodding, I slipped it between my belt and my jeans and continued looking around.

Above a globe on the edge of the desk, John had tacked up three maps of Ashburn to the wall. One showed a topographical representation of the area. Another showed the locations of giant caverns and lakes under the town. The third map was a simple street layout with a red line drawn on it to show the borders of Ashburn proper. I examined the last map the hardest, but I didn't see anything that looked like it represented an exit or a portal leading out of town.

I shook my head and realized how tired I was, as I vowed to revisit the maps later when I had more time and energy.

As I made my way to the exit, I noticed a cape draped over a coat rack that stood to the right of the door. The cape was black with gold edges and inlay, and it glowed red, alive with power. For all I knew, it held the secret to undreamt magical energies, the key to escaping

Ashburn, and a way to defeat Ahriman. But I left it there anyway, mostly because I was pretty sure I'd look ridiculous wearing it. And given the next place I was about to visit, laughter was the last thing I wanted to elicit.

CHAPTER 30

I CHECKED THE address twice.

Turned out, Marco and his gang hung out at a flower shop—or *shoppe,* if I took the sign literally.

Night had fallen, but the store was still lit up, even though the neon sign in the window said it was closed for business.

With a slight turn of my wrist, I pushed open the locked door and stepped in, goggles on, glowing dagger tucked into my belt, and Gus gripped tight in my fist like an ax.

Inside, the store seemed legit—filled with flowers and the heady scent of roses. Julio stood behind the counter, clipping rose stems and wearing an apron with the store's logo on it—a drawing of three green flowers held by a cartoon hand. He didn't look very fierce in his uniform, and judging by the scowl on his face, he knew it.

"We don't have any more business with you today," he said.

"There are a few things I forgot to ask Marco about," I said.

Julio glanced down at the jagged guitar neck in my hand.

"That what you used to take down that big guy outside the bar?" he said, pointing at Gus with his chin.

"That's right," I said. "And I still need to speak to Marco."

Julio shook his head.

"It's after business hours, jefe. Come back tomorrow if you want to talk to the man. And call before you come next time. Marco doesn't like surprises."

Julio was flexing his perceived power since he was in his nest, but fortunately for me, he wasn't wearing his silver pendant.

I approached him, gripping Gus tight enough that my knuckles went white.

"I need to speak to him now."

"What you *need* to do is put that away," he said, pulling out a Glock and holding it up for me to see. "Or I'll put a hole in your chest."

Before I knew what I was doing, I closed the distance between us and my hand went for my dagger. Through the lenses of my goggles, I could see my blade glowing bright red as I sliced through the barrel of Julio's gun like it was a stick of butter.

"Consider this your last chance," I said, touching the dagger's tip to the soft part under his chin.

With eyes wide in fear, he pointed to a door at the rear of the store.

"He's in the back, chilling with some of our people. But you go in there and interrupt him and there's gonna be trouble."

I grinned.

"Your concerns have been noted," I said as I tossed Julio into the wall with a thud and a cloud of drywall dust.

Turning my back on him, I walked to the rear of the store and kicked open the door.

When I stepped into the hall, Santos was sitting on a metal fold-up chair, smoking a cigarette outside another door that must have led to Marco's office. When he saw me, he dug into his pocket for something, but I moved with supernatural speed and introduced the magic-laden Gus to the top of his head in a single, fluid motion. I helped Santos slide to the floor, unconscious, then reached into his pocket. Sure enough, it was another one of the silver pendants with the stylized demon face. The instant I touched it, I felt my power drain away. I had no idea what kind of magic the pendants carried, but the fewer of them the Olmecs had, the better off I was going to be.

With no good options for getting rid of the damn thing, I stood on the chair, pushed up one of the ceiling tiles, and hid the pendant there. Once I stepped down to the floor, I felt better immediately. I got ready to bust in the door, but I heard Rose's voice in my head, telling me to think before acting rashly.

I won't lie. It had felt good to take out my frustrations on Marco's underlings, but I was there to see Marco and to ask him why he'd broken into my house and taken my blood and my bathroom trash.

Taking a deep breath, I reigned in my anger and steadied myself before trying the doorknob. When I stepped into the room, Marco was sitting behind his desk, slouched in a chair, with a string of drool hanging from his lip. His right arm was stretched out in front of him with a hypodermic needle hanging from where he'd injected himself. The vial from the day before was on the desk, now only half-filled with my blood.

Miguel sat in a chair on the other side of the desk, his arm in a cast. That made me grin. A short but muscled man I didn't recognize, with a shaved head and a goatee, stood next to him.

Before either one of them could react, the skin on Marco's face started to ripple and spasm as his skin turned a deep purple-red and his mouth bled from razor sharp teeth growing from his gum line. At first, I wondered if it was a hallucination or an illusion, but Miguel and the other guy saw it too, and it was clear they were more worried about Marco than me.

I braced myself, holding Gus and my glowing dagger in front of me, just before Marco stood up, almost flipping his desk over in the process. He jumped into the air and landed on top of his desk, reaching out for me with hands that ended in three-inch long talons. Miguel pushed himself away, his mouth open and showing his missing teeth, but luckily for him, he was just out of his boss's reach. The new guy didn't move fast enough, though, and in a flash, Marco raked his claws across the man's neck, splattering fresh, bright red blood all over the room.

"Damn, man!" Miguel shouted as he scrambled away, trying to get to his feet. For a second, Marco glared at Miguel with the cold eyes of a reptile, and Miguel shoved his hand down his front pocket, probably trying to find his pendant.

Marco turned and focused on me again. He leapt toward me from the desk but slipped on the blood-slick floor when he landed.

While still on the floor, his face changed into a human's for a few seconds before morphing back into something that was part demon and part human.

When he looked up at me from the floor, tears were running down his disturbing visage.

"Tu sangre," he growled in Spanish. "Your blood is…beautiful."

I glanced over at Miguel, who was pressed up against the wall on the other side of the room, eying the exit.

With caution, I slipped the dagger back under my belt and lowered Gus to my side. Marco sobbed with joy, and to say I was confused would have been an understatement. I'd seen friends and groupies go crazy on mind-altering drugs, but nothing like that before.

"Is that what you do with my blood?" I said. "Is that why you broke into my house tonight? Why did you take my trash?"

Marco looked up, crinkling his eyebrows, confused.

"Did Marie hire you to steal my stuff?" I said. "So she could make a soul jar for me?"

I stared down at Marco, waiting for his answer. Instead of responding, he passed out, and my window for getting information out of him closed.

With Marco out of the picture for the night, I turned to Miguel, who looked at his unconscious boss, then me, and held up his pendant in his clenched hand.

"Why'd you guys break into my house today?" I said, keeping my distance.

He shook his head back and forth sharply.

"That wasn't us, man," he said. "After we left the bookstore, Marco took a hit of your blood, but he said there was something different about it this time—something better—like it was pure. He said we were going to get more of it, but we didn't do nothing to your house. Not yet, at least."

I shook my head.

"When he wakes up tomorrow, tell him if he messes with my house or Sybil or anything that's mine, he'll be sorry. And tell him he needs to find Marie Lacroix and bring her to me, alive."

"That Voodoo chick?" he said. "Word is she's gone. Left town, man."

"I know, but she had to go somewhere, and your gang has connections outside Ashburn. So check around, and tell Marco if he brings her back to me before Sunday, he can have more of my blood—

a lot more. If he doesn't find her, he'll never see another drop."

"He ain't going to like that."

"If you don't tell him what I said, I'll make sure he knows you're the reason he won't be getting any more of my blood."

"Damn, John," he said, but he nodded slowly. "I'll tell him when he wakes up."

"There's one more thing."

I reached into my back pocket, pulled out the folded-up list of orders for the next week, and let it fall so it landed on Marco's unmoving body.

"Make sure you have everything ready for next Friday," I said as I turned to leave.

On the way out of his office, I glanced up at the ceiling tile where I'd hidden the pendant. When I opened the door and stepped into the main store, the place still smelled like flowers, but there was a new scent in the air and a dozen angry gang members waiting for me.

I sighed and drew my dagger again, ready to fight my way out and hoping none of Marco's boys had any more of those damn pendants.

From behind me, Miguel spoke up.

"Everybody chill out," he said. "John and the boss just had a conversation, and now John's leaving. Ain't that right?"

I nodded slowly as the gang members parted to make a path for me. As I walked through them, I dropped my human illusion enough to let them see my fiery red eyes and the sharp horns protruding from the front of my head. I did it partly for effect but also to give them a good reason not to mess with me.

A few of them mumbled while others sent up whispered prayers to gods I'd never heard of. I ignored them, and within seconds stepped into the cool air and took a deep breath.

Then I stopped dead in my tracks.

Standing no more than six feet in front of me in a thin, floral print dress, Marie looked at me with blank, milky eyes.

"Do you know where I live?" she said, straining with every word. Before I could answer, she collapsed in my arms.

CHAPTER 31

I SET MARIE in the Audi's passenger seat, then took a quick look at Marie with my goggles. She was human, or at least she had been, but purplish-gray residue wafted from her body, like supernatural steam.

Halfway to her house, she came to and turned her head toward me, her eyes still mostly closed.

"Did you kill Laura Henders?" I said.

"I can't remember anything," she said. Her voice was listless, and her words came slowly and with effort. "I was making lunch, and then I was outside the flower shop, and I saw you."

I reached over and placed my hand on top of hers. Her flesh was cold.

"Who did this to you?"

"I don't know," she said, struggling to answer my question.

She was hiding something, but I decided to give her a break for the time being—after all, she'd been through enough already. We drove the rest of the way in silence, not speaking again until we pulled into her driveway.

I hit the button to unlock the car door, but she reached over and squeezed my hand.

"Please don't leave me," she said. "I'm afraid."

The digital clock in the dashboard said it was around nine at night, and it wasn't like I had anything else to do other than go back to the house and watch Shadow poop in the back yard.

There was a slim chance Sybil would be home, but given her lifestyle and the fact that it was dark already, she was probably out having her version of fun.

Besides, Marie was in need, and just because she was a zombie and I was in a demon's body didn't mean I didn't have a heart. I got out of the car and walked around to the other side to help her. Up in the yard, her merry band of undead gardeners worked on the same areas of grass they'd been tending since the first day I'd seen them.

We walked up to her front door together. Instead of opening the door, she stood there, staring at the doorknob. At first, I thought she'd noticed the broken lock, but then she turned to me.

"This is where I live," she said, but I couldn't tell whether she was asking me or telling me.

"This is your house," I said as I pushed open the door, and we stepped into the foyer. While she used the powder room, I pulled my goggles off and sat on the bottom of the stairs, rubbing my eyes. As I scanned the lifeless house, I was drawn to the illustration of the Baron as it seemed to stare at me from across the room.

Without realizing it, I started singing a tune in a hushed voice. It was an old song about a guy having a hole where his head was supposed to be, and hearing it made me feel better.

"Was there music just now?" Marie said as she stepped out of the bathroom and staggered toward me.

Before I could answer, she plodded up the stairs, and I followed. The strong smell of sandalwood and jasmine assaulted my nostrils as we entered her bedroom.

"Did you say you would stay?" she said, before shuffling off to the bathroom without waiting for my reply.

I sat on the edge of her bed and shook my head. I hadn't known Marie very well, but she was disturbingly different from the woman I'd met a few days ago. As much as I didn't want it to be true, she looked like and was behaving like a zombie, with only slightly more personality than her gardeners. If what she had told me about her religion was true, someone had taken her ti bon ange. And if I was going to help her, I was going to need assistance from someone who knew a lot more about the undead than me. All I could do was hope Sybil or Rose might know how to save her, if that was even possible.

The only person I wasn't going to ask for help was Oizys.

Marie returned a few minutes later, her mocha brown skin shining in the candlelight as she walked toward me, naked.

For a second, *danger, danger* signs lit up in my head. I wasn't sure how to politely decline advances from a dead person, but thankfully, she ignored me, slipped under the sheets, and rested her head on the pillow.

"I'll stay until you fall asleep."

"You are a good person," she said in a throaty whisper, barely moving her lips.

I nodded and crawled up the bed, until I was lying next to her, on top of the covers. Hesitantly, I reached one hand over and touched her neck, feeling for a pulse. It was there, but barely.

I pulled my hand away and lay very still, staring at the ceiling.

When I woke up, I wasn't sure how much time had passed, but it was still dark, and Marie was asleep next to me. Even with the pallor of death on her cheek, she was still beautiful.

As I quietly picked up my goggles from the end table, she rolled over, still asleep, so that her back was to me. I watched her shoulders, but they barely rose or fell.

Then I heard a loud creaking from downstairs.

I got up, slipped on the goggles, and made sure I had both of my weapons before investigating the noise.

When I made it to the ground floor, I crept into the kitchen. Through a crack in the curtains, I saw the silhouette of a woman standing on Marie's deck.

I thought about calling the Sheriff. He knew about the weird shit that happened in Ashburn, and burglars and trespassers were clearly his jurisdiction. But then I remembered Marie's gardeners and the magic spells protecting her place. Her defenses hadn't stopped whoever was on the deck, which meant the lurker didn't want to hurt Marie.

I unlocked the door with as little noise as possible before turning the knob and opening the door. The woman on the deck turned to face me, and I recognized her at once.

It was Laura Henders, standing in a paper hospital gown, looking at me with cloudy white eyes and dried dirt on the side of her face, like she'd woken up on the ground—or maybe under it.

"I don't mean to be rude," I said, "but the last time I saw you, you were wearing a white blanket."

She made a guttural noise, then stumbled down the stairs and took off running across the lawn, toward the forest that bordered the back of Marie's yard.

I ripped off my goggles so I could see better and chased after her. Even though I felt light and fast in John's body, she made it to the woods before I could catch her.

Within seconds, I was clawing my way through dense tree branches and tall razor grass before ending up on a paved walking trail surrounded and insulated by tall pine trees and dense underbrush on both sides.

I looked up and down the trail, but Laura was nowhere in sight.

As I walked along and tried to catch my breath, dead silence surrounded me. Either the forest was devoid of animal and insect life, or all the critters and animals were keeping their mouths shut for a reason. The crescent moon shone directly overhead, and a thin fog started to gather around my ankles.

Just as I decided to head back to Marie's house, my senses screamed for me to run—to get away as fast as I could.

Before I could move, a loud braying split the muted night.

First, I heard the animal. Then I smelled it.

When I turned around, the giant black goat from The Farm was standing with its horned head bowed and its glowing yellow eyes leveled directly at me.

CHAPTER 32

T HE GOAT'S MOUTH didn't move, but the air around me vibrated with the same unearthly low voice I'd heard at The Farm.

"We have unfinished business, demon," the goat said as it towered above me.

Its eyes glowed a deep amber, and its huge body was so black it seemed to swallow the moonlight. Slowly, it worked its way around to my left. With each step, the creature edged closer, and I crouched down, preparing to meet its attack with my dagger in one hand and Gus in the other. Then I noticed something that made my heart miss a beat. The dagger wasn't glowing. I glanced over at the guitar neck, and it wasn't giving off its god-forged white magic either. I'd gone from being well-armed to facing a goat demon with a dagger and an oversized toothpick.

Before I could figure at what was happening, the goat charged, and I tried to jump out of the way. Even with the speed of a demon, I wasn't quick enough, and one of the goat's massive horns pierced my side as it threw me off the trail and into a patch of dense grass below an old weeping willow.

I jumped to my feet and faced the goat as it approached me again.

"You are different from when first we met so long ago," the voice said. "You are weaker."

I dropped Gus on the ground and pressed my open hand against my wound to staunch the black blood that was oozing out of me. I thought about trying to explain to the goat that I wasn't the same John it hated—that I was sure we could have a great relationship if we could only start over from scratch.

But before I could try my horrible plan, the creature lowered its head and charged.

I stepped to the side again, but this time, I slashed with my dagger as I spun away. The blade wasn't glowing, but it was still sharp and made of iron, and I was rewarded with a spurt of black blood shooting out from the goat's neck.

My victory was short-lived, and before I could ready myself, the animal turned around and charged a third time.

Both of its horns caught me full-on, piercing my chest, as the giant animal picked me up and tossed me into the air again. When I landed, the impact with the earth was so hard, I thought I was close to dying. All the bargaining with Ahriman and selling my soul to him was about to become worthless. I winced as I wondered where my soul would go once I died in John's body, but I was pretty sure I knew the answer, and it wasn't good.

I propped myself up on one arm and waited for the inevitable as the monstrous creature ambled toward me, like a killer who knew his victim was beaten, with no way to escape.

"Finish it," I said. "At least I'll finally get out of this town."

The goat came closer, and with purpose, it placed one of its hooves on my chest, immobilizing me.

"You do not have to die," the voice said, "You need only show me the way out of this prison, where I have been trapped for so many centuries, and I will let you live."

I spit black blood on the ground and laughed.

"You're stepping on the wrong guy," I said. "I don't know the way out. I'm trying to leave Ashburn, too."

As the goat pressed harder on my chest, I heard footsteps to my right and the familiar voice of Oizys's assistant, Blaire.

"Step away, most profane Goat of Mendes," he said.

The goat turned its attention to Blaire, but it didn't lift its hoof.

"I am nothing compared to you," Blaire said with conviction to the goat. "But you know my mistress, and she will see you suffer if you harm this demon."

As if punctuating his final word, Blaire held out a small book in front of him, like a priest showing a Bible to a possessed child.

The goat arched its neck and screamed like a human, the sound piercing my skull and grating against my brain.

With the small book still held high, Blaire turned to me.

"I can save you from this, but you will owe *me* a favor this time," he said. "No matter what I ask."

One of the last things I wanted was to owe someone else a favor, but the absolute last thing I wanted to do was to die.

"I'll owe you big time," I said, with a tight-lipped smile. "Now could you please get on with it? This thing is crushing my chest."

"Do you give your bond?"

"Oh, for crap's sake," I said, closing my eyes and pretending I knew what I was doing. "There. My bond is given."

Blaire nodded, then held the book higher and spoke in a language that sounded to me like garbled sounds with no structure. The goat must have understood them, however, because it lost interest in me and bleated and stomped its front hooves, shaking the ground like thunder. I couldn't see the title written in gold leaf on the book's spine, but it didn't take a genius to realize it was a powerful tome—and way too rare of an item to be owned by a human.

While the goat was distracted, I picked up my dagger, while trying unsuccessfully with my other hand to staunch the bleeding from one of the puncture wounds in my chest.

I tried closing the distance between me and the goat, but before I could stumble very far, the animal glanced at Blaire, weighing its chance of success before backing into the shadow of the weeping willow.

Even with my goggles on, the giant animal blended in with the tree's shadow cast by the moonlight, and when I blinked, the goat was gone.

Blaire rushed to my side and helped me sit down with my back against a small sapling. As I tried catching my breath, I could feel my wounds healing and the pain slowly leaving my body.

I stared blankly at the ground, feeling better by the moment, but stunned.

Blaire looked down at me and grimaced through pursed lips.

"It's not any of my business, but there is something decidedly different about you. You should not have needed my help that much. If you wish to share whatever is happening to you, I would offer you my vow not to divulge your secret to anyone."

For a second, I considered taking him up on his offer, but I ended up keeping my mouth shut. After all, Blaire worked for Oizys, so no matter how good he seemed, and no matter how much he'd just saved my ass, I could never trust him completely.

"I'm fine, but I won't forget what you just did. And before you ask, yes, you are no longer in my debt, and I owe you a huge debt. Whatever I can do, name it."

He shrugged almost effeminately and smiled.

"Trust me. I will. I know you see me as only a lowly servant, but I have big plans, and now I have a way to make those plans come true."

"Where'd you get that?" I said, nodding toward the small black book still clutched in his hand. "Must be pretty powerful to stop that goat in its tracks."

"This volume belongs to my mistress. She does not know that I have borrowed it."

"Like I said, I'm more than grateful for the assist," I said, shaking my head in fake condemnation. "But you know I'm going to have to let Oizys know you took her book. It's only fair to her."

Blaire tried to hide the shiver that ran up his spine. He looked up at me with a slight grin and rosy cheeks.

"Whatever you think is necessary, sir. I completely understand."

CHAPTER 33

B ACK ON THE main neighborhood street, Blaire and I parted ways. I looked down at Gus and then my dagger. Both were glowing like they were supposed to again, so I removed my goggles, exhausted, and headed back to Marie's house.

Pretty soon, I was standing in her driveway, staring up at her darkened window, inhaling the cool, dewy night air.

A part of me wanted to go back up to her room and tell her about chasing Laura off her deck. But, given her current state, I didn't think she'd understand what I was talking about or even care. Plus, as much as I liked Marie, I wasn't excited about falling asleep next to a zombie again. I knew she wasn't interested in eating what little brains I had in my head, but it didn't feel right lying down with the undead. Instead, I decided to go home and wake up the next morning with a succubus from Hell—a much better idea all around.

Before I left, I locked Marie's back door and made sure Laura Henders was nowhere to be seen. After the house was secure, I slipped into the Audi and drove away as quietly as possible, listening to a station that played mellow acoustic remakes of once-popular songs— the perfect backdrop for my tired mood.

The final chord from a cello remake of AC/DC's *Hell's Bells* was still ringing in my ears when I pulled up to John's driveway and into the garage. As I got out of the car, I wondered if my hellhound had pooped in the house or if he'd eaten one of the neighbors. Such was the life of a respectable demon living in the 'burbs.

As I stepped into the living room, Shadow raised his head from the floor, his ears standing at full attention. He looked at me, picked his leash up with his mouth, and stared at me, hopeful.

I shook my head and laughed.

"You don't need a leash in the yard."

He dropped the leash and wagged his tail.

"And I know you can walk through that door without my help any time you want."

He ignored me and gave me his best big-eyed doggie stare. I gave in, rolled my eyes, and opened the back door.

Shadow shot onto the deck, then ran into the middle of the yard. Within a second, he'd taken a dump as big as my head. I turned away, not wanting to even think about what he'd had for dinner.

After letting him sniff around the yard for a few minutes, I gave a low whistle, and he came running right away.

I cursed as I looked at the clock. It was 3:30 in the morning and I was yawning and in desperate need of rest. I didn't expect to see Sybil upstairs, but when I opened the door to the master bedroom, to my surprise, she was asleep under the covers.

I wasn't sure if stealth was one of my new demonic powers or not, but I did my best to brush my teeth and to wash the scent of sandalwood and jasmine from my face before slipping into bed.

Pulling the sheets up to my chin as quietly as possible, I tried not to wake Sybil, but I wasn't successful.

"Thank you for letting the dog out," she said in a flat voice with her back facing me. "Where were you tonight?"

I closed my eyes in the darkness and felt the bliss of promised sleep washing over me.

"Did you deal with Marco?" she said, jolting me awake just as I was dozing off. "You can't let that stand. John wouldn't have."

"I can guess what John would have done. But that isn't me," I said. "I paid Marco a visit, but I don't think he did it."

"Do you have anything else you would like to tell me?"

"I ran into Marie and had to take her home. That's why I'm late."

There was a slight pause.

"She's back?"

I nodded in the dark.

"Did she say why?"

"She couldn't remember anything."

"So you took her home and hung out with her for a while? Watched Netflix?"

"She was pretty shaken up, and I found Laura Henders—the woman who died yesterday—sneaking around her house. Except she was mostly alive tonight and a pretty fast runner. I chased her, but she got away and led me into a trap, of course."

"She's a zombie," Sybil said, flipping onto her back, but still not looking at me. "That's something your friend, Marie, could have done, in case you hadn't thought of that."

"I did think of that possibility, but someone turned Marie into a zombie, too, which pretty much puts her in the clear."

"Anything else?"

"A demonic goat tried to kill me earlier tonight. Did I tell you about the goat? I don't think John and the goat got along very well."

Sybil rolled over and faced me. Even in the dim light, I could see her red eyes simmering like dying coals left in a fire.

"No, you did not tell me anything about meeting, much less fighting, the Goat of Mendes."

"Yeah, that's what Blaire called it," I said, nodding.

"Blaire's involved with this, too?" she said, lifting her head and raising one eyebrow.

"He showed up out of nowhere and saved my ass, for a price, of course."

"You know, the majority of the creatures around here—John could have taken them out easily, mostly because he knew their names. But even John would have thought twice about going up against the Mendes Goat. Without the goat's name, John would never have been able to defeat him on his own."

"Good to know," I said, not wanting to admit I didn't know the real names of the supernatural creatures in Ashburn, including hers.

When I looked over at Sybil, she was staring at the ceiling, silent.

Even though I was beyond tired, I rolled from one side to the other for the next hour, unable to fall asleep.

When the darkness overtook me at last, my dreams were plagued by images of Ahriman and the sounds and smells of the Mendes Goat.

CHAPTER 34

T HE GRUMBLING IN my stomach told me it was late in the morning when I awoke. Because the sun was out, I thought there was a good chance Sybil was in bed, but I was wrong.

She was gone, but as soon as my foot hit the floor, Shadow was there, living up to his name.

"You're not as scary as you think," I said with a grin, but when I reached down to pet him, he dropped his head and curled his lip.

Without thinking, I pointed a finger at him.

"No," I said in a stern voice. To my surprise, my digit remained attached, and Shadow sat down and offered me the top of his head, willingly.

"Good dog," I said as I rubbed his cranium.

I'd spent the night in John and Sybil's bedroom three times so far, but I'd never really taken a good look at it with my goggles. I checked out every wall, the closets, and under the bed, but I didn't find anything magical.

I slipped off the goggles and snooped around the old-fashioned way. Other than John's choice of reading material, which ranged from epic fantasy to non-fiction books about science, I didn't find any personal items that told me anything about who John was, or why he'd given his life for mine. The most interesting parts of the bedroom were the wooden bedposts and the deep grooves worn into them.

I pulled open the nightstand drawer and was greeted with myriad sex toys, handcuffs, and spiky instruments that could easily have doubled as torture devices. I shut the drawer and hoped Sybil wasn't in the habit of using them.

Next, I went into the bathroom with Shadow at my heels. I rummaged through the cabinet drawers and searched under the sink. The only thing out of the ordinary was his medicine cabinet, but only because it was devoid of medications—one of the benefits, I supposed, of being a demon.

With a shake of my head, I put on my jeans and a solid black tee-shirt and made my way downstairs to continue my search.

The living room was littered with innocuous knick knacks, including a small statue of the Buddha, a pair of blue marble bookmarks shaped like owls, a Chinese Pi disk, and fifty or so small notebooks of various sizes and designs. I thumbed through a couple of them, but they were all empty, and their spines were unbroken.

All in all, John and Sybil had kept a messy house with far too many stains of unknown origins on the carpets and walls.

I was about to brew some java to start my day, but I stopped when I noticed a red glow in the corner of my eye. When I turned to look at it, it disappeared. And as soon as I turned away, I saw it again. This time, I slipped on my goggles before turning to face it. When I did, the door to the basement stairs shimmered with red waves of magic.

Opening the door and flipping on the stairwell light, I descended into the basement with Shadow close behind me. At the bottom of the staircase, I stood with my mouth open, stunned as I stared at the once-empty basement.

I'd been prepared to see any number of things down there, like a dead body, more blood stains, or even a torture chamber. What I found instead was a fully stocked recording studio filled with instruments and gear.

All my lamenting about not having a guitar, and there'd been half a dozen of them in the house the whole time. For a second, I worried that the studio was an illusion or a dream.

But when I lowered my goggles, it was still there.

It wasn't as nice as my setup at home, but there was a complete drum set in the corner, some bass guitars and amps, a PA system, two mics on stands, and a recording booth.

And at the center of it all sat John's collection of guitars.

I walked over to the Oriental rug and the comfy leather chair he'd set up as his playing area. My fingers trailed across the heads of the Les Paul, the Tele, the Strat, the PRS, the Rickenbacker, and the Schecter Hellraiser. On the other side of the basement, I saw two hard-shell guitar cases that likely held his acoustics. One had the Martin logo stenciled on it, and the other was a Taylor. Seeing all the guitars together in one place took my breath away more than any of the supernatural horror and wonder I'd encountered thus far.

I was in a place as close to Heaven as I was likely to find in Ashburn. They were all amazing instruments, but I couldn't take my eyes off the Schecter.

I know other guitar players would have told me I was crazy, but there was something about the way the Hellraiser played and the noises I could squeeze out of it that I loved.

I picked up the heavy guitar, plugged it into the amp, and cranked up the dials.

Making myself comfortable in the throne-like chair, I hit a chord, and my ears were rewarded with a full, earthy blend of perfectly tuned strings that shook the room and made Shadow jump.

As my fingers moved across the mother-of-pearl inlaid neck, I went through some major pentatonic scales, then transitioned to one of my favorite tunes—one I'd written just after *Yeah, Yeah* had gone to the top of the charts. It was called *Stellar Invasion*, and back then I'd been convinced that anything I wrote would go gold. It turned out the world hadn't been ready for a five-minute opus about a celestial being who bends the fabric of space-time and eats planets at will. I admit, I might have taken a couple of questionable edibles while composing that one, but even decades later and completely sober, I still loved it.

I sang the first verse while my guitar gently wept. Then I moved into the chorus, letting my voice rise and crescendo.

A grin spread over my face as I thought about writing an entire album about Ashburn—a series of songs that would follow the adventures of a hero who walked into a small suburban town filled with forgotten gods, angels with broken wings, and rock-and-roll demons, all imprisoned by a powerful being for some unknown, diabolical purpose.

I stopped playing *Stellar Invasion* and noodled around with some new ideas, searching for the right riff around which I could build the first song. After half an hour of playing, mostly with my eyes closed, a melodic spine emerged.

Then Shadow's ears perked up, and he gave a piercing alert bark, and my fingers stopped. Two seconds later, I heard the doorbell ring over the hum of the amp.

I turned the volume knob on the Schecter to zero and put the guitar back in its rack before trudging upstairs to find out who was there. I didn't like being interrupted when I was in creative mode, and with each step I fantasized about the person at the door being a magazine salesman or someone else Shadow might find tasty.

Instead, when I made it the door and looked out, Oizys was standing there wearing a white silk blouse buttoned to her neck with her arms crossed in front of her.

I opened the door, but before she could say anything, I held up the palm of my hand.

"I know what you're going to say—that I messed up by letting Marie escape, but surprise—I ran into her last night. She's safe and sound and back in her house, in Ashburn, Virginia. I'm not even sure she ever left."

Oizys uncrossed her arms while Shadow growled menacingly behind my legs.

"You spoke with Marie?" she asked.

"We had a good talk last night, and trust me, she's not going anywhere."

Oizys crinkled her eyebrows and pushed her way past me. As soon as she was in the house, my vicious hellhound was nowhere to be seen.

Maybe I left out a couple of key points regarding Marie, like the fact she was a zombie. But essentially, I'd told Oizys the truth. Marie hadn't seemed like she wanted to go anywhere or do anything other than sleep. She was officially off my most-wanted list, whereas Oizys had moved to the top.

"I'm glad you're convinced the Voodoo priestess won't be leaving us anytime soon. Strangely enough, I'm forced to agree with you. But

I came here to tell you about something else—another dead human."

Even though Oizys was a demon, I could read her face. She was keeping something from me and enjoying the suspense way too much.

"Who died?" I asked sharply, doing my best to stare her down.

"If you're going to be ungrateful about this," she said in a tone of contempt, "I won't waste my energy being delicate. Early this morning, just before sunrise, a runner found Marie's dead body on the walking trail behind her house. I thought you would like to know, since the two of you had such a pleasant time yesterday."

CHAPTER 35

I HEARD WHAT Oizys told me, but I didn't believe her. Sure, the last time I'd seen Marie, she'd been a zombie, with only half of her soul and no discernible pulse. But she hadn't been completely dead. And she'd needed my help. For all I knew, she still needed me, and I was going to find out.

"Who did it?" I asked, keeping my face devoid of emotion as I rubbed the back of my neck to ease the mounting tension. "Do you know how she died?"

Oizys shrugged her shoulders.

"I wasn't fortunate enough to view the body," she said with a grin.

I stepped up to Oizys, certain my demonic rage was showing and not caring one bit.

"Where is she now?"

Oizys's eyebrows went up again, showing mild surprise.

"I do not keep track of such mundane things. She might still be in Ashburn, at the Police Station, but I imagine your Sheriff friend would know for sure. But really, John, I am quite shocked you care so much for one of *them*. I hope you're not going soft on me."

"I just need to know what happened to her," I said as I walked past Oizys and opened the door. "And who did it. It's my job."

She frowned but moved to leave.

"I had something else I wanted to share with you," she said as she stepped through the doorway.

"Tell me later," I said.

"But this one is fun," she said. "I thought you'd like to know Blaire has been properly punished for his oversight regarding my package yesterday. I assure you, it won't happen again. Although, in a way, I hope it does. You should have heard him scream. It was delicious."

"I'm sure he enjoyed whatever you gave him," I muttered, as I put my hand on the door, ready to close it in her face.

"He usually does," she said with a sigh. "Usually."

I analyzed the movements on Oizys's face, as if each were a series of frames frozen in time. She was trying to tell me something about Blaire, but whatever it was would have to wait.

"Thanks for that bonus piece of news," I said as I closed the door on her.

"You can come out now, you big baby," I yelled into the air.

I waited but didn't see Shadow anywhere.

"Fine, but I'm going to run an errand and then head over to the store, if you—"

Before I could finish, Shadow bounded past me, almost tripping me on his way to the door.

He sat there, wagging his tail, with his leash in his mouth.

"We're working now. We'll go for a walk later."

He kept the leash in his jaws as he followed me into the garage and hopped into the passenger seat.

I started up the engine, wondering why I was bringing him along at all.

"Why'd you hide from her?" I asked as I backed out of the driveway. "You're a friggin' hellhound. She's supposed to be afraid of *you.*"

Shadow whimpered and lowered his head.

"Ah, you're killing me," I said, as I gunned the engine and headed for the main road.

On the way, I decided to turn into Marie's community. Maybe I was hoping to see her outside checking on her eternal gardeners, but as I neared her house, I saw two police cars at her curb and an officer sealing her door with crime scene tape. I thought about asking one of the cops where the local police station was, even though that would have seemed an odd thing for John to ask. But I kept driving when I saw Oizys flirting with one of the officers.

As I drove past, Shadow growled, and Oizys turned to look at me with a gleam in her eye, like she had somehow heard him.

I hit the gas and left the scene shrinking behind me in my rear-view mirror.

"Time to visit the morgue," I said as I used the car's nav system to locate the nearest police station.

Five minutes later, I parked between two Sheriff's cruisers. Being around cops always made me nervous, even when I wasn't doing anything wrong. But walking into a crowded police station felt twice as bad.

The lobby was guarded by two cops who peered at me through narrowed eyes as I walked in with Shadow trotting behind me. I waited for them to tell me that dogs weren't allowed, but they ignored him and kept their eyes on me. At least I'd left Gus and my dagger in the trunk.

The one police officer was an older man with a white mustache and a sharpness to his eyes that told me he'd seen a lot and was bored sitting behind a desk. The other guy was younger and skinny. The way he was trying to mask his expression of contempt told me he was looking for trouble and probably pulling receptionist duty as punishment for his latest screw up.

What can I say? I'm quick to judge people, but I'm also hardly ever wrong.

I looked the old guy in his eyes and pretended to be polite.

"Good evening, officer. A friend of my mine passed away last night. A Marie Lacroix? I was told she was found on one of the walking paths near her house. And I was wondering if there was any way I could see her one last time. It would really mean a lot if I could tell her goodbye."

The old guy nodded then looked away and typed something into his laptop, one finger at a time.

"Are you a family member?" the younger cop said. "You don't look like one to me. And we don't allow dogs in here."

Shadow's ears flattened, and he fixed his gaze on the skinny police officer.

"Marie and I were very close," I said. "And I really need to see her."

"What you *need* to do is put that dog on a leash and get it out of here," the skinny officer said.

"Shut it, Allen," the older cop said, looking at me but clearly speaking to his partner. "Looks like your friend's here until the morning, John. I can take you back if you want."

The older cop knew me, which explained why he was cooperating. Before I could thank him, Allen put his hand on the older cop's shoulder.

"You know the rules, Charlie. He can't go back there. Either him and his dog leave, or I'm sounding the alarm."

"I appreciate your help," I said to Charlie as I ignored his red-faced partner.

Charlie nodded, but his eyes were glazed over and he'd turned pale.

"Are you feeling all right?" I said.

"You, shut up," Allen said to me. "And Charlie, what the hell? Maybe you *are* sick if you think you're taking this asshole and his mutt back there to see one of the peepsicles."

I wanted to ignore Allen the asshole so badly, but something inside me snapped, and I turned on him, letting the smallest amount of my demon rage show in my eyes.

"What is your problem?" I said. "Charlie is going to take me and my dog to see my friend. Do you really have a problem with that?"

I was ready for him to pull his gun or to sound the alarm. But instead, he broke into a genuine smile and sat back in his chair.

"That sounds perfect to me, sir," he said, turning to his computer and humming a tune. "I'm very sorry for your loss, and I hope you have a good rest of your day."

I raised an eyebrow and cocked my head as Charlie stood up and motioned for me to follow him.

He led me through two security doors, swiping his access card and punching in his PIN. We stopped outside a room with glass double doors and a wall placard that read, *Medical Examiner.*

"She's in drawer 12B," Charlie said with a smile that felt out of place among the dead. "I'll wait outside, but you take all the time you need."

I nodded slowly as Charlie swiped his badge and opened the glass doors. Cold air from the room rushed out to greet me, and Charlie motioned for me to enter.

I studied his eyes before going anywhere. They were still glazed over, and he seemed to be somewhere else mentally.

"Let me ask you a question, Charlie."

"Sure thing," he said.

"What would you do, hypothetically speaking, if I told you that you were sleepy and that you should take a nap in one of the cadaver drawers?"

"I'd get some sleep, I suppose," he said without a pause. "Do you want me to go to sleep right now? Am I tired?"

"No, you're perfectly fine. In fact, you feel great and well rested."

Charlie took a deep breath and smiled, looking invigorated, just like I'd said he was.

"I have one last question," I said. "If I asked you to kill yourself right now, what would you do?"

"Off the top of my head, I can think of a couple different ways to do it. But my gun or my knife would be the easiest. Whichever is best for you."

"There's no need," I said. "I was only wondering. You can wait out here for me. That will be fine."

He nodded and stepped back.

I entered the morgue and added what had just happened between me and Officer Charlie to the list of things I had to ask Sybil about one day.

After locating drawer 12B, I grabbed the handle and pulled until the stainless-steel platform rolled toward me and was fully extended.

Unfortunately, Marie's body wasn't on it.

I heard Shadow growl, followed by a familiar voice behind me.

"Guess your friend wasn't as dead as we thought she was," Sheriff Boreman said. "Seems we've been getting a lot of that lately."

CHAPTER 36

T HE SHERIFF STOOD a few feet away from me with his hands
on his hips. Even though I was on his turf, his face showed a tint
of fear that spoiled his attempt at looking confident and in charge of
the situation.

Shadow lay down on the floor and licked one of his paws, ignoring
the Sheriff completely.

"I was getting ready to come find you," the Sheriff said. "An hour
ago, the medical examiner showed up to start his preliminary review
of your friend's body. But the drawer was empty, as you can see. I was
hoping one of the newbies had screwed something up, but everything
was in order on our end. I downloaded the video from the security
cam to my phone so you could see what happened for yourself."

The video showed the back of Marie in a paper gown as she walked
toward the exit. She moved a little stiffer than usual, but otherwise she
looked unharmed and well—just as I'd left her. On the bottom of the
screen, the time stamp indicated she'd escaped only an hour ago.

"I really thought she was one of us," the Sheriff said. "A human, I
mean."

"She was," I said. "But she dabbled in—certain things."

"You mean, Voodoo. I had to talk to her twice last year about
slaughtering chickens in her kitchen. Ended up citing her for a few
health code violations. It made for a good headline in the local
newspapers, but it wasn't much of a big deal. Freaked out the
neighbors more than anything else."

"I'm sure the HOA didn't like it either," I said.

"Let me ask you something," the Sheriff said, ignoring my dig at Oizys. "Do I need to be worried about your friend walking around loose in my county?"

I didn't know how to answer his question. My experience with zombies was limited to watching them do fake yard work outside Marie's house, so I told the Sheriff what he wanted to hear.

"She's no harm to anyone," I said, probably lying but thinking John would have been proud of me.

My assurance satisfied the Sheriff, as his shoulders relaxed and his posture slackened.

"You look like you could use some sleep," I said.

"Don't," he said sharply, before turning his head to avoid my eyes. "Don't pretend to give a shit about me—or any of us. I know the deal here, and I don't like it. But it is what it is. Just take care of your mess and don't let this kind of thing happen again. I'd hate for word to get out that there's something weird going on around here. Rumors like that might draw a lot of unwanted attention, if you know what I mean."

"If I didn't know any better, I'd swear you just threatened me," I said.

"All I did was make a statement."

"Has anyone else seen this video?"

"I erased it on the server," he said. "Nothing ever gets really deleted nowadays, but somebody'd have to be looking pretty hard to find it."

"Make sure no one does," I said with a snarl.

The Sheriff tensed up—exactly the effect I was going for.

"I'll show myself out," I said, before I remembered what else I'd wanted to ask him. "Any progress regarding Laura Henders?"

"Not much. Her permanent address was in Sterling. I don't know why she was walking around Ashburn by herself. I figure she was visiting someone, but no one has come forward."

"Do you still have her body, or did your men lose hers, too?"

His look confirmed what I already knew—that Laura had gone missing just like Marie. But his face convinced me he didn't know any more than he was telling. Someone or something was working behind the scenes, manipulating the situation, and getting two people killed in the process—and neither one of us knew who that was.

I walked out of the station, nodding to Charlie on the way out and glaring at Allen.

Five minutes later, I pulled into the parking lot outside Ancient Pages. Despite a grumble of protest from Shadow, I locked him in the bookstore with a fresh bowl of water and hoped I wasn't going to return to find a monster-sized poop in one of my reading chairs.

I couldn't get Marie off my mind, and I wasn't hungry, but I needed to talk to someone I could trust, and the best contender was Rose.

I opened the door to Bangrak Thai and waited to be seated. The place was full, and for a second I was afraid there wouldn't be an open table or that Rose would be too busy to talk.

Within a few seconds, a young waitress with a nervous smile greeted me.

"Any room left for me?" I said with my best attempt at a smile.

"We always have a table for you. Please follow me, and I will prepare for you a very special lunch."

She seated me at a small table close to the kitchen, then turned to leave.

"I know she's busy," I said. "But could you tell Rose I need to talk to her?"

The server's face turned to a friendly frown as she bowed her head.

"I am very sorry, but she is away, visiting her sister."

"Where does her sister live?" I asked, not wanting to hear the answer.

The server shook her head.

"They live…together."

"I thought you said she was visiting her sister."

The server nodded and looked pleased.

"Yes, that is right," she said with enthusiasm.

Confused, I gave up and ordered a dish of flat noodles that showed up five minutes later. As I picked at my food, I did my best to sort through everything in my head.

Someone had broken into my house and stolen my blood—and my bathroom trash—and it wasn't Marco, the gang leader who was actually addicted to my blood. A giant black goat had tried to kill me.

The head of the local HOA lied to me at least twice I knew of. And, counting Marie, two humans had died and been turned into zombies since I'd started my new job.

I didn't know how John had performed during his first week as Ahriman's enforcer, but I had a feeling he'd done much better than me. I reminded myself again that I wasn't John and that his job had been forced on me. I'd done what I could do to uphold Ahriman's commandments, and it had amounted to a big fat hill of beans. My next step was to go home, play guitar, and drink.

Ahriman could take his job and shove it.

As soon as I thought that, my guts flipped and a wave of anxiety flooded my body, screaming at me—telling me there was something I was missing or a piece of the puzzle I wasn't seeing. I didn't care about solving any mysteries, but I could hear the echo of Ahriman whispering my true name in my ear, and I knew I had to continue.

I'd talk to Rose when she returned, but for the time being, I decided to see the one person in Ashburn who might know more than her. He wasn't a big talker, but he was next door, and he was always in.

CHAPTER 37

I ENTERED THE bookstore's hidden back room, this time with Shadow at my heel.

"I'm home, honey," I said, hoping I spoke loud enough for Walt to hear me. As expected, the only answer I received was the faint scratch-scratch-scratching of his pen from deep inside the spatially impossible room.

Weaving between the piles of books and papers, I made my way back to his workspace, or his prison, depending on how you looked at it. He was in the same position, hunched over and writing, but the pile of finished pages next to his foot was in danger of toppling over. I picked up the stack of his work without so much as a nod from the shackled scribbler.

"I don't know how you write all the time like that," I said. "The last album signing I did, I got tired after my first twenty signatures."

I carried the papers to a table that backed to a set of shelves lining the nearest wall. On the middle shelf, a stack of four thick, oversized, leather-bound books stood out from the rest of the paper in the room. I picked up the first one and opened it. It was like a scrapbook inside, filled with bits of paper, each resembling the folded-up scrap I carried in my pocket from Abby the Imp. Each of the notes in the book contained words or symbols hand-written by Walt. The only difference between the piece of paper the imp had given me and the ones in the book was that under each of the pasted-on scraps was a handwritten name carefully printed in blue ink. Chaz's name was written beneath one of the pieces of paper that contained marks from an unknown, ancient alphabet comprised of lines and circles. In the upper right corner of the book's page, the word *Ahriman* was printed in bold, but the space above the name was blank.

For a second, I wondered whether the scrap of paper in my pocket held the secrets to Ahriman's name, but if it had, I was sure John would have used that knowledge to take down his boss and leave Ashburn a long time ago.

Even so, my heart sped up when I realized what I held in my hands. Walt's seemingly chaotic writings contained the true names of the supernatural beings in Ashburn, and the book paired those names with their owners wherever John had figured out the connection.

I turned the page and saw Oizys's name printed near the top. Above it, John had pasted a long piece of torn paper with strange letters scrawled across it. I smiled even though I didn't recognize the language in which her true name was written. I closed my eyes, took a deep breath, and exhaled. The instant I opened my eyes, I tried reading her name as quickly as I could, hoping that some part of John's memory would kick in.

It didn't.

I flipped through another dozen pages in the book, searching for any mention of the Mendes Goat, Sybil, or Marie, but to no avail.

Still, I'd found the secret to John's ability to control and intimidate the supernatural population of Ashburn—his own personal Rosetta Stone.

Too bad I couldn't read it.

I placed the oversized book back where I'd found it and walked away from Walt without a word. I hadn't found the answers I'd come for, but I still knew more than before.

When I closed the door to the secret room behind me, a wave of anxiety flowed through me—the same feeling I used to get when I'd leave my house and not be able to remember if I'd turned off the burners in the kitchen.

A low throbbing began in my cranium as I walked toward the front of the store where a man and his child were waiting outside, peeking at me through the window.

I opened the door and watched their faces blossom with hope right before Shadow and I stepped outside, and I locked the door behind me.

"Excuse me," the man said, trying to get my attention.

"I'm on a coffee break," I said, slipping my goggles on to shield my eyes from the sun that was a lot higher in the sky than it should have been for that time of day. I felt bad about not letting the man and his kid into the store, but I had a feeling John hadn't run much of a book-selling business anyway.

And besides, I hadn't been completely lying to the man. The morning had clearly gotten away from me, and I was in desperate need of some java.

CHAPTER 38

A S I WALKED along the sidewalk heading for the Moon Dollarz, I entertained myself by trying to explain the concept of coffee to Shadow.

"It's a magic drink. It makes you hyperactive and focused at the same time."

Shadow cocked his head and looked up at me just as flashing blue and white lights lit up the store window on my right.

When I looked over, Sheriff Boreman was stopped at the curb in one of his cruisers and was motioning for me to join him.

"Miss me?" I said with a forced smile as I walked up to his passenger-side window.

"We got another one," he said. "You'd better follow me."

Before I could say anything, he hit his siren once and pulled a tight, three-point turn. I stared longingly at the Moon Dollarz sign as his car pulled away.

"This is going to be a terrible afternoon," I said to Shadow as I made my way into the parking lot toward the Audi.

The Sheriff waited at the exit just long enough for me to catch up before he took off at full speed.

Together, we raced up Claiborne then turned up Truro Parish Drive with our tires squealing. As I braced myself for another murder scene, I felt a sense of failure that was probably not deserved. It had been my job to keep Ashburn's human population safe from its supernatural neighbors. I also remembered Rose's warning about not breaking the rules too often. A sinking dread flowed through me, because I was pretty sure Ahriman was going to notice three human corpses, even though officially, Laura and Marie weren't really dead.

I followed the Sheriff through an all-way stop sign as we turned into a neighborhood I was all too familiar with. He pulled over next to two other police cruisers at the mouth to one of the walking trails that cut through a patch of thick woods. I stepped out of the car, put Shadow on his leash because there were so many people around, and hurried to catch up with the Sheriff. With each step, the forest surroundings became more and more familiar, until at last we reached the same clearing where Blaire had saved me from the Mendes Goat the night before.

I stayed close to the Sheriff as he forced a path through the crowd of emergency workers.

"Give us the space for a few minutes," he said as two of his deputies and a man with a digital camera stepped away.

The Sheriff and I stood over the motionless body that was face down in the grass. When I saw that the dead guy wore a well-fitted suit, my arm hairs stood straight up.

"We identified him from his wallet—Blaire Howard. Worked for the local HOA. For Oizys."

"Can I see his face?" I asked. The Sheriff called over two men wearing latex gloves. They set their bags down and finished photographing the dead body before gently turning it onto its back.

When I saw what was left of Blaire's face, I grimaced and had to force myself not to puke.

"Jesus," the Sheriff said as he took out a cloth rag and coughed into it.

Blaire's face had been eaten away, and his mid-section was in tatters. Even though I had to force myself to do so, I bent down and got in close enough to see the details of his face. I looked for as long as I could stand, holding my breath, but I didn't see a single speck of yellow-orange powder anywhere on him. Something had attacked and mutilated Blaire, and the results were savage. That was bad enough, but I was also stressed because whoever or whatever killed Blaire wasn't the same person or creature that had turned Laura and Marie into zombies. And that meant I had two supernatural killers to look for when I couldn't even find one.

Staring at his corpse, Blaire's wounds didn't match anything I'd read about to do with Voodoo or even heard of before. I was no expert, but the scene in front of me looked more like an animal mauling than anything else.

"This is going to sound strange," I said. "But could you have your men search for hoof prints in the area?"

"Like from a demon or from a goat?" the Sheriff said, his face red with anger.

"Maybe both," I said, backing away from what was left of Blaire.

The Sheriff followed me, shaking his head and growling.

"I know what you are, John. And I know I'm not in much of a place to make any demands, but you're the one who has to take care of this. I appreciate that you're a lot easier to work with lately. I really am thankful for that, but I think you might be losing your edge, too. Normally, you would have taken care of things by now, and I'm getting a little worried. Do I need to be worried?"

"I'll take care of it," I said. "Just like I always do."

Hoping I sounded more confident than I was, I led Shadow back to the car. I wanted to walk away and lose myself in some music, but I was sure Ahriman's spell wouldn't let me do that, so I didn't even try.

I kept repeating in my head that I wasn't a detective or a demon enforcer. I was only a once-famous musician, who was good at writing verses and choruses, and not much else. And that was it. Verse. Chorus. Verse. Chorus. Bridge.

I stopped walking, and Shadow looked up at me with his tongue hanging out of his mouth.

A bridge. That was exactly what I needed—something that linked Laura, Marie, and Blaire. If I had that, I'd have somewhere to start, at least. But unless Blaire got up and joined the ranks of the living dead, I couldn't think of anything they all had in common.

Except Oizys.

CHAPTER 39

O IZYS HAD BEEN the one who told me about both Laura's and Marie's death, and she'd practically told me she'd done something awful to Blaire. I wanted to find Oizys, grab her by the throat, and make her confess to stealing Laura's and Marie's souls. For all I knew, she'd been responsible for Blaire's death as well, even though that piece didn't feel right. She certainly wasn't going to win any awards for boss of the year, but Blaire's wounds weren't what I would have expected from her.

I went home and dropped off Shadow at the house, then hopped back in the car, and decided to follow Oizys to see if I could learn something. That approach had always worked with cheating husbands, so I went back to what I knew and waited for Oizys to show her hand.

After getting back on Claiborne and heading for the Nature Center, I entered the Nature Center parking lot with caution.

With my goggles on, I could clearly see the fiery sigils floating above the building, but more importantly, I saw a pink VW Beetle, with MAKUHRT tags parked up front. I didn't need to be a demon or a detective to figure that one out. So I parked far away from her car while maintaining a line of sight with her office window.

I felt a little like a peeping Tom as I watched her sitting at her desk, stroking and smiling at the Hummel figurine I'd delivered to Blaire.

I squinted and tried to figure out exactly what she was doing as the statuette began crawling around on her desk like a living creature. With a huge smile, Oizys reached into her top desk drawer and took out a small silver hammer. She tapped it lightly on the figurine's tiny, painted foot, then raised her hammer high, like she was lining up for a Major League swing.

She brought the mallet down directly on top of the porcelain foot and smashed it to bits.

That was bad enough, but the figurine screeched in pain so loudly I could hear her through the window. With each cry of agony, Oizys's shoulders relaxed a little more, and her mouth opened into a soft, round shape as she soaked up the tiny statue's suffering.

The figurine squirmed and tried to get away. But Oizys picked it up, licked the jagged edges where the foot had once been, and dropped the Hummel into her side desk drawer before gently shutting and locking it.

After she sat for a few moments, she stood up, straightened her schoolmarm's skirt and blouse, then slipped into her suit top and left the office.

I slouched down into the driver's seat just as Oizys got into her car, revved the engine, and took off.

The last time I'd tailed someone, I'd been in my thirties and following a scrawny little married man who liked to pick up dates downtown. He'd been easy to follow, mainly because he didn't think anyone knew about his secret life and because he spent most of his energy looking at the women.

As I started up the car and pulled back onto Claiborne, I reminded myself that Oizys wasn't a cheating husband and that she likely had the same heightened powers as me. As I followed her, I stayed far enough back that I was only a dot in her rear-view mirror.

As it turned out, doing that in the suburbs was hard as hell.

Still, she didn't seem to notice me, and after she turned into a housing subdivision I was unfamiliar with, she pulled up to a curb and parked.

With a spring in her step, she almost bounced her way to the front door of a double-large McMansion and rang the bell. As she waited for someone to answer, I scoped the house with its perfectly kept lawn and shrubs. The full stone facade and the outdoor accent floodlights made my lip curl.

Oizys tapped her foot and rang the doorbell again. When she turned her body, I could see she was holding a paper-sized manila envelope. Maybe it was an HOA violation notice she was hand delivering so she could soak up the homeowner's distress in person.

After a minute, a woman opened the door, and just as I'd guessed, Oizys handed her the envelope and waited as she opened it and read the letter within.

As the homeowner started to gesture excitedly, Oizys shook her head and grinned. The woman grew more irate, but Oizys clasped her hands together, gave the woman her best fake smile, and shrugged.

I had no idea what the violation was, but Oizys was enjoying the shit out of giving it to the homeowner.

After five minutes of arguing, the woman stepped back into her house and slammed the door. When Oizys turned around, I could've seen her wider-than-possible smile from a hundred yards away as I slouched down in my seat, trying to become invisible.

I heard Oizys revving the VW's engine before pulling away. I started the car and followed her carefully to another house in the same neighborhood.

The McMansion she parked in front of this time looked pretty much the same as the first one she'd visited. The only real differences were that the new house was at the end of a pipe stem and had a large white rock sitting in its front yard.

I got out of the car and made my way into the strip of dense woods that lined the right side of the pipe stem.

Oizys seemed to be treating the woman who came to the door in a much nicer manner than she had the previous homeowner. I couldn't hear what they were saying, but I could read the woman's face. To my surprise, she looked excited to see Oizys, although for the life of me, I couldn't imagine why.

The woman's excitement soon turned to anxiety, however, as Oizys pointed to the large white rock in front of the woman's house, shaking her finger at the homeowner like an elementary school teacher.

The woman slouched her narrow shoulders, bowed her head, and nodded. Oizys turned around and left, once again with a big smile on her face, but this one seemed more devious than before.

I wasn't sure why, but my gut told me, in more ways than one, to stay at the house instead of continuing to follow Oizys.

It was still light outside, so I waited for the HOA demon to leave, then went back to my car and turned on the radio, preparing to wait until nightfall before checking out the house.

Finding nothing worth listening to on the radio, I played with the buttons on the car's control panel. When I hit the *Media* button, a menu of artists popped up on the screen in the dashboard. John had been an asshole, but his taste in music wasn't too bad.

I had tons of choices, and as I scrolled through the list of artists, I found it difficult to pick one. Finally, I settled on some classic rock and tapped my foot as a driving beat from one of the most incredible rock drummers of all time filled the car like the wings of a Valkyrie's horse flapping its way to Valhalla.

Just as I was getting into the song and belting out my best falsetto singing voice, a box truck pulled into the pipe stem and parked in front of the woman's house.

Three men ambled out of the vehicle. One made his way to the front door and knocked, and the other two opened the back of the truck. Within minutes, all three of the men were moving large boxes of all different sizes and shapes into the house.

After ten minutes of unloading the boxes, the workers went inside and didn't come out for almost an hour.

Twilight was setting in by the time the truck drove away. After another thirty minutes, it was dark enough that I felt comfortable getting closer to get a better look at what was going on.

I felt exposed, expecting that someone would see me, but I tried to remember who I was now. John wouldn't have cared about someone noticing him. In fact, he probably would have knocked down the door and taken a look at whatever he wanted to see without even asking.

But I wasn't John, as I told myself at least hourly. Instead, I walked slowly to the front of the house and checked over both shoulders—something criminals always seemed to do, but which never seemed to work. I ducked into the space between the bushes and the side of the house and tried getting a quick look inside, but the window blinds were closed. I crouched down and waited for it to get a little darker, then I vaulted their fence and lay down on their lawn, face-down.

Just like my own McMansion, the place had two small, ground-level windows that looked into the basement. There was light shining from both of them as I shimmied closer to take a look.

I wasn't sure what I expected to find, but what I saw was closer to a modern-day dungeon than a suburban basement. Two poles had been installed in the middle of the floor and connected to the ceiling. I also saw a machine that looked like a rack, a couple of wooden stocks, iron manacles attached to chains that had been bolted to the walls, and a table filled with whips and floggers.

In the midst of everything, the woman who'd spoken with Oizys and the woman's husband folded up empty boxes and stacked them away neatly into a closet.

I turned from the window and sat with my back against the side of the house. If a human husband and wife wanted to turn their basement into a sex dungeon, that was their choice. After all, we lived in America, where people were still free to do shit like that if they wanted.

But had it been a coincidence that Oizys showed up right before the dungeon equipment was delivered?

Unlikely.

That's when a large piece of the puzzle fell into place. I'd been spending a lot of time trying to figure out what had happened to Laura Henders and worrying about Marie trying to leave town. But what if I should have been watching Oizys instead? What if she were the one really trying to escape?

Since Oizys harvested her power from the suffering of others, torturing homeowners in a dungeon seemed like something that would make her absolutely giddy. If she could gather enough power from their collective pain, it could also make her strong enough to break through Ahriman's magical shield and free herself.

That would explain why Oizys had been so eager to have me think about and investigate everyone but her.

I remembered back to when I'd asked Oizys if she wanted to leave Ashburn. With hindsight, her answer now seemed ridiculous, as she claimed to be content making the lives of Ashburn homeowners as miserable as possible.

After another half an hour, I got up and walked back to the

sidewalk and to the car. I thought about being more John-like and confronting the couple, demanding an explanation for why they were setting up a dungeon on a Saturday night in my town.

Instead, I shook my head and settled into the car, waiting for the victims to arrive, but no one showed. After a while, the lights in the house went out, and I decided to go home.

By the time I pulled into John's garage, I was looking forward to seeing Shadow and Sybil. As expected, Shadow was waiting for me, his leash in his mouth and his tail wagging hard.

I greeted him with genuine excitement and rubbed his head before letting him into the back yard.

It wasn't yet midnight, but when I was done with Shadow, I made my way upstairs, ready to crash. When I stepped into the bedroom, Sybil was there, sitting up, naked in bed with her arms crossed over her ample bosom.

"Are you trying to go back on our deal?" she said. "We were supposed to find a way out of Ashburn together. But you and Shadow have been running around a lot without me."

"You're never here," I said. "I've checked lots of times, but you're always out doing something I probably don't even want to know about. And yes, you and I are going to get out of here, together—one day. But we can't leave right now."

"You want to stay?" she said through her scowl.

"Of course not," I said. "But I need more time to figure out what to do about Ahriman. Don't worry, I'm still taking you with me when I finally get out of Ashburn. A promise is a promise."

She grinned ever so slightly, then let her hands drop, revealing her ample breasts for a split second before she slid under the sheets.

I took off my clothes and set my goggles on the nightstand, but hesitated before joining her. My body told me to hurry up and get into the bed, but my instinct for self-preservation was stronger.

"Have you already eaten tonight?" I asked.

She laughed, a light girlish giggle that sounded eerie coming from the lips of a fully-grown succubus.

"I had a light snack before you came home," she said. "Don't worry. I'm saving my appetite for later."

And with that, Shadow slid under the bed to settle in for the night on the carpet, and I slid under the sheets to give my demon girlfriend a hug.

The hug quickly turned into more than that, of course, and before I knew it, we were wrapped up in each other. As long as I kept the image of her demonic face out of my head, rolling around with her was pretty amazing. I could totally see how her kind were able to tempt men into their beds and suck the life force from their souls. And to be honest, as she kissed my neck, I imagined there were plenty of worse ways someone could die.

An hour later, after our carnal passions had been fully satiated, we settled into a session of quiet pillow talk.

"I think Oizys is the one trying to escape somehow," I said. "The whole Voodoo priestess thing was just a distraction."

Sybil drew back and crinkled up her eyebrows, doubting me.

So I told her about Blaire being dead and me following Oizys and seeing the dungeon being set up in the couple's basement. Instead of getting on board with my theory, Sybil chuckled.

"I'm no fan of Oizys," she said, "but she really loves it here. And she's never even hinted at leaving in the past. Maybe that couple you saw likes a little pain with their pleasure, and Oizys just wanted to join in on the fun."

I lay back on the bed and took a deep breath, thinking.

"You're better than John was in the sack," she said, touching my chest with her taloned forefinger. "I just wanted you to know."

"I'm not sure what to say," I said.

She leaned in and kissed me again.

"Don't say anything," she said as she got up and walked to the bathroom, her powerful body gleaming with each purposeful step.

When she returned, she slipped back into bed and rested her head on my chest in a show of affection I hadn't been expecting.

"Not going out tonight?" I said.

She kissed my chest gently, then looked into my eyes.

"I'd like to stay with you for the rest of the night, if that's okay. I never wanted to be here much when John was around, but you're different."

"That sounds great," I said. "But if you want to fool around again, I'm going to need a nap."

"I'll be here when you wake up," she said as she snuggled closer.

As soon as I closed my eyes, I began to fall into the oblivion of sleep. My brain sorted through the events of the evening and lingered far too long on the image of Blaire missing most of his face. Just before I passed out, I replayed the details of my passionate evening with Sybil and of our discussion afterward. I was starting to like her, but there was something that didn't connect about why she wasn't feeding tonight—some detail she had mentioned that I couldn't recall.

"You said you were saving your appetite for later?" I said in a slurred voice as I held on to consciousness by a thread.

She laughed as the darkness of sleep finally claimed me. I heard her response right before I passed out, like it was coming to me from the far end of a pitch-black tunnel.

"I'm saving up my appetite for the party tomorrow night," she said. "Food always tastes better when I'm really hungry."

CHAPTER 40

I HAD FINISHED the album earlier that evening, and I hated every one of the new songs, but at least Ahriman was gone. Even so, I couldn't sleep.

At first, I'd felt light and free when he left, but my elation was short-lived. Soon after, the sickness crawled through my body, taking control of my internal systems again. It felt like I'd been slammed with an instant case of the flu, only a thousand times worse. The cancer was making up for being kept at bay with an unnatural vengeance.

I leaned over the edge of the bed and coughed up blood—a lot of it—and I was sure I was about to die, despite Ahriman's promises.

I lay back on my studio's hospital bed and struggled to take a full breath, but I only managed a shallow, raspy inhalation. And as I clung to life, a familiar dark presence appeared at the foot of my bed in the shape of a man with large, curled horns.

"Our deal," I managed to say.

"I am keeping my end of our agreement," Ahriman said. "The album will be released tomorrow, and when you wake up, as I promised, you will no longer be dying of cancer."

"Or of anything else," I said, suddenly frantic at the idea that he was tricking me and planning my sudden death from another illness.

He chuckled.

"As I have said, you will not die of any human disease," he said. "Now rest. Tomorrow is an important day for both of us."

I hated the way he seemed so happy while I was in such pain, but

I resigned myself to sleep and comforted myself with thoughts of waking up cured and healthy, with a brand-new chance at life.

As the room around me faded, Ahriman played the recording of *Blood Blister*, the first single from the new album—his tune about the end of the world.

How appropriate, I thought, as its heavy-handed electronic drums kicked in.

In a final moment of panic, I became terrified of falling asleep, fearing that giving in to my exhaustion would be the same as surrendering to death.

I fought the blackness until the song's chorus rang out.

When the world ends
With a wound like a whisper
When the world ends
Through the pain I will miss her
When the world ends
It will break like a blister
When the world ends
All my blood will go with her

And then, at last, the darkness washed over me, and I slept.

Once unconscious, I had a vivid dream. Someone lifted my spirit from my body, and instead of letting it rise to the heavens or plunge straight down to Hell, they pulled it to the side. And with a brave cry, they dove into my body and took my place. Although for what reason, I had no idea.

CHAPTER 41

T HE INSTANT I woke, I turned to Sybil and blurted out a
question my mind must have been working on while I was asleep.

"What party are you going to tonight?"

"Good morning to you, too," she said with a kiss. "I hope you got
plenty of rest, because I'm feeling horny again. I'm not getting up this
early for nothing, you know."

"Tell me about the party," I said.

"It's nothing," she said, but her face gave off plenty of micro-tells.
She was embarrassed about something, which was something I didn't
expect from her.

"Hanging out with some friends?" I said. "A few demons getting
together for tea and biscuits or maybe a good old-fashioned
possession?"

"What is wrong with you?" she said. "It's just a human party with
some local swingers celebrating the start of summer. The men are
looking for something more extreme than what they can get at home.
And the wives want to show off their toned asses and implants to men
who appreciate them."

My eyebrows raised.

"That's why you didn't eat last night? Because there's going to be
plenty of humans to snack on tonight?"

She slapped me on the chest just hard enough that I couldn't tell whether she was being playful or trying to remind me of how strong she was.

"Don't worry," she said. "There will be plenty of out-of-towners there tonight."

"Don't you think Ahriman might notice if you eat someone?"

"Darling, stop," she said. "I only play with people who don't live here. And I pick single people or ones who won't be missed…very much. Ahriman only cares about humans who live here. As long as I pace myself and don't make too much of a mess, tourists are usually fair game. Remember Hillary? She didn't live in Ashburn, and Ahriman didn't show up when I ate her heart, did he?"

"John let you kill tourists?"

"Sometimes he joined in and dined with me. It was the closest thing we ever had to a date night."

I inhaled deeply, trying to process what she was telling me.

"I know what you think of me," Sybil said. "I saw how you looked at my real face and how much I disgust you. I can read faces too. But I am what I am, and I have to eat human hearts—the more innocent, the better. If I don't, I get weak, and being weak in Ashburn is dangerous, especially when you're the enforcer's girlfriend. Dating John didn't make me very popular."

I looked away and shook my head. I didn't want anything to happen to her. She didn't deserve that. But I also didn't want a bunch of innocent partygoers to lose their lives just because they didn't live here.

"I know John didn't use to care, but if I see you trying to kill someone tonight, I'll have to stop you."

She smiled.

"Sorry, babe. But even if you could carry through with that threat, you're not invited to this party. Nobody wants Ahriman's enforcer watching over them. They want to relax and have fun."

"Who would know I work for Ahriman? I thought you said it was a human party."

"Mostly human."

"If supernaturals are going to be there, and they don't want me to show, that must mean they're going to break Ahriman's laws."

She shrugged.

"Technically, most of the supernaturals will only be breaking one of his commandments."

"Which one is that?"

"The one about hurting humans," she said after a pause. "That's why a lot of the swingers go to these parties in the first place—to hurt and to *be* hurt."

"Where's the party being held, Sybil?"

"I don't know yet. It rotates from house to house. They email guests right before the party starts and put a white rock in front of the house that's hosting, so it's easy to find."

"The house with the dungeon in the basement had a big white boulder in front of it."

Sybil rubbed her hands together and grinned.

"Oh, that's great!" she said. "That means I won't have to bring my own toys tonight. The parties where the hosts go all out and take the time to decorate and prepare are always the best ones."

"I'm glad to hear my first party's going to be a good one," I said.

"I told you, you aren't on the invite list," she said, her face stern.

I sneered and glanced at the ceiling before leveling my eyes on her.

"My name is John Starling—enforcer to his demonic awesomeness, the great Ahriman. That means Ashburn is my town and I can go anywhere I please, including a party full of sexual deviants, if I so choose."

Sybil exhaled heavily.

"I know you're getting stronger," she said. "Strong enough that I can't stop you if you really want to go. But they'll have guards there and defenses to keep out the unwanted masses, and tonight, that will include you."

"Don't worry," I said. "I have a plan, and Oizys isn't going to like it."

"You think Oizys is up to something?"

"She gets her power from human suffering," I said. "I think she's going to use the equipment in that dungeon in ways your swinger friends aren't prepared for—to do some real injury and harm to them, so she can get the hell out of Ashburn. I also think three people have died, or mostly died, to keep me distracted from what she's really planning. And I have to stop her."

I was trying to sound confident, but I had no idea how I was going to prevent Oizys from doing anything.

"Do what you need to do," I said as I got out of bed. "I'm going to feed Shadow, then I have some things I need to take care of before the party tonight."

Sybil was quiet while I dressed but held out her hand as I was about to leave.

"If you've made up your mind about this, maybe we should go together. We said we were in this as partners, and that we're gonna leave Ashburn together one day, right?"

I nodded and put my hands on her shoulders.

"We *are* in this together," I said, "And I could really use your help."

"What can I do?" she said with a nod.

"Go to the party before me. Scope the place out. Try to find out what's going on, and more than anything, keep track of Oizys until I show up."

"Will you come find me when you get there?"

"You can count on it," I said with a grin. "But I don't think you're going to have a hard time figuring out when I arrive."

CHAPTER 42

S YBIL SAID THE party started at ten, so I had all day to prepare, and that included making a few social calls.

First stop was Oizys herself. I didn't expect anything to come from it, but if she knew I was onto her, I thought there'd be a small chance she'd give up her plans without a fight.

When I parked outside the Nature Center, her car wasn't there, but I went inside anyway, with Shadow at my heel.

"Unless he's a service animal, that dog is not allowed in here," a nasally female voice called out from my left. I looked over and saw a short, roundish woman with a helmet of orange-blonde hair.

"I don't suppose Oizys is around," I said.

She shook her head, but her hair didn't move.

"She's off for the weekend and out of the office all next week. Perhaps I could assist you with something…after you remove your pet."

She was telling the truth about Oizys, as far as she knew it, but I disliked her anyway. Shadow made a low, gurgling sound that let me know he agreed with my assessment.

"Thanks for nothing," I said, before turning to leave.

The Oizys trip was a bust, and next on my list was Marco. Ten minutes later, I pulled up to La Flower Shoppe. When I stepped into the store with Shadow once again by my side, the regulars were there, sorting flowers. The instant they saw us, Miguel, Julio, and Santos set down their stems, slipped on their pendants, and prepared for a fight.

I raised my hands and forced a smile—something I'd never been very good at.

"Not today, boys," I said as I let my glowing red eyes burn through my facade. "I'm here with a business deal for Marco."

Miguel glanced at Shadow, then shot me a dirty look as he headed to the back of the store. When he returned with his boss, I tried to read Marco's body movements and his demeanor, but all I saw was the face of a junkie who barely had himself under control.

"What do you want, John? I already sent out the orders for next week. It's too late to make any changes."

"I want to hire your gang for the night," I said.

He laughed.

"The great demon enforcer and his pet hellhound need the Olmecs? You really *are* a lot funnier than usual."

"You won't have to do much," I said. "Just get me to a party and wait for me outside."

"Like a taxi?" he said.

"Something like that."

"Is it a birthday party with ponies and cake and hot soccer moms? Or maybe one of those formal events at the Kennedy Center. Oh, I'm sorry. I forgot, you can't go to the Kennedy Center, because it's not in Ashburn."

He stepped closer—the power of his pendant making me weak. He wasn't a demon, but I could see fire in his eyes all the same.

"I hope you're not talking about that swingers thing tonight. You know you're not invited to those, hijo."

"This is my town, and I'm giving myself an invitation," I said. "I've been working really hard lately, and I need to let off some steam."

Marco tilted his head left, then right, cracking his neck.

"Those parties always have their own security. That kind of taxi ride don't come cheap."

"If your boys aren't up for it, I can ask someone else."

"We can do it. I just don't know if I want to yet. What are you paying with?"

I looked into his eyes, past the bravado and spoke to the addict crouched inside. He was talking tough, but I could tell he was drooling at the thought of tasting more of my blood.

"You know what I'm offering," I said.

Marco licked his cracked lips.

"I still have some of your shit left over from yesterday," he said, trying to drive down the demand side of the equation.

"First off, no you don't," I said. "Secondly, I'll give you two vials right now in good faith, but that's my final offer."

His mouth moved—looking for another tough guy line to throw in my face, but his inner junkie pushed to the front of the line and took over the negotiations.

"Two now plus two more after the job is over."

I wasn't sure how much blood I could safely lose, but if the night went the way I was thinking it might, I was going to need Marco's help to get inside.

"Two vials now and one after the job. Take it or leave it."

"You just bought yourself a ride," he said, snapping his fingers at Santos. "Get me a kit."

Within seconds, the shop was closed for business, and the veins in my arm were pumping out the precious substance Marco craved so much. When both of the glass containers were full, Marco capped them off and pulled them close to his chest like they were filled with gold.

Before he could stash them away, I grabbed his arm.

"One more thing," I said, leaning in close. "You can't shoot up yet. I need you clean and in charge of your people tonight. If you don't agree to that, I'll smash those vials right now, and get someone else to help me."

He huffed then pulled away from me, placing each container of my blood into its own protective case.

"You worry about your plans for the party, and I'll take care of things on my end. Entiende?"

"Yeah, I understand," I said. "But if you show up high, I'll know, and that will be the last of my blood you'll ever get. Entiende?"

A look of strained panic shot across his face—an addict facing a dilemma.

"I told you not to worry," he said, but his voice cracked at the end.

"What time you want us there?"

"Meet me at eleven, a block down from the party. I assume you're on their email list?"

"Don't worry about what lists I'm on," he said with a dark laugh. "But after we get you settled in, I might sample some of the local treats myself. Sometimes, the Ashburn ladies get in the mood for a bad boy like me, you know?"

"You don't get to go inside unless I say so. You're working for me tonight, not partying."

"Any other demands you want to make before you and your ugly dog leave me alone?" he said with a scowl.

"You should come prepared for more than their usual security."

"What does that mean?" he said.

"I don't know what to expect, but make sure everyone wears their pendants. And if you see a big black goat that talks—"

Marco shook his head.

"If I see the goat you're talking about, we're *out* of there, and I'm keeping your blood for my trouble. You can deal with that monster on your own."

I was going to push back on him, but instead, I nodded, turned, and walked out the door. The truth was I really *didn't* know what to expect. For all I knew, Oizys had only hired a couple of beefy bouncers or off-duty cops to work the door. But given everything she'd already gone through to keep me from finding out about her plans, my gut told me to be prepared for something a bit more substantial.

As I drove away with Shadow in the passenger seat, I tuned in the classic rap station and smiled as Mike D and the boys shouted at me through the speakers, telling me to fight for my right to party. Maybe I was reading too much into it, but as I belted out the words to the chorus, they gave me the boost I needed for the fight ahead.

As Shadow howled along next to me, I laughed and pressed down on the accelerator as we sped to the bookstore. A few minutes later, I screeched into the parking lot and set Shadow up in the store with a fresh bowl of water.

"I'll be back in a few," I said as my trusty pup settled on the floor and rested his chin on his two front paws, looking bored.

Next door at Bangrak Thai, the server sat me at one of the booths, but as I'd feared, Rose was still visiting her sister. With a sigh, I ordered the Drunken Noodles and prepared to stock up on some carbs for later on.

After shoveling the savory food down my throat, I returned to the bookstore, sat down in one of the reading chairs, and rubbed Shadow's blocky head.

Since I was running early, I picked up "The Serpent and the Rainbow" from the end table. Whether it was coincidence or fate, the page I turned to showed a photo of a gaunt man with dirt on his face and rags for clothing—a documented Haitian zombie. Everything about him seemed alive, except his eyes. They were lifeless and hazed over, just like Laura's and Marie's.

I'd seen plenty of zombie movies and TV shows, but they were always about flesh-eating monsters with an insatiable drive to devour living flesh. The man in the photo—just like Laura and Marie—was different.

According to the passage in the book, spirit possession and the act of zombification represented the Voodoo religion's darker side. When a Voodoo sorcerer—a *bokor*—wanted to force someone to become his unwilling slave, he administered a special powder to his victim. Within minutes, the person died, or at least it would appear that way. After the funeral, the bokor would visit the grave and raise the body from the dead. When the victim stepped out of the ground, they weren't the same person. They were without their soul—a zombie damned to roam the land of the living, compelled to carry out the bokor's commands.

Western science concluded the victims were given a powerful toxin to simulate death and were later *raised* from the dead by the bokor as the poison wore off. But those of the faith still believed.

I closed the book and shook my head. A week ago, I would have taken the civilized explanation as the truth without a second thought. But after everything I'd seen, I believed Marie and Laura Henders were real zombies—not completely dead but missing the part of their soul that made them fully human. That was disturbing enough, but what bothered me the most was an unanswered question. If Marie and Laura were zombies, who was the bokor who'd made them, and why was he or she helping Oizys by distracting me?

I had a feeling I'd find out the answer to that and more at the party, but first I had some serious prep work to do, so I closed the book and got busy.

CHAPTER 43

I POPPED OPEN the Audi's trunk and picked up Gus and my dagger, along with a large metal file and a small hatchet I'd snagged from John's garage. Through the lenses of my goggles, I could see pure white magic coming off of Gus like steam, and I smiled.

Even though Chaz was only a god of pig farmers, he was still a god, and having a weapon that was oozing magic from a deity had to be a good thing.

When I stepped back into the bookstore, it was already noon as I turned the sign to *Closed*. In the five days since I'd arrived, I hadn't sold a single book, and I'd spoken to only one customer. I promised myself that if I survived the night, I'd do something about that.

But at that moment, I had more important things to tend to, so I headed straight for the rear hallway, with Shadow following silently behind me. A second later, I stepped into the hidden room and was greeted by the sound of Walt's writing.

I made my way through the maze of stacked papers and books to his desk. He still had a way to go before needing more paper, but I didn't know how the night was going to turn out. So I set Gus, the dagger, and the tools on the table and slapped another twelve inches of paper down for Walt to use.

When I looked over his shoulder, I saw what I expected—a large sheet of paper filled with words and symbols I didn't understand. I shrugged and walked over to the leather books with the names in them and opened the first one, turning to the page with Oizys's name on it.

"Any chance you want to tell me how to pronounce this?"

As expected, Walt didn't even acknowledge my question.

I flipped through the book and exhaled loudly. All that knowledge and power in my hands, and none of it was within my reach. I closed the tome, took a deep breath, and began my preparations.

The main thing I had to do besides getting my courage up was to turn Gus into a proper weapon. First, I dug out the frets and the rest of the hardware from the wood with a screwdriver. After a few whacks from the hatchet and a lot of filing, the jagged guitar neck started to look more like a giant, sharpened stake or a short wooden spear.

With a nod of satisfaction, I set the new and improved Gus next to the dagger and went looking for something to help me carry them.

In one corner of the room, I found pieces of rolled-up, thick leather. I'd held a lot of jobs in my day, but a tailor hadn't been one of them, and I had no idea how to sew. But my dagger cut easily through the material, and in half an hour I'd fashioned two crude loops and attached them to my belt. They weren't pretty, but they held Gus and the dagger securely and left my hands free to do other things.

With my weapons at my side and my goggles on my head, Shadow and I left the hidden room to wait until it was time to meet Marco. When I stepped through the hidden door and into the store, I furrowed my brow, confused because night had already fallen.

That was the second occasion time had gone wonky when I'd been inside the room. I'd only been in there for a little more than an hour, but when I checked my watch, it was late, and I only had fifteen minutes before my meet-up with Marco and his gang.

I cursed as I raced to lock up the store and ran to the car, Shadow prancing effortlessly behind me.

Once I was at the wheel and Shadow was in the passenger seat, I sped out of the parking lot and pulled up to the stoplight at Claiborne. The light was red, but there wasn't any traffic, so I blew through the signal and burned rubber. I was so intent on driving that I didn't even take the time to find the perfect song for the trip. Instead, I turned up the tune that was playing as loud as it would go and listened as Oingo Boingo sang about going to a dead man's party.

Hilarious.

Five minutes later, I parked along the curb some ways down from the party and got out of the car. As I stood under the streetlamp's yellow light, I knew I looked foolish in my outfit, but I hadn't dressed to impress. I'd been going for a functional, badass vibe, and I thought I achieved that look quite nicely.

Shadow sat on my foot as we waited. Two minutes later, his ears stood straight up, and I heard footsteps coming toward us. Marco emerged from the darkness—good to his word after all—with a dozen members of his gang in tow. Miguel, Santos, and Julio were up front—the usual suspects—but the rest of his guys were new to me, and each of them looked every bit as hard as I suspected they were.

"I hope you're ready to boogie," Marco said as he stepped up to me with a smile. "Because your bodyguards are here, pendejo."

I nodded and turned with Marco as we started walking toward the house. As uncertain as I was about the way the evening would turn out, I felt pretty good knowing Marco and his group of thugs had my back. I didn't know what kind of security Oizys had hired, but if I'd been assigned to guard the door and saw us coming, I'd have stepped aside and let me in without a second thought.

As we walked down the lamp-lit street, I was ready for anything—for full-on fiery demons or hordes of hellhounds. But I wasn't prepared for the dozen slow moving figures that ambled toward us from the front yard.

As they passed under one of the street lamps, I saw Laura Henders leading the group. On either side of her were my two friends from outside the pub, the formerly dead Buddy and Paul. Their bodies looked the same, but as they shuffled along in silence, their milky white eyes told me someone had upgraded them from possessed morons to mindless zombies. And of course, behind them were my favorite zombie gardeners. At least they were finally getting a break from their lawn duties.

For a second, I was hopeful Marie was with them, but when I scanned the group, she was nowhere to be seen.

CHAPTER 44

I KNEW THE creatures coming at us weren't real people anymore. But, something inside me—a part of my soul that was still far from demonic—revolted at the thought of hurting them. I'd never met Laura while she was alive, but I felt close to her, maybe because she was trying to survive in a situation not of her own choosing—just like me.

The gang members behind me didn't share my warm and fuzzy thoughts about the living dead, however. Before I could say anything, three of them ran ahead and swung baseball bats into the crowd of zombies, aiming for their heads. Four of the zombies went down in the first thirty seconds as Marco's men jumped on them and ended their undead lives forever by stabbing iron-bladed knives through their skulls. Three more of Marco's thugs sprinted past me and attacked Buddy and Paul, hitting them with bats and stabbing and slicing at them with knives.

They broke one of Paul's arms and dealt blows to his head that would have killed him if he hadn't been dead already. A few seconds later, Buddy fell under their barrage and was quickly ended by Marco's men. But Paul fought on with supernatural determination despite the damage to his physical body.

Even when his left leg was broken at an unnatural angle, Paul grabbed one of Marco's guys and slammed him into the asphalt of the street. The gang member's skull made a loud pop as it split against the pavement.

While Buddy was face down, struggling for his undead existence, I watched what they were doing to Laura the way a scared kid views his first horror movie. She was still holding herself together, despite being cut badly in three places. One of the wounds was so deep, it looked like her arm was about to fall off. Even so, no blood poured out of her, and like Paul, she continued to fight, trying her hardest to reach me.

Just when I thought Laura was finished, she raised her functioning arm and ripped out one of the gang member's trachea. The men backed away from her after that. They still positioned themselves between Laura and me, but they gave her plenty of room.

Marco's guys were doing exactly what I'd asked, but I couldn't watch them give up their lives for me without trying to help. So I cursed and jumped into the fray, with Shadow right behind me, ears down and growling. I drew Gus and looked for an opening as Shadow jumped into the air and landed on the chest of one of the zombies that was coming straight for me.

The silver pendants weren't affecting the zombies at all. But as soon as I was mixing it up nice and close with Marco's guys, my supernatural strength faded. I kept moving and swinging Gus as hard as I could, but my godly guitar neck wasn't nearly as effective as usual.

I clubbed one of the undead creatures in the head, and he staggered backward, but as I looked over my shoulder, I saw Laura coming at me through a break in the crowd. She lunged for me, her eyes milky white and glazed over.

"I'm sorry about this," I said as I knelt in front of her and thrusted the sharp end of Gus up through her throat and into her brain. She looked down at me like a confused animal before she slumped to the ground, fully dead at last.

I felt sick in my stomach, but I knew I'd done the right thing. Even so, it still sucked.

While Marco's men took care of the remaining zombies, I turned from Laura and set a path straight for the front door of the house. The entrance looked like any other door in the neighborhood, with one major difference. A mountain of a man in a tight tee-shirt was guarding it.

Santos passed me on the left and jumped high in the air, a large knife raised above his head. He landed on a large zombie I hadn't seen, pushing the undead guy's head back as far as it would go and exposing its neck. With a flick of his wrist, Santos drove his knife's iron edge under the creature's chin and up into its gray matter.

"You need us to take care of the bouncer, too?" he said as he turned to me with a savage smile.

"I've got this. Just wait for me out here," I said as I sprinted toward the door. The big man tensed, ready for a fight as I jumped the last five feet and landed on the porch, standing unearthly still in front of him.

"Invitation," he said in a slow, deep voice, trying to sound intimidating.

I looked him dead in his eyes, my strength returning with each second, now that I was away from the pendants.

"I left it in my other pair of jeans," I said as I stepped to move past him.

"No invitation, no—" was all he had a chance to utter before I swatted him away with a flick of my wrist. He shot through the air and landed in the bushes, unmoving.

I forced my heart rate to slow and got my breathing under control. The noises of the party in full swing seeped into the evening air, and I could smell the mass of humanity behind the door. Shadow sat down next to me with his back to the entrance and sniffed the air.

I carefully turned the doorknob and stepped into the foyer, motioning for Shadow to stay on the porch and stand guard. For once, he did what I wanted and remained outside.

Smart dog.

When I closed the door behind me, the noise in the house fell several decibels as everyone stopped what they were doing and turned to look at me. The only sound I heard was the thumping of drums and an overdone bass line while a guy rapped about carrying a stick and not being afraid to use it.

"How appropriate," I said under my breath as my hand grazed the god stick hanging from my belt.

Using my goggles, I scanned the crowd. There were a few demons in the back of the room trying to hide from me, but most of the guests were human. Even so, they were the ones shooting me the exaggerated looks of shock and contempt.

At first, I didn't understand how a bunch of regular people knew who I was. But I finally figured out they weren't gawking at me because I was Ahriman's hated demon enforcer. They were glaring at me because I was the only one in the room who was still fully dressed.

246

CHAPTER 45

A S MY DAD used to say, *When in Rome, do as the Romans.* And in
this case, being a Roman meant losing most of my clothes. So I
forced a smile and stripped down to my boxer briefs. I was okay with
being mostly naked, but I slipped my goggles back into place and
synched up my belt so it hung low on my hip to make sure Gus and
my dagger stayed by my side.

Yes, I looked ridiculous, like a lame member of the Village People.
But I wasn't about to go up against Oizys unarmed, no matter how
many partygoers were passively judging my fashion sense.

Fortunately, once I was appropriately undressed, most people
ignored me and went back to their conversations and their foreplay or
whatever else they'd been up to before I'd arrived.

"I should have brought a backpack," I said as I stood there with
my jeans and my shirt in my hands.

A curvy nude woman waved at me from behind a table in the foyer.

"You can check those here," she said loud enough to be heard over
the music. I forced a smile, walked over, and handed her my clothes.

"Good evening. My name is Samantha," she said with a fake giggle.
"I remember how nervous I was at my first one of these. But I assure
you, everyone here is very friendly. Start talking to someone who looks
interesting, and you'll have a new friend soon enough. Just make sure
you follow the house rules. Oh, and if you'd like to be on our mailing

list, leave your email address on the sign-in sheet."

I leaned in closer, so I didn't have to shout.

"Remind me of those rules, Samantha."

"No touching unless you know the person well or they have specifically asked to be touched," she said in a practiced manner. "Also, please make liberal use of the male and female condoms located in the ornamental wicker baskets conveniently located throughout the residence. Unprotected intercourse is strictly prohibited, even if it's with your spouse or significant other."

She moved close enough that her lips brushed my ear.

"I'm required to say that last part. But I'm sure you'll find most acts are allowed at the discretion of the hosts, as long as everyone involved fully consents."

"How are things laid out tonight?" I asked. "Finger foods in the kitchen. Drinks at the bar. Dungeon in the basement?"

"You are so clever," she said, standing up straight and touching her naked bosom with one hand. "Are you sure you haven't been to one of our parties before? And, yes, we have an assortment of designated specialty areas for our guests. Upstairs, private rooms are available on a first come, first served basis. The master bedroom is locked and off limits, of course, but three guest rooms are in play.

"As you have already noted, the basement is set up as our main activity room this evening, complete with multiple S&M stations and plenty of both standard and extreme toys for everyone's pleasure. We maintain strict levels of hygiene, but I strongly advise following the condom rule with all toys. Two dance poles are also available, each with a strict 230-pound weight limit. And of course, our trademark orgy room is set up tonight with a maximum capacity of 30, due to size constraints and building codes, you understand. Lastly, on this floor, we have a clothing check—that's me—and a full bar in the kitchen that is included with the price of admission, and—"

Her brow crinkled with concern.

"I'm sorry sir, but are you here with someone else—a woman, perhaps? I don't mean to be rude, but single men are strictly forbidden. The gentleman at the door should have explained this to you before you were allowed entrance. Rules are rules, I'm afraid."

"I am well aware of the importance of rules," I said as I let my eyes glow red with the power of hellfire. "That's exactly why I'm here."

When Samantha saw what I was, her eyes opened wide and her face tightened, but she wasn't frightened the way she should have been. She was one hundred percent human, but I wasn't the first supernatural creature she'd seen, and I wondered how many other humans in Ashburn knew the truth.

"My apologies," she said with a quiver that struggled to become a smile. "I didn't realize you were—one of them. Of course, you are welcome here without a companion. Please enjoy your visit and let me know if I can be of further assistance. There are several women—and men—here tonight who would be more than happy to—"

"Who's throwing this party?" I said. "Who owns this house?"

She frowned, and her left hand started to shake.

"Jack and Melissa are your hosts for the evening," she said, smiling. "We don't usually divulge the last names of those kind enough to invite us into their home, but I can assure you they are both trustworthy and discreet."

"Does everyone here know about—my kind?"

"Oh, no sir," she said with a vigorous shake of her head. "I work for Ms. Oizys, serving at this and other supernatural functions as one of her trusted and official minions. I assure you there are very few humans here tonight who know of your existence."

"Where is Oizys now?" I asked, even though I was pretty sure I knew the answer to my question.

"The last I saw her, she was downstairs in the activity room."

With a nod, I turned away and walked toward the main living room. I made it as far as the leather couch before a squatty man wearing a black leather vest and chaps bumped into me. He started to apologize, but then he recognized me.

"What a surprise finding you here," Chaz said. "I spoke with your girlfriend downstairs just a few minutes ago. I have never been very keen on she-demons, but I must say, Sybil is one succubus who is A-OK in my book."

"It's good to see you too," I said, looking over his head and scanning the room. "You said Sybil was in the basement?"

He nodded, then leaned closer so I could hear him over the thumping of the music.

"You know many women," he said. "I was wondering if you had any suggestions for someone with whom I might get along. A lady who likes music and nature, perhaps? A nice girl. But not too nice, if you know what I mean. Oh, and a human is fine with me. I am not prejudiced. But no fallen angels. They are too much drama."

"I'll see who I run into tonight," I said as I mentally filed his request at the very end of my to-do list.

Chaz nodded with a smile and was about to leave me alone. But then he glanced at my hip, and his smile soured into a frown.

"Is that all that remains of the guitar I gave you?" he asked, pointing at Gus. "I put a piece of my spirit into that instrument."

I started to explain, but Chaz's face turned dark and sullen, and his eyes opened wide, unblinking.

"You were not invited to this party," he said in a deep, disembodied voice that rattled my gut.

"Look, I'm sorry about the guitar," I said as I realized something was very wrong with my old buddy Chaz. I had no idea whether or not a demon was capable of possessing a god, but Chaz's eyes were crazy and wild like Miguel's had been outside the pub, and I could tell he wasn't in control anymore.

Chaz-not-Chaz grabbed a drink from a person standing next to him and chugged the glass down in one shot. Although impressive, it seemed an odd thing for a possessed god to do.

"Now it is time for you to die," he said.

Before I understood what was happening, Chaz lunged at me with god-like speed, grabbed my throat with one hand, and drew his other hand back, ready to strike. His fist glowed so brightly with white magic that it left spots in my vision. While my brain was still figuring out what to do, my body reacted, twisting in the direction of Chaz's grip and striking the inside of his elbow as hard as I could. He released my throat as his arm went numb, and I unsheathed my dagger, its edge glowing a deep blood red.

I didn't want to hurt Chaz. After all, he was sort of a friend, and it wasn't his fault his body was being used by an invading spirit to kill me. Suppressing my instinct, I held out my blade and barely touched his chest. As soon as the metal made contact, Chaz was thrown across the room, sending partiers scrambling out of the way.

I didn't know who or what was pulling Chaz's strings, but at the top of the list was a certain demonic goat who seemed to hate me. My other guess was Oizys herself. I had to assume that if I could possess people, she could, too. And if for some reason she and the Mendes Goat were working together—well…then, shit.

Before I could finish my thought, Chaz literally flew across the room and slammed into me so hard that I broke half-way through the opposite wall. As I sat on the floor, trying to clear my head, naked people stampeded toward the exits only to discover the front and back doors were suddenly gone—vanished. Soon, twenty-some people were bunched up at both ends of the house, fighting each other to escape through doors that were no longer there.

"Check the windows," someone yelled.

One of the more ambitious naked people pulled back a gauzy pink curtain to reveal a solid wall where the window should have been.

The entire house had turned into a trap—one set by Oizys.

I picked up my dagger and stood ready to face Chaz again. I'd set out to stop Oizys from leaving town, but I was more worried at the moment about a possessed god trying to kick my ass and a gaggle of frenzied humans who might end up as collateral damage.

Chaz floated slowly toward me, a wild, maniacal smile plastered on his face. I held the glowing red dagger with one hand and drew Gus with the other.

Anger churned in my gut, and I let all vestiges of my human guise slip away as my internal magic filled my veins like electricity. I welcomed the rise of my demonic nature as it spread through me and steeled me for battle.

Chaz saw the change spreading through me and reached into his vest pocket. He pulled out a horrid, flesh-colored rope that looked like it was woven from animal innards. It crackled with white energy, just like Gus, and I backed away, wary of what his new weapon could do. Faster than I could see, he lashed out with the rope, using it like a whip and wrapping it tightly around my neck. It pulsed with a life of its own as he jerked me toward him like a dog on a leash. The rope burned into my neck, and for a second I panicked. I stabbed at it with my dagger, but that only resulted in red and white sparks and a spray of animal intestines.

As the rope tightened, blackness crept in from the sides of my vision. In a move of desperation, I hefted Gus as high as I could and brought its wooden edge down hard on the rope. The sharpened neck sliced through the woven flesh with ease, and I fell backward onto the floor, with the end of Chaz's rope still wrapped around my neck.

I ripped the disgusting cord from me and looked up to see Chaz slumped over on the floor, unmoving. I crawled to him and turned him onto his back. Just as I did, someone smashed a heavy bottle over my head. It hurt about as much as an empty Solo cup, but it still pissed me off.

I looked up and saw a mostly naked, middle-aged man standing over me, with that same crazy look Chaz had been sporting only moments ago.

This guy had huge shoulders and a hard, protruding gut that made me think he used to be a football player. I snarled and coiled myself, ready to take him out, but I stopped cold as my stomach erupted in pain. It was Ahriman's frickin' spell. I thought it was only there to compel me to enforce his commandments. But I was wrong. It was also there to keep me from breaking them, and that meant I couldn't kill or harm any of my human attackers.

Maybe I could have fought through the pain and punched the guy anyway, but the momentary pause gave my logical side a chance to engage. If I hit my attacker with even a fraction of my strength, he'd be dead as soon as whatever was possessing him left. My opponent, however, didn't share my concerns. He squatted over top of me and started punching me in my face and stomach. He gave it all he had, but his blows were like falling snow on my demon flesh.

I held up my hand and smacked his head just hard enough to knock him out without doing any lasting damage.

An instant later, another human came at me from behind. When I turned to face him, he fainted.

It happened again, and again—each human with the same crazy smile and wide-open eyes. The expression passed from one face to the next as dozens of naked partygoers took their best shot at me, one-by-one, before each crumpled to the ground, discarded by whatever evil spirit was inside them.

I swatted each person away as I tried to make sense of what was going on. Chaz had been a good choice, filled with godly powers to use against me, but the people being thrown at me now were useless.

Or were they?

Sure, they couldn't hurt me, but they were great at doing one thing—distracting me from why I'd come to the party in the first place—to stop Oizys from leaving.

CHAPTER 46

FISTS, FEET, AND elbows tried to stop me from reaching the door to the basement stairs. None of them really hurt, but they slowed me down.

When I finally made it there, I fought my way into the stairwell and pulled the door shut behind me. I went to lock it, but I cursed out loud as I realized the lock was on the other side of the door.

I saw the blade of my dagger pulsing with crimson magic and moved it to the doorknob. When the two metals touched, the brass doorknob turned bright red and melted in place. I knew it wouldn't hold back the people on the other side of the door forever, but I hoped it would buy me enough time to find Oizys.

As I went down the stairs two-at-a-time, my ears were bombarded by loud crunk music playing in the basement.

When I turned the corner of the stairs, I almost collided with a horned demon licking the neck of a beautiful nude blonde woman. I was sure she couldn't see the demon's true form and that she had no idea what she was getting herself into. When the demon recognized me as another of his kind, he growled. But his eyebrows rose, and his forked tail stiffened when he realized who I was.

He flattened himself against the wall, trying to blend into the shadows as he shoved the woman between him and me, using her as a human shield—the kind of classy move I expected from a demon.

I ignored him but dragged the bewildered woman along with me as I continued on to the basement.

At the bottom of the stairs, the woman broke free and ran away, which was fine by me, because at least she was safe—relatively speaking. I had problems of my own to deal with as I stood, slack-jawed, taking in the unexpected scene in front of me.

I'd shown up ready to stop Oizys from hurting innocent people and using their energy to escape Ashburn. By the sparse light of the room's low-wattage lamps, I saw the torture machines, the tables, and the poles as I remembered them. But the fifty suburbanites wearing only their smiles and various pieces of glow-stick jewelry didn't look like they were suffering very much.

In fact, I was the only one who looked like he wasn't enjoying himself.

I swore out loud, confused and wondering if I'd gotten everything wrong about Marie and Oizys. Then I reminded myself that something supernatural had just used Chaz and two dozen humans to try to stop me from making it to the basement.

That hadn't been my imagination, and the gnawing in my gut was real, too.

There was something happening or about to happen at the party that someone or something didn't want me to know about, and that meant it needed stopping. I just didn't know what *it* was yet.

As I scanned the mass of dimly lit, naked bodies, I didn't see Sybil or Oizys anywhere. Not wanting to start another panic, I secured my dagger and waded into the crowd as the intense music pounded mercilessly at my ears.

A few feet inside the basement, I passed a side room filled with intertwined naked people on the floor. I hadn't been a rock star for very long, but I recognized a good old-fashioned orgy when I saw one. I stepped in and looked closer with my goggles and wasn't shocked to see a few horns and snaking tails mixed in with the tangle of human body parts. But the pair of wings in the back of the orgy surprised me—a little bit.

And there, in the middle of the sea of undulating flesh, I finally spotted Sybil.

She was entwined with two women and a man doing various penetrative things to each other. The scene itself didn't shock me, but the pang in my chest caught me by surprise, even though I knew my emotions made no sense. After all, she was a succubus. Having sex with humans was what she did. And technically speaking, I wasn't even her boyfriend. But—there it was—the ugly head of jealousy and being hurt was making an appearance in what passed for my heart.

As if sensing my presence, Sybil raised her head from between a set of thighs and stared at me with glowing red eyes. Her forked tongue draped over her pointed fangs, and a drop of bright red blood dripped from her chin. I pulled my goggles from my face so I could see her in her human guise. Her face was once again beautiful, and she was smiling at me, but the blood on her chin—that was still there.

We held each other's gaze as the song in the room changed to a sensuous jam with a slow and steady drop-beat.

I wanted to ask Sybil if she knew what was going on—if she'd discovered anything about Oizys. But she disappeared into the mass of flesh, and I let her be. As I continued walking around, I waited for someone or something to jump out and grab me, but nothing did.

Weaving through the naked people, I could smell their humanity with every breath. To my right, a woman was on the floor being held down and tickled while someone else pleasured her with his hand. At one point, I passed by a guy sitting with his ankles tied to the legs of a chair and his arms tied behind his back. A woman was kneeling between his legs, but instead of doing what I'd expect in that situation, she was performing terrible acts with a long stainless-steel rod. It looked like torture to me, but his face showed nothing but ecstasy. If Oizys was in the room, she wasn't getting any power from him at all.

And then, to my right, I heard the *whap, whap, whap* of leather hitting flesh.

I followed the noise to a wall of sweaty male backs and pressed myself in between them to see what was going on.

They were standing, bunched around a wide, low-to-the-ground, wooden table, on which a naked woman with welts on her back and shoulders was tied face-down. She was being beaten by a skinny man wearing nothing but Army boots, and she moaned and cried so loudly, I could hear her above the din of the music.

I moved to grab the man—to stop him from hurting her, but as I did, Oizys turned her head and gazed up at me with glassy eyes.

From the mixed expression of agony and ecstasy on her face, she was enjoying everything being done to her. She certainly didn't look like she was trying to escape. As far as the men were concerned, maybe their abhorrent behavior was their way of paying the HOA lady back for too many neighborhood fines and fees.

Confused, I stepped back, forgetting everything I thought I knew about Oizys and trying to figure out what the hell was really going on.

Just then, the song overhead ended, and another one began. I didn't recognize the tune, but it wasn't an American pop song, that was for sure. Instead, the music had a primal feel to it, consisting mainly of heavy drums and percussion. And as if on cue, the energy in the room amped up as everyone started having sex with the frenzy of wild animals. Some were in groups while others watched and had fun by themselves. But everyone joined in. Oizys flashed me a contented smile as the whip cracked against her back once again.

The entire basement was a sea of horny suburbanites indulging in their fantasies and rutting on the floor and up against the walls.

I allowed myself a short laugh as I noted the untouched basket of male and female condoms on the floor, next to Oizys's table. But my moment of humor was short-lived as I reminded myself to stay sharp—that something was lurking somewhere, as yet to unfold.

And then it happened.

The writhing bodies parted in front of me to reveal a lone figure moving toward me—the head gardener I'd last seen tending to Marie's imaginary flowers.

His skin was a glistening deep ebony like I remembered it, but his face was painted white to look like a skull. He held a thick cane in one hand, and in the other, a half-empty bottle of rum. But most notably, he was naked except for a ragged black tuxedo jacket, top hat, and a pair of sunglasses with only one lens. Through the hole where the other lens should have been, a single milky white eye glared at me. The gardener was still a zombie, but his face wore a wry grin, showing something I'd never seen on an undead face before—emotion.

The gardener broke into a full smile as he neared me. The instant before he spoke, I recognized him from the drawing in Marie's house—the one of her loa—the Baron to whom she prayed and made all her sacrifices.

"Why are you still here?" the gardener said in a deep voice that rattled my insides. "I will not tell you this again. You were *not* invited to my party."

CHAPTER 47

T HE BARON STOPPED a few feet away from me. I pulled out
Gus and my dagger—not sure either would be of any use—and
waited for him to attack.

Instead, he took a long swig from his bottle of rum and laughed.

When I blinked, he disappeared, and someone to my left sucker
punched me in the jaw.

I looked at the guy who'd just clocked me and tried to ignore the
fact that the only thing he was wearing was an unbuttoned leather vest,
a cowboy hat, and a pair of fancy red boots.

He stumbled forward and threw another punch that I swatted aside
with ease. I raised Gus, ready to strike, but I stopped myself, even
before Ahriman's spell kicked in. The man wasn't my real enemy.

With a sharp exhale, I sheathed my weapons and picked up Mr.
Cowboy, ignoring the clamminess of his sweat-slick skin. His limbs
flailed around in the air before I slammed him against the drywall just
hard enough to knock him out.

No sooner was he on the floor than a short, naked woman kicked
me in my ass—literally—which hurt my pride more than my butt. One
look at her and the way she dropped into a fighting stance told me
she'd taken one-too-many kick boxing classes.

I raised my hand out of instinct, but I stopped myself again, not
wanting to hurt her. Of course, she wasn't worried about hurting me
at all. She swung her leg around, but when she landed her kick, I heard
the snap of her shin as it broke against my bone. When she tried to

put her weight on her leg, she fell, but with her face set in a snarl, she struggled like a mad person, still trying to attack me from the floor.

A second later, her eyebrows knitted in pain as the Baron's spirit released its hold on her body.

I turned, ready for my next attacker, but paused as an elderly woman ran at me from the middle of the room.

"Oh, come on," I said out loud. "I'm not going to fight an old lady."

I stood with my arms akimbo, waiting for her to arrive. But when she was only a few feet from me, her crazy eyes returned to normal and her legs went out from under her.

She slid to a stop when she collided with me. When she looked up, I saw a glint of recognition.

"This is no way to treat a customer," she yelled as I shrugged and turned away, guessing it would be a while before she visited the bookstore again and not really caring.

An instant later, a young, muscled guy with a crew cut came at me from the right and landed a fist to my throat. Unlike the others, he fought like a soldier and knew how to throw a punch.

If I'd been a human, I would've been dead right away. As it was, his strike made me cough.

Once.

With a grunt, I picked up Mr. Crewcut and tossed him gently into a decorative column, deciding I'd had enough.

As much as I didn't like leaving my body unattended, I needed time to think, and I couldn't do that with a different possessed human getting in my way every few seconds. I needed room to breathe and to figure out my next move.

Running as fast as I could, I pushed through the crowd of men standing around Oizys and noted the biggest guy there as I dropped to the ground and slid under the wooden table. Once I was hidden by the table, I reached out and touched the big guy's ankle. In a flash, my spirit poured into him, leaving John's body alone and unprotected but mostly hidden.

Inside my head, I heard a muffled *what the hell's going on* from Chip—the name of the man I'd just possessed. I turned him away from Oizys and scanned the room, looking for the Baron.

Instead, I saw the soldier I'd just slammed. He was up again, with that crazy look in his eyes that let me know the Baron was still in command. He sniffed the air and made a straight line for the table where John's body was stashed. I tucked my chin and rammed Chip's shoulder into the soldier's side as hard as I could, which sent him tumbling to the carpet.

What ensued next was odd, to say the least.

I fought like a madman, using Chip's fists to pound the soldier. I'd chosen well, because even though Chip was older and more out-of-shape than my opponent, he had the shoulders and hands of a boxer and knew how to take a hit. I threw a flurry of left jabs, keeping the soldier at bay. While he was busy watching my lead hand, I came around with a hard right hook to his ribcage.

Crack, crack went his ribs as he sucked in air, trying to fill his lungs. With one more front kick, he was out of it for the rest of the night. On his way to the floor, he started screaming, and I turned around, waiting for the Baron to possess someone else.

I turned and turned, waiting for someone, anyone to attack, but no one did, and that worried me more than anything else.

Then I felt a chill in my spine, and I knew the Baron was behind me. Before I could make Chip's body turn around, the gardener picked me up and slammed me to the floor.

I didn't know how badly Chip was hurt, but I couldn't move, and I was pretty sure he was going to need spinal surgery—or at least a really good chiropractor. I raised my head in time to see the back of the gardener as he walked toward Oizys's table.

If the Baron made it to John's unprotected body, he'd rip it to pieces without a struggle. I still wasn't the biggest fan of living inside the shell of a demon, but it was the closest thing I had to a body of my own, and I wasn't about to lose it.

The gardener made it to the group of men surrounding Oizys and began tossing them aside, one at a time. With the way clear, he paused and stared at Oizys's ravaged, naked body. Then he looked at the floor, focusing on John's outstretched arm that jutted out from under the table.

Still unable to stand, I reached over with Chip's hand and touched the woman closest to me. For a split second, I shared her body—the wife of a senior vice president for a government consulting firm—a man who'd stopped paying attention to her long ago.

I made her dive forward and touch the person farthest away from her she could still reach. Suddenly, my soul was in the body of a middle-aged man who worked at Moon Dollarz and spent most of his energy trying to have sex with his customers.

The man lurched forward and touched the next person, and that person did the same, until, like I was riding a stream of spiritual electricity, the gardener himself was within reach.

I watched through the eyes of a stranger as the gardener's hand inched closer to John's arm.

Before the gardener could touch it, I grabbed his ankle, and in an instant, the world became very confusing.

CHAPTER 48

I T WAS DIFFICULT to make sense of things in that first moment. But my spirit and the Baron's spirit were together inside the body of the gardener—a man who'd already lost his soul—his ti bon ange—and had become a zombie. None of the gardener's personality remained, and his voice in his own head was weaker than mine or the Baron's.

From the outside, it must have looked like the gardener was losing his mind or having a seizure. On the inside, things weren't much better, because the spirit world was the Baron's domain, and I barely knew what I was doing.

There were no punches thrown or kicks landed, but the Baron raged against me, trying to force me out of the gardener's body, while I resisted through willpower alone. It only took a few seconds before I started to lose my tenuous hold on the gardener's body. I looked around through his eyes, as the fear of being exorcised and spending eternity as a disembodied spirit grew inside me.

You and I should not be fighting, he said. *We are both prisoners here and have a common foe. Abandon the body of my follower and come with me. We can leave this place together.*

I heard his words as clear as if they were my own thoughts, but that wasn't all. The two of us shared a single body and a single mind, and before he could block me from learning the truth, I learned everything.

I saw the Baron's soul inside Marie's body as she traded with Sue the farmer, paying her with a bottle that contained a tuft of black hair, a small waxen figure, and her ti bon ange. I saw the Baron using Marie and her animal sacrifices to build his power so he could influence the physical world and kill Laura Henders. With rage, I learned her death was only meant to distract John and to give the Baron another zombie to do his bidding while he prepared for the party. I didn't see any memories of Oizys and the Baron together. As best as I could figure, the only thing she was guilty of was being herself and suspecting something was up but letting her hatred for Marie cloud her ability to figure out what was really going on.

Marie hadn't been the one trying to get the Baron to help her escape from Ashburn. It had been the other way around. The Baron was trying to leave town, and everyone at the party was providing him with the energy he needed to do it.

As I struggled to digest my revelation, I could feel the Baron gathering his strength for a final push to cast me out of the gardener's body. My only hope was that, amid his fury, he'd slacked off on his control of the gardener's body.

With a single thought, I made the gardener drop to his knees and touch John's outstretched hand just as the Baron blasted my spirit with all his power.

As soon as the connection was made with John's body, I pulled a little spiritual jujitsu, and let the Baron push me out of the gardener and back into John's empty, demonic shell.

Home once again, I pulled John's hand away and rolled out from under the opposite end of the table. I jumped to my feet, ready to face the Baron, but he was gone.

I cursed and turned just as Sybil stepped up to me, naked and drenched in sweat.

"It's the Baron," I said. "He's the one trying to escape from Ashburn."

She grinned as she moved in close, her body undulating with the rhythm of the drum-laden music that filled the basement.

"Is that who's behind all of this?" she said in a slurred voice, like she was drunk on something. "John didn't pay much attention to him or the other spirits. Usually, they keep to their own, scaring the locals at Halloween, messing with tarot cards and Ouija boards, but not doing much more."

"He's got a lot more than magic tricks planned for tonight," I said. "He's feeding off the sexual energy from the party."

She laughed.

"I'll bet he is! I've never felt so much erotic juju in one place, and that's saying a lot. But at least everyone's having a good time. It's not a bad way to go, really."

"What do you mean, it's not a bad way *to go?*"

"Look around. Humans are normally so boring they don't give off enough magic to light a candle. But tonight's different. Everyone here is generating lots of sex magic, and now that the Baron has a hold of that energy, he'll pull on it like a string, until there's nothing left of these people. He doesn't really have a choice, though. He'll need everything they can give him to break through Ahriman's wards."

I looked around and knew she was right. I could feel the power leaving people's bodies as each of them climaxed in ecstasy only to start again and again, never satiated, in an endless loop of desire.

"I could *make* them stop fornicating," she said with a cold grin. "That would cut off his power source and solve our problem."

"You know I can't let you harm them," I yelled over the din of the music, as my stomach twitched.

"You're much nicer than John, but not nearly as fun," she said as she leaned into me and started rubbing my chest.

"Is it always this hard for you to focus on something besides sex?" I said.

"I'm a succubus. Abstaining from temptations of the flesh is not my strong point. But I have to admit, I am finding it more difficult than usual to concentrate tonight."

I exhaled a long breath as she wrapped herself around me, pressing her naked body against mine.

"How do we stop an orgy in its tracks without hurting anyone?" I said. "Can we call the police for that?"

She shook her head and pointed at two Sheriff's Deputies indulging in the pleasures of a soccer mom dressed as a cheerleader.

"How about a hellhound?" I said. "If Shadow showed up in his true form, that might scare them enough to do the trick."

"I believe you're not allowed to expose the truth to humans," she said, even as Ahriman's spell wrenched my stomach to remind me she was right. "I don't think that would work anyway. Everyone here is in some sort of a trance."

And like someone had pulled a shroud of stupidity from my brain, I knew exactly what I had to do. It wasn't the sex I had to stop.

It was the music.

CHAPTER 49

I HUGGED SYBIL, which I think scared the crap out of her "You're amazing," I shouted as someone turned up the music in the basement even louder.

"Of course I am," she said.

"No, I mean what you said about everyone being in a trance. We have to stop the music. Find the speakers."

"And then what?"

I smiled.

"You should like this part. Rip them to shreds."

"Very funny," she said as she walked off, elbowing her way through a couple trying to have sex while standing up.

I made my way to the nearest wall, stepping through the writhing sea of humanity as best as I could. At one point, I paused and cocked my head to the left when I saw the little old lady who'd run into me earlier having more sex than I thought her heart could stand. I knew senior citizens needed love, too, but I still grimaced and turned away.

I tried hopelessly to zero in on the source of the music, but it was too loud and bouncing off the walls. Instead, I scanned the room until I spotted a tiny box speaker mounted to the wall above two men and a woman who were busy going at it.

Without hesitation, I rushed over to the threesome and pulled out my dagger. Their eyes remained glossed over as I stabbed the speaker above their heads, sending a spray of sparks raining down on them.

They didn't even pause.

Unfortunately, with only one speaker out of commission, the music was still too loud.

I turned around and saw Sybil on the opposite side of the room—a crushed speaker held high in her hand. That was two down, but the place was still rocking, and with each minute, the Baron was growing in power.

I searched along the wall until I found another speaker hidden behind one of the lamps. When I looked up, I saw Sybil ripping another speaker out of the wall as well.

At this point, the music was noticeably quieter, and I started to think we had a chance. Then, just as I spotted one of the last speakers sitting in the middle of a basket of condoms, I felt the presence of someone coming toward me.

I raised Gus, ready for anything, but when I looked up, I saw Marie walking confidently toward me, naked and as beautiful as ever—except for her milky white eyes.

People always say the soul is in the eyes, but that's not true. The soul is in the muscles and everything around the eyes. I know this, because even though her eyes were dead, I could still see pain and sadness on her face.

"You came for me," she said. "I knew you would."

"I thought you were dead."

She laughed the same gentle way I remembered. I breathed deep the smell of her skin and her hair, and my head reeled with intoxication like it always did when I was around her.

Wordless, she moved closer until her breath was gentle on my ear. Even though we stood in the middle of a sea of naked bodies, it felt as if we were alone.

"Come with me," she said. "We can leave this place together. My loa will protect us from Ahriman."

She moved her hand to my belt.

"All you have to do is—nothing," she said with a smile before she kissed me deeply. I closed my eyes, and any foothold I had with the real world was lost.

As we kissed, the moans and groans of pleasure around us grew louder and more frantic. It was like the entire room was riding a single, shared wave of sexuality. But even though the mounting energy meant the Baron was close to making his move, I couldn't tear myself away from Marie.

I was lost in her, hopeless, until somewhere from my left, I heard someone talking to me—telling me to snap out of it.

"Pay attention," the voice said. "Pay attention."

I tried half-heartedly to focus on the warning, but I couldn't ignore Marie—until I realized somewhere in my swirling thoughts that the voice belonged to Sybil.

"That's not Marie anymore," she screamed.

I blinked, trying to break the spell I was under, but my passion argued with me, telling me Sybil was jealous because Marie was the one rubbing my chest and kissing my neck instead of her.

Marie stepped back and leveled the gaze of her dead white eyes on me, then raised a bottle of rum and took a giant swig. I shook my head and narrowed my eyes. The bottle was the same one the Baron had been holding. I shook my head again and again, then closed my eyes and tried to listen only to Sybil's voice.

When I opened my eyes again, I still saw Marie in front of me. But she was different. Her rosy cheeks were gone, replaced with cold, pale skin, and her sensuous smile had turned to a slightly parted mouth with gray lips.

I tried not to think about the fact that I'd just been kissing a zombie and held her at arm's length as she struggled to embrace me. I pushed Marie's hollow shell away as people writhed on all sides of me to the rhythm coming through the last remaining speaker.

She came toward me again, but my lust for her had been replaced with sorrow and dread. I put my hand up, ready to stop her as gently as I could, because whatever she'd become wasn't her fault.

But before she reached me, Sybil stepped in and lifted Marie off the ground by her neck.

"Don't hurt her," I said.

Sybil looked at me, then dropped Marie, letting her body hit the carpeted basement floor with a thud.

"She's already as good as dead," she said in a voice devoid of sympathy.

I didn't know whether zombies could be knocked unconscious or not, but Marie didn't move.

"I told you not to hurt her," I said, but Sybil ignored me and stared at Marie's motionless body, the bottle of rum by her side, draining its remaining liquid onto the carpet.

Then she reached over to the final speaker that was sitting in the basket of unused condoms and crushed it in one hand.

At last, the music stopped, and when I raised my head, all I could hear was the buzzing in my ears.

I expected to see a bunch of very confused, naked suburbanites running for the door, but instead, everyone was sleeping. Other than the sounds of snoring, and the soft moaning from a barely awake Oizys, a dead silence filled the room.

Then I heard footsteps and saw the gardener appear, dressed in his top hat and tuxedo jacket, walking toward us. He used his cane to pick his way through the piles of sleeping humans.

He came to a stop a few feet from me, and I tensed, tired and worn, but ready for another fight if that's what it came to.

Instead of attacking, he smiled and looked at me through the open lens in his sunglasses.

"I believe our relationship began on a sour note," he said. "Let us try this again, shall we? I will go first."

CHAPTER 50

"AS I MENTIONED before, you and I have much in common," the Baron said. "We are both slaves to Ahriman. And neither of us wish to live out the rest of eternity in this place."

I couldn't argue with him on that point, and I'm sure that's what he was counting on.

"Do you understand what a loa is?" he said. "What do you truly know about my kind?"

"Only what she told me," I said, glancing down at Marie's unmoving body on the floor. "She worshipped you, and you had her fooled into thinking you cared about her. That was her mistake."

The Baron ignored my dig.

"We loa are the spirits of the ancestors of the living. We listen to messages from worshippers like Marie—their hopes and their prayers—and we deliver them to Bondye, the one true god. But because of Ahriman, I am unable to fulfill my duty."

"People are used to having their prayers ignored."

The Baron's milky white eye took on a faraway gaze.

"I used to answer them," he said. "I was their champion with Bondye, until I came here one day and never left. Now I can only listen to the distant cries of my descendants. Their voices give me just enough power to sustain myself, but not enough to break free of this place."

"You seem pretty strong right now."

"Tonight is different. St. John's Eve. The beginning of summer when people turn to thoughts and deeds of the flesh. It is my favorite time of the year."

"Are they ever going to wake up?" I said, motioning to the crowd of sleeping people.

He shrugged.

"Not in this world," he said. "But fear not. Each of them will live on in one form or another. This will not be the end of them. They are serving a higher purpose. My descendants will praise their names for generations to come."

"That's not good enough," I said.

The Baron grinned and stared me down, the same way the picture of him in Marie's house used to follow me.

"I have enough power to take you with me," he said. "You and your woman can leave the confines of Ashburn tonight and be free at last."

Sybil hesitated when he made the offer, but she knew the same thing I did. The Baron was lying.

"That's mighty nice of you," I said. "But I really have to insist you stay. It's nothing personal, but I've got a job to do."

The Baron shook his head and grinned.

"You will not stop me."

He might have been right, but I wasn't about to give up. Even so, if I was going to have any chance of defeating him, I'd need every ounce of power I could muster. So I let my human guise drop completely and went into full-on demon mode for the first time. My hardened muscles were suddenly covered in rough, dark red skin. My feet had talons instead of toes; and my forked tail swung slowly by my side with a life of its own. Swirls of red magic engulfed my hands, and my fiery eyes glowed with power. Most of all, I could feel the weight of black, razor-sharp, curved horns protruding from my forehead.

I was no longer David Steele, the musician. I was John Starling, the demon enforcer, and I was about to kick some spirit ass.

I drew my dagger and took a single step toward the Baron. The blade had worked before when the Baron had possessed Chaz, and I was hoping it would work again.

As I closed in on the Baron, he blew a cloud of something glittery at my face. I shut my eyes as my exposed flesh was attacked by what felt like a thousand mosquitos all at once. When I carefully reopened my eyes, my arms and chest were covered in tiny shards of glass. The Baron laughed when he saw the confusion on my face, and he smiled when I came at him with my dagger.

"Your weapons are nothing to me," he said, swatting my blade away with his cane.

He was right; my dagger was useless. All I could figure was that the blade's demonic magic had worked earlier because the Baron had been in the body of a god. If I were going to beat him now, in the body of one of his followers, I needed some magic that was a little more…noble.

I sheathed my blade and pulled out Gus, crackling with its white energy, and the Baron stopped laughing.

When I swung it at his head, he stopped smiling.

But he remained perfectly still as Gus sped toward him. An instant before the holy weapon was about to hit its mark, the Baron moved out of the way as fast as the wind. An instant later, I felt my neck hairs stand up, then felt a burst of pain shoot through me as he struck the back of my legs with his cane.

I howled in agony, like someone had just scraped my nervous system with a rusty piece of metal.

"Somehow, you wield the power of a god," he said. "But you are still only a demon. Nothing more. The cold, hard iron of my cane can burn you like you were back in Hell."

The skin on the back of my legs was sizzling like a steak on a grill, but I pushed past the pain and lunged for him. Once again, he moved so quickly that by the time I was there, he was gone.

He appeared again to my right, and as I turned to face him, Sybil made her move, lashing out at him with her claws. The Baron turned and raised his iron cane to fend her off.

"No!" I said as Sybil ducked and barely missed having her head bashed in. Before he could recover from over-swinging, she was on him, clawing and ripping at his torso, shredding his black tuxedo jacket and opening several deep gashes in his chest.

She was doing a lot of damage to the body, but no blood was

coming out, and the Baron wasn't slowing down.

"Nothing you do to this body can hurt me," he said with a booming voice. "This is only a shell. I am a loa—a spirit—and I shall be held captive no longer."

Purple energy crackled around him, throwing Sybil to the ground as he moved toward the back door.

I dove for his legs, but as soon as I touched him, I was thrown across the room, landing on top of some very unfortunate naked people, who still didn't wake up even when I crashed into them.

I pulled myself up and charged at the fleeing Baron with Gus held out in front of me. I was rewarded when the sharpened weapon sliced through the Baron's magic with a burst of white energy and cut into the center of his back. The gardener's body staggered—his central nervous system clearly damaged—but my best shot barely slowed him down.

"He's a spirit," Sybil said, coming up behind me. "This is not the way to defeat him."

"I'm open to your ideas," I said, exasperated, as the Baron opened the back door and stepped outside into the muggy night air.

Sybil and I followed him up the cement stairs that led to the backyard, still helpless to stop him. Even though I knew it wouldn't do any good, I stabbed him with Gus again, as hard as I could, and one more time for good luck, because I had no other choice. But just as Sybil had said, despite the horrible damage I was inflicting on his physical form, he continued, unhindered, into the middle of the yard.

I tried to tackle him again, but was thrown back, this time landing on a patch of lush, wet grass. I hadn't been able to hold on to him for more than an instant, but for that brief moment when our bodies connected, I'd felt the power of his spirit again.

As I lay sprawled out on the grass, trying to catch my breath, the Baron dropped his cane, raised his hands to the night sky, and began chanting in a language I'd never heard before.

And that was when I finally came up with a plan.

CHAPTER 51

"**D**ON'T LET HIM leave," I said as I raced down the concrete stairs and into the basement. I slid across the carpet and landed next to Marie's unmoving body. I wondered if any piece of her was still alive, but checking on her would have to wait. I snagged the nearly empty bottle of rum lying next to her and raced back outside to join Sybil.

By the time I made it back, the Baron was three feet off the ground and fully aglow with purple magic. And Sybil was snarling mad.

"You left to get a drink?" Sybil said through gritted teeth as she eyed the bottle in my hand. "And how the hell am I supposed to keep him from leaving? If I could do that, we wouldn't be having this problem."

I rolled my eyes, then shook my head. I wanted to tell her my plan, but if I did that, the Baron would hear me as well.

Instead, I put my fingers between my teeth and whistled as loudly as I could—hoping Shadow would hear.

Before the sound of my whistle had faded, Shadow was standing at my feet, wagging his tail and glancing at me expectantly, ready to go for a ride.

"I know you don't understand me," I said, kneeling down in front of him and petting his head. "But this is very important. Please, I need you to bring me my pants."

Shadow cocked his head and whimpered once.

I pointed to the underwear I was wearing and nodded.

"Pants. Go get my pants, boy."

Shadow wagged his tail excitedly, then blinked out of existence. Gone.

I looked up and saw the Baron rising ever higher. The purple magic that surrounded him had sprouted into dozens of thin streams that arced into the air and stretched back into the house.

A few seconds later, Shadow returned with what looked like a human femur bone in his mouth. He dropped it in front of me and barked.

"He doesn't understand that much English, you know," Sybil said in exasperation.

"I need my pants," I growled at her, frustrated, still not wanting to speak my plan out loud.

She sighed.

"Ask him if he wants to go for a walk."

The Baron was five feet above the ground, his arms outstretched to either side of him.

"I don't have time to take him for a walk," I said.

"Just do it. Trust me."

I reached down and rubbed Shadow's chest. "Do you want to go for a walk, boy? Who wants to go for a walk?"

With that, Shadow dropped down with his front paws extended and his rump up in the air. Then he disappeared, leaving me and Sybil alone with the Baron.

"He left again," I shouted at Sybil. "That's not helping very much!"

Shadow was gone for what felt like an eternity, but within seconds he reappeared, sitting in front of me with his leash and my pants in his slobbery mouth. He stretched his neck forward and dropped everything at my feet.

"Good boy," Sybil said, glaring at me.

I knelt down and pulled the scrap of paper from the back pocket of my jeans. I unfolded it and scanned the indecipherable language scrawled in Walt's handwriting.

"What the hell is that?" Sybil said.

"A gift from John, I think," I said. Taking one last look at the markings on the paper, I rolled it up and dropped it in the bottle. The paper sunk into the eighth-of-an-inch of rum at the bottom of the bottle, but its ink didn't run. Walt must have used one hell of a pen. I shook the bottle, and the dampened paper stuck to the inside of the glass.

"I hope you aren't trying to make a Kanari," she said. "It takes a master practitioner of Voodoo and a very specific ritual to create a proper soul jar."

I grinned like a madman and shook my head. I looked up at the Baron who had moved even higher into the air amidst a shower of red and purple sparks.

"He's breaking through the first of Ahriman's spells," she said.

"I'm going to try to bring him down, but if that doesn't work, I need you to toss this up to me, when I say so," I said, and handed her the bottle. "And be ready to seal it up."

"With what?" she said, taking the bottle from me.

"Be creative. And watch your head, I don't want to land on you."

She furrowed her eyebrows—confused—but before she could ask me any questions, I crouched down and jumped high into the air, aiming for the Baron's bare legs. As soon as I touched his foot, my spirit jumped into the gardener's body once again. I watched through the gardener's eyes as John's body plummeted to the yard below and Sybil jumped to one side just in time to avoid being crushed.

My offer for you to join me has expired, demon. Now I command you to be gone.

The irony wasn't lost on me that the Baron was trying to exorcise me from the gardener's body. Luckily for me, his efforts were just as effective as when I'd tried to control Ahriman. Without my real name, he had no hope of getting rid of me that easily.

But the sheer force of his spirit kept pushing at me, forcing me out a little at a time, just like the last time we'd battled for control over the gardener's body. As my grasp began to slip, a feeling grew in my stomach, but it wasn't Ahriman's spell this time.

It was fear.

I didn't know much about being a demon yet, and I was especially ignorant about how to move around as a disembodied spirit—which is what I was about to become if the Baron succeeded in forcing me out. Worse, I had no idea how to get back to John's body without touching it.

For all I knew, as soon as the Baron exorcised me, my spirit would sail around loose like a balloon in the wind, forever lost.

With no other option, I focused on Sybil and the ground below and willed the Baron's body to descend. But we continued to rise.

I have met many a demon far greater than you in the spirit realm, and I have conquered them all, he said. *Let go and rejoin your body while you still can, or I will force your ti bon ange to serve me for an eternity of torment.*

People don't make threats when they really have the upper hand, and his words of bravado let me know that some part of him was worried.

I concentrated harder, visualizing my feet touching the cool, damp blades of the grass below. As the moments passed, the gardener's body began to lower so slowly I almost didn't notice. It took all of my might to descend only a few inches, but at least we were going in the right direction.

I was winging it, hoping my willpower was enough to get me back to the ground and closer to Sybil, but the spirit world was Baron's home. And although I pushed harder than I'd ever tried before, our descent stopped, and we started to rise again.

I screamed inside the gardener's head, my spirit flailing like a child throwing a tantrum. But nothing I did made any difference.

Almost drained of energy, I knew I had to try my plan before it was too late.

While the Baron was busy pushing my soul away, sucking the last bits of sexual energy from the sleeping partygoers, and breaking through Ahriman's first magical barrier, I made the gardener talk—something the Baron hadn't been expecting.

"Sybil," I said. "Throw me the bottle."

Without hesitation, she heaved the bottle skyward, complete with Walt's little scrap of paper. I reached out and caught it before the Baron knew what was happening. And as soon as I grabbed it, I held the bottle in front of the gardener's face.

I saw the strange symbols, and so did the Baron. And just like a person trying not to think about something they've been told not to think about, the Baron read the word out loud in his head.

And I heard it.

I didn't know what the sounds meant, but I had a pretty good idea he'd just inadvertently spoken his real name. I'd always been good at memorizing lyrics and I had near-perfect pitch, so I spit his name back at him, sound-for-sound in my head and commanded him to do my bidding.

Hear me, mighty loa. By the power of your name, I command you to enter this bottle, where you shall stay until I release you.

I'd like to say I heard him screaming in agony as his spirit was sucked into the bottle, but in reality, he was there one moment, sharing the gardener's head with me, and the next moment, he was gone.

The gardener seemed to barely notice the difference, but I felt it immediately. I was stuck inside a zombie's head and most importantly, I didn't know how to keep us aloft.

Instantly, the gardener, still clutching the empty bottle of rum, free-fell to the ground and landed next to Sybil's feet, a few feet away from John's body.

The ground was soft and grassy, but the gardener was already broken, and his body would barely move for me as Sybil grabbed the bottle and held it close to her ample bosom.

"Close it," I managed to say, as I struggled to stretch the gardener's arm far enough to reach John's body.

My hand was almost there when Sybil grabbed it.

"David, I need to know something."

"Can you ask me later?" I said.

"Do you really promise to take me with you when you leave?"

"I said I would."

"That's not an answer. Give me your oath."

I forced my head up and looked at her, but when I saw her face, my anger drained away. She looked soft and vulnerable, and even though I knew it was an illusion to make her appear human, all I saw in front of me was someone afraid of being left behind again.

"I give you my oath," I said and closed my eyes, even as I felt the gardener's heart stutter and stall. Without the Baron to animate him, his body was near the end of its existence.

I set my head down and waited, unsure of what would happen to my soul when the gardener finally passed.

Then I felt Sybil lifting my hand and placing it on John's arm.

Instantly, my soul fled the dying gardener's shell and returned to John's body.

After taking a few deep breaths, I sat up and looked at Sybil and the bottle she held in front of her.

Something seemed odd, and as I narrowed my eyes, I could see what looked like a piece of pink latex covering the lip of the bottle.

"Is that a condom?" I said.

"You told me to be creative."

It looked ridiculous, but it worked like a charm.

As we both silently watched the bottle for signs of the Baron trying to escape, we saw none—only a purple swirl of smoke writhing and twisting behind the glass—the Baron's spirit bound by my command and unable to leave the prison of my makeshift soul jar.

After a few minutes, my heart rate calmed down, and I became acutely aware that Sybil and I were sitting in someone's back yard, mostly naked.

"I'm getting hungry," Sybil said as she stared at my tight boxer briefs.

I looked back at her, and for a moment, I felt a pang of affection. Yes, she ripped out human hearts and ate them. And yes, her demonic existence revolved around destroying men with her sexuality. She was a succubus, through and through. But she'd stuck by me and had been there when I needed her most, and she was *my* succubus.

And that was all that mattered at that moment.

CHAPTER 52

I SLIPPED INTO my pants, then walked down the concrete stairs with Sybil, back into the basement. Shadow followed close behind us with his leash still in his mouth, while naked people everywhere woke up, exhausted and befuddled, but satisfied.

Sudden movement from the far side of the room caught my eye, and when I turned, I saw Raziel, buck naked, stepping out of the orgy room. He yawned and grinned—and then he spotted me.

"Breathe a word of this, demon," he said in a voice filled with hatred, "and I shall see you destroyed and banished to eternal pain in ways you cannot imagine."

Sybil and I looked at each other and laughed.

"Don't worry," I said. "I won't tell Dad what you've been up to."

Raziel snarled and balled his hands into fists. It looked for a moment like he was going to attack me, but all he did was flex, close his wings in front of him, and disappear into nothingness.

"Are all angels that friendly?" I asked Sybil.

She shrugged.

"They're usually in better moods, especially after an orgy."

As we continued our way through the basement, stepping around people as they stood up and stretched, I didn't sense any fear in the room—just a lot of confusion as people tried to remember what they'd done that night and with whom.

Even the men who'd been taking out their anger on Oizys had dropped their whips and were looking around bewildered and lost.

I walked past the men and undid Oizys's restraints. She lay there, completely naked, the skin of her torso and her thighs crisscrossed with welts and bruises. She looked a mess, but the relaxed smile on her face was one-hundred-percent genuine.

"What the hell is wrong with you?" I said. I knew my words were out of character for John, but I didn't care.

If Oizys noticed, she didn't say anything. She just sighed and slowly sat up.

"That was delicious," she said.

I shook my head as the guests made their way to the ground floor to retrieve their clothes from Samantha.

One person, however, didn't move at all, even though her eyes were open as she stared at the ceiling.

Marie.

Even though I'd just defeated a powerful loa, I was still woefully inexperienced with the workings of Voodoo. But I understood enough to know she'd been a casualty of the Baron's plans and that she'd never be herself again without her ti bon ange.

I held the liquor bottle with the Baron's spirit trapped inside close to my face.

"You'll make this right somehow," I said. "Or you'll be the one who suffers for an eternity."

I leaned down and helped Marie get to her feet. She moved like an automaton, but at least she wasn't under the Baron's control anymore.

"Can you find something for her to wear?" I asked Sybil. I half expected her to be annoyed by my request, but she nodded, and together we went upstairs in search of Marie's dress.

When we finally made it through the line, Samantha grinned sheepishly at me, then wiped all emotion from her face when she saw Sybil. A minute later, she handed the rest of our clothes back to us, and we dressed in the foyer.

As we walked out, Samantha pointed at the bottle of rum with the pink condom for a top.

"I'm sorry sir, but you can't leave here with an open bottle. Club rules."

"Don't you remember me?" I said.

"I'm afraid not, but it doesn't matter who you are, sir. Rules are rules."

Whether it was because the Baron's hypnotic music had stopped or because some other unknown magic was at play, I was happy she didn't know who I was.

I turned around and walked away, bottle still in hand, with Sybil, Marie, and my little hellhound by my side.

I was surprised to see Marco and his boys outside, still there, waiting for me like he said they'd be.

"I was wondering where your mutt went," he said as Shadow gave him a low growl. "I hope you and your friends had a good time, because you look like shit warmed over."

"Thanks for waiting," I said.

He laughed and held out his hand, palm upward.

"I'm not going anywhere until you pay me what you owe."

Sybil started to say something, but I motioned for her to stand down.

Without words, I held out my right arm and let one of Marco's guys drain me of another vial of the black stuff running through my veins.

Once Marco had what he wanted, he and his Olmecs left in silence.

Marie stood next to me, expressionless, as Oizys came out the front door, walking with a limp. She winced with each step and avoided eye contact with me.

"You were wrong about Marie," I said.

She shrugged and kept moving.

"Then again, if it weren't for you, I never would have ended up here tonight, and I wouldn't have stopped the Baron from escaping."

It was her turn to grin and nod.

"Then you still owe me," she said as she walked past us.

"I'm ready to go home," I said, looking at Sybil.

We walked toward my car, with Marie following—a blank expression on her face the whole time. Seeing her like that made me wonder how much I'd really helped her by foiling the Baron's plans. My head told me I'd done the best I could, but my heart knew I'd been too late to save her.

Shadow pranced along next to me, his leash in his mouth and his tail wagging. I wondered if he realized that he'd saved the day. Even though he likely didn't, I promised to take him on the longest walk of his life as soon as I woke up the next day.

"I had a good time tonight," Sybil said with a grin.

My eyes widened even though I tried to keep a straight face.

"That was your idea of a good time?"

"I've had worse," she said in a whisper.

That wasn't the last time I wondered what kind of evil jerk the real John must have been to her, and I decided I didn't feel bad at all about him ending up in my cancer-ridden body. He probably deserved that and a lot more.

"What are you going to do with the Baron?" she asked as I opened the car door for her.

"I'm not sure, but I have an idea I think is going to be a win-win-*lose* proposition."

CHAPTER 53

T HE NEXT DAY, I woke up early, left Sybil in bed sound asleep, and checked on Marie in the guest room. She was lying there in the same position we'd left her the night before, her eyes open, her body apparently no longer requiring sleep. I'd insisted Marie stay in the guest room, despite Sybil's suggestion that she sleep in bed with us. Even though she denied it, I think the idea of it turned her on, because—well, that's just how Sybil was.

After giving Shadow a rack of frozen ribs, I took him for a long walk around the neighborhood.

When we returned, I tried to get him to join me in the car, but he refused. I didn't think his powers included being psychic, but it sure seemed like he knew where I was heading.

And to be honest, I couldn't blame him for not wanting to go with me. I didn't want to go either, but I had to.

During the ten-minute drive to The Farm, I tried to put myself in a positive mental state. It had been a pretty rough night, but in the end, I'd stopped the Baron from escaping and had done the best I could to uphold Ahriman's commandments.

Of course, there'd been some casualties along the way.

Laura Henders had been turned into a zombie by the Baron and had later lost her undead life at the hands of the Olmecs. Blaire had been killed by something pretty powerful, and although I had no evidence, I suspected he'd been a victim of his helpful nature and the Mendes Goat—the same creature I was on my way to see.

And then there was Marie. Unlike Laura and Blaire, she actually lived in Ashburn, but technically, she wasn't fully dead. She was a zombie without the Baron being around anymore to control her, which sucked for her, but meant Ahriman probably didn't care. But I did, and it was for her sake I parked on the side of the street, walked past the road-side store that was closed for the day, and started down the path in the early morning dew.

With each step closer to the barn, a dark foreboding filled me like a nightmare I didn't want to revisit.

Finally, I stood in front of the double doors to the barn, this time without my faithful hellhound. The only thing in my hand was the bottle containing the Baron's spirit.

What I was about to try would have been a lot easier if I'd known the Mendes Goat's real name, but with the deal I was about to offer, I hoped I wouldn't need it.

I stepped into the barn and did my best not to jump when the door slammed shut behind me. Inside, the three human farm hands working with one of the horses stopped in their tracks, suddenly frozen and unresponsive.

Blackness covered my mind like a heavy stage curtain when I heard a familiar, dark voice in my head and saw the giant black goat step out from one of the stables. He stared me down with glowing yellow eyes, clearly not happy I was there.

"You are in violation of our agreement again, enforcer," he said in an unholy deep voice that emanated from one of the farm hands.

"I was hoping we could come up with a new arrangement."

Silence.

"Here's my proposition," I said, trying to keep my voice strong as I raised my free hand and pointed to the barn's wooden shelf with the glass jars on it. "I want the Kanari that contains Marie's soul."

"It is one of my favorites," the voice said.

"You stole it from her."

"She gave it willingly as payment. What do you offer in exchange?"

I held up the bottle with the Baron's spirit trapped inside. I wasn't certain, but the goat seemed surprised.

"You know what this is," I said. "The Baron's spirit is worth much more than that of a mere human."

"If you are attempting to deceive me—"

"I'm telling the truth, and I want to make things right between us." The voice laughed.

"I do not know who or what you are, but you are not Ahriman's enforcer, and as such, you do not know my true name, which means you have no power over me. Tell me why I should not simply kill you."

"You could try," I said. "But you didn't do a very good job last time. And even though I may not be the guy you're used to dealing with, I'm definitely Ahriman's enforcer now. I carry all of his authority, and I have all the powers and knowledge of my predecessor."

"Then why not take what you want?"

"I'm running things differently in Ashburn from now on. If I have to, I *will* destroy you. But at the moment, there's no need for that, since we both have something each other wants. You have Marie's soul, and I have the Baron's, complete with his true name written down on a sheet of paper inside the bottle. He's a powerful loa, and he'd be yours to command. Frankly, I think you're getting the better deal here. Or we can fight to the death right now. It's your choice."

It was a long wait for the Goat of Mendes to decide our fate, but five minutes later, I walked away from the barn, still alive and holding Marie's soul in my unsteady hands.

CHAPTER 54

I SAT IN John's garage for half an hour, trying to figure out how to put Marie's soul back where it belonged. In the end, I realized the only person who could help me was probably Marie herself.

When I finally got my nerve up to enter the house, Sybil and Marie were sitting at the table in the breakfast nook, two cups of black coffee in front of them. But Marie's cup remained untouched.

"How is she?" I said.

"Ask her yourself," Sybil said as she raised her mug toward the motionless Marie. "She can talk. And she seems to know what's going on—more or less."

I sat down next to Marie, but she kept her eyes on Sybil.

From under the table, Shadow grumbled like he wanted to say something.

"You have to tell her what you want her to do," Sybil said in a quiet voice.

"Marie," I said. "Can you look at me, please?"

She turned her gaze until it rested on me. Her light brown eyes that had mesmerized me when I first met her were still gone—replaced by two milky, vacant orbs.

"I have something for you," I said, placing the Kanari in front of her. "But, I don't know how to do what needs to be done. I could try, but I'm afraid I'd only get one shot at it, and I don't want to take any chances. Can you tell me what to do?"

"Only the one who removed it can replace it," she said slowly, as she strained with each word.

I felt my eyes water up. Her answer was the one I'd been afraid of hearing.

"There has to be another way," I said, looking to Sybil for hope—anything at all—but she turned away and shook her head. "Maybe I should've let the Baron escape and take you with him. I'm sorry."

I wasn't expecting a reply, but I saw the struggle on Marie's face as she tried to form her words.

"He would not have taken me with him," she said. "I know this now."

Marie reached out, picked up the Kanari with her ti bon ange trapped inside, and hugged it close to her chest like it was her child.

"Thank you," she said as she handed the Kanari back to me with care. "Keep this safe for me, please."

I nodded as I took the Kanari, keenly aware she was trusting me to protect her very soul.

"I know where it will be safe until we can figure out how to return it to you."

She nodded slightly, and a tear rolled down her cheek.

"I was right about you after all," she said. "You *are* more than a demon. You are also a good man."

EPILOGUE

E VEN BEFORE I could see him, I knew Ahriman had entered the crowded bar and was about to ruin my night of watching my Ashburn neighbors belt out their favorite tunes through the wonder of the karaoke machine.

He sat down in the chair opposite mine, a specter of death waiting for me to speak.

"I don't think I'm cut out for this job," I said, doing my best not to let my face show how much I wanted to attack him.

"Nonsense," he said. "You will do exactly what I ask of you."

"I did the best I could this week, but—"

"I was watching. You performed—adequately. You should go home now, make some of your beloved music, and enjoy the charms of your girlfriend. Have a little fun or read a book. Hell, walk that damn dog of yours. And try to get enough rest so you're ready the next time you are needed to perform your duties."

He raised an espresso cup that hadn't been there a moment before and took a sip.

I still had lots of questions, but before I could say anything, there was a break in the karaoke music, and I heard the beginning of the beat I hated so much—the one from my posthumous hit, *Blood Blister*—as a plump brunette took the microphone and prepared to sing.

I shook my head, glanced up at the flat-screen TV mounted above the bar, and saw something that made my night even worse.

The late-night television host was interviewing none other than the famous one-hit wonder who'd finally made a comeback after almost fifty years—the one, the only, the used-to-be-famous, David Steele.

He was interviewing—me.

I turned to Ahriman, ready to barrage him with angry accusations of foul play, but he was no longer there.

My head reeling, I watched as a healthy version of me joked and laughed with the television host and held up a full-sized album cover of my latest release. A few minutes later, my impersonator walked over to the small studio stage, strapped on my favorite guitar, and took the mic, ready to perform.

I felt paralyzed and sick to my stomach.

Since I'd arrived, I'd assumed John was the one who'd gotten the raw end of our deal—that no matter how much I didn't want to be stuck in Ashburn, at least it wasn't as bad as dying, trapped in my old body.

But I'd been wrong about that—dead wrong.

Ahriman and John had tricked me into coming to Ashburn, inhabiting John's body, and taking over his job. I didn't know the reasons for their actions yet, but I was going to find out. And when I did, I'd leave Ashburn for good and reclaim my identity, even if I had to destroy Ahriman and John to do it.

I picked up my shot of Maker's Mark and took a sip. When I set the glass back down on the sticky tabletop, the slide guitar from one of my favorite songs began playing in my head. After the first verse, the chorus started up, and I nodded at the truthfulness of its catchy lyrics before downing the rest of the shot.

I motioned for the server to bring me another one as I thought about the wicked people in the world and how they were doomed to never rest until they closed their eyes for good. As I turned back to the TV, I gave a dark laugh and wondered if I was destined to share their fate.

The End

ABOUT THE AUTHOR

Mike grew up as a military brat, traveling around the world and the country before landing as an adult in the suburbs outside of Washington, D.C. He currently lives with his writing buddies, Elsa and Baloo, the wonderful pups who make sure he takes plenty of breaks.

Word-of-mouth is crucial for any author to succeed. If you enjoyed "Ashburn," please leave an honest review online by going to the "Ashburn" product page where you purchased this book. Even if it's only a line or two, it would mean a lot.

For more information about Mike and his books, to buy directly from the author, or to sign up for Mike's e-mail list, please visit:

writerlayne.com